In the Heart of the Heart of the Country

Books by

William H. Gass

In the Heart
of the Heart
of the Country

and other stories by

William H. Gass

Nonpareil Books

DAVID R. GODINE
Publisher · Boston

This is a NONPAREIL BOOK first published in 1981 by
David R. Godine, Publisher, Inc.
300 Massachusetts Avenue
Boston, Massachusetts 02115

Library of Congress Cataloging in Publication Data

Gass, William H.   1924–
    In the heart of the heart of the country and other
stories.

    (A Nonpareil book; no. 21)
    Reprint of the 1st ed. published in 1968 by Harper &
Row, New York.
    CONTENTS: The Pedersen kid.–Mrs. Mean.–Icicles.
—[etc.]
    I. Title. II. Series: Nonpareil books; no. 21.
[PS3557.A84515   1981]   813'.54   80-83962
ISBN 0-87923-374-5

Third printing, April 1989
Printed in the United States of America

For Joanne, Oliver, and Allan

ACKNOWLEDGMENTS. These stories originally appeared, in somewhat different form, in the following magazines: "The Pedersen Kid" in *MSS,* "Mrs. Mean" in *Accent,* "Icicles" in *Perspective,* "Order of Insects" in *The Minnesota Review,* and "In the Heart of the Heart of the Country" in *New American Review.* I should like to thank the editors for permission to reprint.

Contents

A Revised & Expanded Preface

Few of the stories one has it in one's self to speak get spoken, because the heart rarely confesses to intelligence its deeper needs; and few of the stories one has at the top of one's head to tell get told, because the mind does not always possess the voice for them. Even when the voice is there, and the tongue is limber as if with liquor or with love, where is that sensitive, admiring, other pair of ears?

No court commands our entertainments, requires our flattery, needs our loyal enlargements or memorializing lies. Fame is not a whore we can ring up. The public spends its money at the movies. It fills stadia with cheers; dances to organized noise; while books die quietly, and more rapidly than their authors. Mammon has no interest in our service.

Literature once held families together better than quarreling. It carved a common ancestry simply from vibrating air, peopling an often empty and forgotten past with gods, demons, worthy enemies and proper heroes, until it became largely responsible for that pride we sometimes still take in being Athenian or Basque, a follower or fan. Think of the myths we've wrapped around Lincoln, that figure we have made a fiction in order to make him immortal. Think of the satisfaction there is in supporting a winning team of any kind. It's no small gift, this sense of worth which reaches us ahead of any action of our own, like hair at birth, and makes brilliant enterprises possible.

Some of the stories in this book have been alive (such is the brevity of story-life these days—like the photographer's flash) a long time (no time at all, of course, for Flaubert's *Un Coeur Simple* is now one hundred years old); no, not long by immortal measure, yet a surprising while, nevertheless, like the landed fish who startles us with a late flop. Now I'm to place a few words in front of them—these tales without plot or people, I've been told—and I wonder whether they should serve as muffled drums or slowed steps do: to ready respect before the coming of the hearse.

Perhaps it is the case with many fabrications, but I am struck by how easily they might not have been at all; how really unreasonably provisional their entire existence is. The same for us all, you say? aren't we accidents of genes and conditions of acidity ourselves, of elemental woove and wovvle? the product of opportunity and inclination, simple negligence and malice? Yes. O. Yes. Of course. But we burgeon as easily as water falls. We grow meanly like a cancer. Wasted acres testify to the undiminished requirements of our needs. Suppose it were otherwise, and a mother had to make her child's every cell. How many of us, in that case, would reach complete existence?

What of these excruciating passivities of print, then? If I break a dish, physics takes charge of my freedom like a warden, and there's no finger-smear of mine in the scatter of its bits. My cat's grassy urps, alas, show more of me than the shavings in my sharpener. However, these—these litters of language—they could not exist without the stubborn sustainment of my will . . . amazing to contemplate . . . a commonplace to encounter. So consciously composed, these stories are naturally laden with indebtedness, as though they had been to Hawaii, and encircled by exotic blooms. If my hero's hair is red as rust, to whom goes the credit—a recessive gene in my grandmother's unmentionable make-up? And all those authors I have lain with—loved—left—which ones are to blame for my page-long shopping lists, my vulgarized lingo, my tin pan prose? whose blood beats in the baby when none will claim paternity and the mother is unknown?

To be born unencumbered is not the complete advantage one might immediately imagine. Although the struggle to free one's youthful self of religion, relatives, and region is thereby greatly simplified, since there are no complicated cuffs to be unclasped, no subtle knots to be untied, the self in question is as vague and vaguely messy as a smudged line. I was born in a place as empty of distinction as my writing desk. When I wrote most of these stories, it was a dining table, featureless as Fargo. And I was born through a time so unnoteworthy in the locality that public memory starved, though I was scarcely six weeks old when I was floated out of North Dakota like Moses in a wicker basket. Alas . . . the resemblance was a brief and shallow one, because my basket was placed on the back seat of an old Dodge which tunnelled through twelve hundred miles of gravel dust to surface at the sooty industrial city in Ohio where my father was to teach and eventually to clench his bones together in a painful, accusatory claw.

Obscurely born (rumors circulated secretly like poorly printed money: was I caesarian? a breech? were those forceps marks on the back of my little red neck? was my papa playing baseball when my mother pushed me screaming into being? was I supposed to care that I was born obscurely?) of parents who hardly honored their heritage even by the bother of forcibly forgetting it; and who had many prejudices but few beliefs (the town I grew quickly older in appeared to be full of nigs, micks, wops, spicks, bohunks, polacks, kikes; on the public walks, in the halls of the high school, one could not be too careful of the profaned lips of water fountains); thus while there was much to complain of, just as there is in any family—much to resist—it was all quite particular, palpable, concrete. Good little clerk, my father hated workers, blacks, and Jews, the way he expected women to hate worms. There wasn't a faith to embrace or an ideology to spurn, unless perhaps it was the general suggestion of something poisonously Republican, or a periodical's respect for certain Trade Marks. And I remember resolving, while on long walks or during summer reveries or while deep in the night's bed, not to be like that, when *that* was whatever was around me: Warren, Ohio—factory smoke, depression, household gloom, resentments, illness, ugliness, despair, etcetera, and littleness, above all, smallness, the encroachment of the lean and meager. I won't be like that, I said, and naturally I grew in special hidden ways to be more like that than anyone could possibly imagine, or myself admit. Even as a grown man I was still desperately boasting that I'd choose another cunt to come from. Well, Balzac wanted his *de,* and I wanted my anonymity.

School was a dull time in the beginning; I was a slow student, my achievement intermittent and unpredictable as a loose wire. I decorated my days with extravagant, outrageous lies. Yet I was reading Malory, too, and listening to Guinevere bid Launcelot adieu:

> For as well as I have loved thee, mine heart will not serve me to see thee; for through thee and me is the flower of kings and knights destroyed. Therefore, Sir Launcelot, go to thy realm, and there take

thee a wife, and live with her with joy and bliss, and I pray thee heartily pray for me to our Lord, that I may amend my misliving.

Amend my misliving. And everything in me then said: I want to be like that—like that aching phrase. So oddly, at a time when no one any longer allowed reading or writing to give them face, place, or history, I was forced to form myself from sounds and syllables: not merely my soul, as we used to say, but guts too, a body I knew was mine because, in response to the work which became whatever of me there was, it angrily ulcerated.

I read with the hungry rage of a forest blaze.

I wanted to be a fireman, I recall, but by eight I'd given up that very real cliché for an equally unreal one: I wanted to become a writer.

. . . *a what?* Well, a writer wasn't whatever Warren was. A writer was whatever Malory was when he wrote down his ee's: *mine heart will not serve me to see thee.* And that's what I wanted to be—a string of stresses.

. . . *a what?*

The contemporary American writer is in no way a part of the social and political scene. He is therefore not muzzled, for no one fears his bite; nor is he called upon to compose. Whatever work he does must proceed from a reckless inner need. The world does not beckon, nor does it greatly reward. This is not a boast or a complaint. It is a fact. Serious writing must nowadays be written for the sake of the art. The condition I describe is not extraordinary. Certain scientists, philosophers, historians, and many mathematicians do the same, advancing their causes as they can. One must be satisfied with that.

Unlike this preface, then, which pretends to the presence of your eye, these stories emerged from my blank insides to die in another darkness. I willed their existence, but I don't know why. Except that in some dim way I wanted, myself, to have a soul, a special speech, a style. I wanted to feel responsible where I could bear to be responsible, and to make a sheet of steel from a flimsy page—something that would not soon weary itself out of shape as everything else I had known (I thought) always had. They appeared in the world obscurely, too—slow brief bit by bit, through gritted teeth and much despairing; and if any person were to suffer such a birth, we'd see the skull come out on Thursday, skin appear by week's end, liver later, jaws arrive just after eating. And no one of us, least of all the owner of the opening it inched from, would know what species the creature would eventually contrive to copy and to claim. Because I wrote these stories without imagining there would be readers to sustain them, they exist now as if readerless (strange species indeed, like the flat, pigmentless fish of deep seas, or the blind, transparent shrimp of coastal caves), although a reader now and then lets light fall on them from that other, less real world of common life and pleasant ordinary things.

Occasionally one's companion, in a rare mood of

love, will say: 'Bill, tell about the time you told off
that trucker at the truck stop'; but Bill's audience
knows he's no emperor of anecdote, like Stanley
Elkin, and they will expect at best not to be bored,
pallidly amused, not edified or elevated, not ce-
mented or composed; and occasionally one's children will still want a story told them, improvised on
the spot, not merely read or from a flabby memory
recited. Then they will beg far better than a dog.

Tell us a story, fawfaw. Tell us a lonely story.
Tell us a long and lonely story about the sticky-
handed giants who had no homes, because we want
to cry. Tell us the story of the overfriendly lions.
Tell us the story of the sad and barkless dog. Tell
us, fawfaw, tell us, because we want to cry. Tell us
of the long bridge and the short wagon and the tall
tollkeeper and the tall tollkeeper's high horse and
the tiny brown tail of the tall tollkeeper's high horse
that couldn't swish away blue flies . . . because we
want to cry. We want to cry.

Well which? . . . which shall I tell you the story
of to make you sad so you will cry?

Oh don't do that, fawfaw. We want to cry. Don't
make us sad. We merely want to cry. Tell us a
lonely story. Tell us about the giants. Tell us about
the lions. Tell us about the dog. But do not make
us sad, fawfaw, just make us cry.

Well which? . . . which then shall I tell you if you
want to cry? . . . which, the story of?

Woods.

Woods. I knew it would be woods. I knew it
would be woods when you said tell of the giants
and the lions and the dog. I knew it would be woods

when you said tell me of the long bridge and the short wagon and the thin road running to the bridge which the wagon rode over.

There's no thin road in the story, fawfaw. No. There's no thin road.

Oh. Well. Maybe there's a fat hog? a fat hog squatting on a large log? a large log lying in the thin road running to the bridge which the wagon rolls over.

No, fawfaw, of course not. You know there's no thin road, and therefore there can scarcely be any large log lying in any thin road, and therefore there can hardly be any fat hog squatting on any large log lying in any thin road. No. There can't be because there isn't. And because hogs don't squat, ever. And on logs, no, never. So.

Oh. Well. Perhaps there's a thin snake? Perhaps he sunning himself on a wide rock resting by the side of the road that runs to the brook the bridge goes over?

No. You're hateful and you're horrid. You know there is no road like that. There never never was. There was always only the long bridge and the short wagon and the tall tollkeeper and the tall toll-keeper's high horse that couldn't swish away blue flies. We remember. We remember about that. We want to hear about woods.

Woods. I knew it would be woods. You want to cry.

No. We no longer want to cry. We did but now we don't, but we still want to hear about woods, so say about the woods now, say about them.

Oh. Well. Woods. Anyway, I knew it would be woods.

Well then tell about them. Tell about woods.

You remember about the woods as well as I. I know about you. You remember about the woods.

Yes. Certainly. We remember about woods. We remember everything about them. We remember them entirely and wholly, absolutely and altogether. Because we do, because of that, we want to hear everything again. We want to hear it through from end to end, fawfaw. Mind. You're not to leave out. You're not to put in. We remember wholly about woods, and that is why we want to hear about them right now, and so say about it, and say how it was, and why it was, and all about it.

Woods. Well then. Well then woods. Well . . .

Rhythmic, repetitious, patterned, built of simple phrases like small square blocks (draw me a clown, build me a castle, fold me a hat, sail my paper plane), with magical and imaginary logic, their facts nailed carefully to clouds, often teasing, these stories were fond possessions which fondly possessed their possessor like our dolls . . . remember? And the best ones were those which sounded, when you heard them for the first time, as if you had heard them many times before. Of course, the paragraphs I just placed on the page are not the beginning of any such story; they are *about* the character and quality and construction of such stories, and therefore do not resemble the child's mind or mortality at all.

After those stories which we once employed to hold the ears of children came those calculated to

suspend—not just you or me, but everyone—our
souls like white rags in a line of wash; and these
were written to manipulate a kind of universal
mechanism in our psyches: the Gothic romance
played upon passivity, just as nursie stories put girls
in their place, while the hard-eyed private eye became a hard and fancy phallus. In my adolescence
I forsook Malory to pursue simpleminded empa-
thies. I read of G–8 and his Battle Aces, about Doc
Savage and the Shadow. Threats, entanglements,
and bloody extrications followed one another with
increasing amplitude and gratifying rapidity. Plots
lay over my life like a treasure hunter's map. The
solace they contained was as immense as it was
deceitful, since there was always a way out. I now
wonder whether this glut of blood and mindless action didn't stamp all story for me as trivial, childish,
and cheap. Later I painfully advanced on Thomas
Wolfe and like him made the world a Whitman Sam-
pler and a list of sweets. I also ranted against that
mysterious enemy, the other sex, because I wasn't
whatever I thought women wanted my own sexual-
ity to be.

If Gertrude Stein understood first principles, and
borrowed much of her magical hypnotic beat from
children's tales (everything but woods and witches),
Kafka grasped the second ones with an unholy
hand. He simply did not specialize in extrications.

He had come from the ship at dawn, eager to see
the sights of the city—he had heard there were so
many—and perhaps, one never knew, to turn a

penny of the honest kind through wine and conver-
sation. Hardly had he crossed the docks and entered
one of the narrow streets that lead from the water-
front when nine sergeants of police, running out of
doorways, caught him in a plastic net, bobbing their
silver epaulets and swaying their silver cords across
their chests with the exertion; and he was carried
head down over the right shoulder of the largest, a
man terribly strong, so that all he saw around him
as he bounced against the fellow's buttocks were
nine pairs of superb trousers and the eighteen shining shoes that darted out of them, their silver laces
shaking, while on the road he saw patches of brilliantly iridescent oil. He was slung so steeply that
his head several times struck the pavement until he
cruelly bent his neck. Once he remembered to cry
out but a jounce made him bite his tongue and he
choked upon saliva. Blood collected above his eyes,
making him sick and afraid to speak. In this condition he was brought before a magistrate who ques-
tioned him at once.

He tried to answer but the magistrate only stared,
his head wagging constantly so that powder drifted
from his wig. The questions continued, receiving
the same answers as before. But the blood in your
cheeks, cried the magistrate, bring me a basin! All
he could do was plead. The magistrate rose angrily
and hurled his wig at him, clouds of powder rising,
forcing him to sneeze. The magistrate produced a
portfolio of photographs which he shook one after
the other so the images seemed to blur. There! What
do you say to that, sir? what do you say to these?
At last in terrible vexation he shouted back: you
are crazy, crazy, a creature in my nightmare; and
one of the sergeants thereupon entered to strike him

on the hands and about the face with a watch strap while the magistrate repeated peevishly: he has no dignity, this one, look at his nose.

Franz Kafka and Lewis Carroll, Lawrence Sterne and Tobias Smollett, James Joyce and Marcel Proust, Thomas Mann and William Faulkner, André Gide and Joseph Conrad: what could a poor beginner do? And from whose grip was it easier to escape—the graceless hack's or the artful great's?

In any case, break loose. Begin. And I began by telling a story to entertain a toothache. To entertain a toothache there has to be lots of incident, some excitement, much menace. When I decided to write the story down, I called it 'And Slowly Comes the Spring,' because that fragmentary phrase seemed somehow appropriate and poetic (it wasn't); but it was some weeks before I began to erase the plot to make a fiction of it, since one can't count on the ear of an everlasting toothache. I titled it, then, 'The Pedersen Kid,' and because I believed it was good for me (it turned out, it was), I tried to formulate a set of requirements for the story as clear and rigorous as those of the sonnet. From the outset, however, I was far too concerned with theme. I hadn't discovered yet what I would later find was an iron law of composition for me: the exasperatingly slow search among the words I had already written for the words which were to come, and the necessity for continuous revision, so that each work would seem simply the first paragraph rewritten, swollen with sometimes years of scrutiny around that initial verbal wound, one of the sort you hope, as François

Mauriac has so beautifully written, 'the members of a particular race of mortals can never cease to bleed.'

But what do beginners know? too much. It is what they think they know that makes them beginners. Anyway, here are some of the instructions I drew up (or laid down) for myself during that January of its commencement nearly twenty-five— no—nearly thirty years ago.

> The problem is to present evil as a visitation—sudden, mysterious, violent, inexplicable. All should be subordinated to that end. The physical representation must be spare and staccato; the mental representation must be flowing and a bit repetitious; the dialogue realistic but musical. A ritual effect is needed. It falls, I think, into three parts, each part dividing itself into three. The first part is composed of the discovery of the boy, the discovery of what the boy has seen, the discovery (worst of all) that they will have to do something. The second part is composed of efforts—the effort made to reach the farm; the effort needed to build a tunnel; the effort made to gain the house from the barn. The point here is that the trio, who have come this far only through the social pressure of each other, and in shaky bravado, must go on, knowing that they are ignorant of causes—of the force itself—('He ain't there'). But the shooting leaves Jorge alone in the house. The pressure which had moved him this far is removed, and the pressure of fear—the threat of death—substituted. The third part contains Jorge's attempt to escape and his unwilling stalk through the house, his wait through the blizzard and the night, and his rescue in the morning. The force has

gone as it came. The Pedersens are missing and the great moral effort of the Jorgensens, compelled at every step as it was, is wasted and for nothing.

Though I dropped the rescue, I did not so much depart from this conception as complicate it, covering the moral layer with a frost of epistemological doubt. In any case, during the actual writing, the management of monosyllables, the alternation of short and long sentences, the emotional integrity of the paragraph, the elevation of the most ordinary diction into some semblance of poetry, became my fanatical concern.

Working through the summer, I finished the story in September, and it was seven or eight years after that—and you can imagine how many editorial rejections (it seemed like hundreds; I can still hear the flat slap of the ms. on the front step, the sting of shame in my cheeks, my humiliation, doubts, confusion; I heard the laughter of thousands); and you can imagine how many well-meant sympathies, mailed like cards at Christmas, how many broken chairs and bitter bottles and household quarrels, black thoughts and stubborn resolutions, intervened—before John Gardner generously published it in his magazine, *MSS*.

One must begin, but one must know how to end. It is a knowledge I have altogether lost. 'The Pedersen Kid' had an end I could aim at. Like death, I knew it would come. Like death, I did not know how I would face it. That the rest of these stories are short; that *Omensetter's Luck* is long and *The Tunnel,* as it is turning out, under endless excavation: these are things I had no inkling of when I began. I realize, too, that each one was written with full knowledge of the public failure of the others; hence written with worsening nerves. I explored this, tried that, but like an ignorant and careless gardener, I never knew what sort of seed I had sown, so I was surprised by the height of its growth, the character of its bloom.

Writing and reading, like male and female, pain and pleasure, are close but divergent. Although writing itself may be a partial substitute for sexual expression (during adolescence, at any rate), sexual curiosity propelled my reading like a rocket. Over how many dry pages did I pass in search of water? Beyond the next paragraph, around the turn of the page, an oasis of sensuality would materialize, fuzzy in the desert light at first, but then clear, precise, and detailed as a dirty drawing. My sexual puzzles would undo like bras, mysteries would fall away like underpants passing the knees. Alas! such a hot breath blew upon the page that every oasis withered. What did I learn from Pierre Louÿs? Balzac? Jules Romain? . . . *their* puzzles and *their* mysteries, *their* confusions and *their* lies. I didn't understand. I didn't realize. I wanted dirt or purity, innocence or cynicism, never the muddy mix, the flat balance, the even tones of truth. I carried a critic with me everywhere who rose to applaud the passionate passages with a shameless lack of discrimination, and during the throbbing din it made I couldn't honestly feel or sharply sense or clearly think. Of course, sexual curiosity remains the third lure of reading, yet what an enormous amount of the body's beautiful blushing is wasted on the silliest puerilities when writers write for the reasons readers read.

He wondered how her breasts were really formed. Guess, she said. Did the nipple rise like a rainspot on a pond, and were the hollows of her thighs like cups which would contain his kisses? Imagine what will pleasure you, she said. Her clothing always fought him off. His fingers could not construct the rest of what they touched, even when one, slipping beneath the boundary of her underwear, traversed a sacred edge. She would permit him every liberty so long as cloth was wrapped like a bandage between them, but his hands or his lips or his eyes on anything but customary flesh caused her to stiffen, sucking at her breath until it drew like a bubbly straw. He realized he was as much ice water as a wound. One day, indeed, she had taken all her upper garments off but a soft thin blouse of greenish Celanese, and through its yielding threads he had compressed her. His protests were useless. Guess, she always said. And finally when he had with sufficient and extraordinary bitterness complained how hard her teasing was on him, she'd firmly ordered his phallus from its trousers as you might order a dog from a tree. Dear thing, she said; I'll free you of me. Ultimately, this became their love, like shaking hands, and he had eventually accepted the procedure because, as he explained, it was so like the world. She smiled at this and slowly shook her head: you still have your dream, she said, and I have my surprise.

The material that makes up a story must be placed

under terrible compression, but it cannot simply release its meaning like a joke does. It must be epiphanous, yet remain an enigma. Its shortness must have a formal function: the deepening of the understanding, the darkening of the design.

In a sense, 'Mrs. Mean' is a story of sexual curiosity translated, again, into the epistemological, although it had its beginning in an observation I never used.

> 3 August '54. The following tableau at the House of Many Children: father is going to work and is standing by the car talking with his wife. He is tall, thin, dark, heavily bearded so that, though he shaves, he always has a heavy shadow, almost blue, across the sides of his face and chin. She is large, great breasted, fat, pig-eyed, fair. The children annoy father who yells at them in a deep carrying voice, cuffs one hard and shoos the rest away with a vigorous outward motion of his arms (like chickens). The children flee, crying and screaming and carrying on. Then father departs. Mama waves and when he's gunned the car furiously away (it stalls twice), she turns to the house; the children's heads pop into place. She makes her voice deep and gruff like his and shouts at them. She swings at one or two (missing widely), and makes his shooing motion with her arms. The children roar delightedly. She goes in and they all troupe gaily behind her.

I was to observe this scene, played with only slight variations, many times, and what interested me about it, finally, was the triangle formed by mother, children, and private-public me; but I didn't

begin to invent a narrative Eye, my journal tells
me, until July 12, 1955, when the first words of the
story appear in an unwhelped form. Empty of any
persuasive detail, the focus wrong, order inept,
rhythms lame, these initial early sentences are aim-
less, toneless, figureless, thin.

> We call her Mrs. Mean, my wife and I. Our view
> of her, as our view of her husband and each of all
> her children, is a porch view. We can only surmise
> what her life is like inside her little house, but on
> warm, close Sunday afternoons, while we try the
> porch to stay cool and watch her hobbling in the
> hot sun, stick in hand to beat her children, we think
> a lot about it.

I notice that by November I have begun writing
little encouraging notes to myself: buck up, old boy,
and so on. It has become a drab affair, like the
writing of all my fictions. Imagine an adultery as
full of false starts, procrastination, indecision, poor
excuses, impotence, and, above all, *plans.*

> The idea I must keep in mind is how I can (a) tell
> the story of the public Mr. & Mrs. Mean, as seen
> by the 'I' of the story, (b) make 'I' more than a
> pronoun—rather a pronounced personality, (c)
> slowly, imperceptibly shift from the factual report-
> ing of it to the imaginative projections of 'I.' The
> problem is as knotty as PK, and as nice. The ending
> will be, of course, unsatisfactory, as it will end in
> the imagination, not in the fact, as if the imagination
> had filled in the gaps between facts with more *facts,*
> whereas only fancies are there. All stories ought to
> end unsatisfactorily.

A month later I had a page, and I completed the piece at some unspecified time in 1957.

I write down these dates, now, and gaze across these temporal gaps with a kind of dumb wonder, because I am compelled to acknowledge again the absurd manner in which my stories have been shovelled together: hodge against podge, like those cathedrals which have Baroque porches, Gothic naves, and Romanesque crypts; since the work on them always went slowly; time passed, then passed again, bishops and princes lost interest; funds ran out; men died; shells shattered their radiant windows; they became victims of theft, fire, priests, architects, wind; and because they were put in service while they were still being built, the pavement was gone, the pillars in a state of lurch, by the time the dome was ready for its gilt or the tower for its tolling bell; so the difficulty for me was plain enough: as an author I naturally desired to change, develop, grow, while each story in its turn wanted the writer who'd begun it to stick around like a faithful father to the end. This dilemma, like drink, nearly destroyed the work of Malcolm Lowry. The absurdity enlarges like the nose of a clown, too, when one realizes that the structure which eventually gets mortared and plastered and hammered together more nearly resembles some *maison de convenence* than even the most modest church. Still, needs are served as much by the humble and ridiculous as by the lordly and sublime.

In any event, it became necessary (it is always

necessary) to rewrite earlier sections of whatever I found myself finally trapped in, according to the standards and style of the part presently underway; because, though time may appear to pass within a story, the story itself must seem to have leaked like a blot from a single shake of the pen.

And when you retrace your steps, even if it's your intention to change them, the path you've already worn down deepens; it is increasingly difficult to escape your first mistakes, really to see a fresh new way of solving some repeating problem; while certain points along the route, like places where you've fallen often, threaten your nerve, so that you are inclined to seek trails around the mountain which won't require you to climb in the cold and cross it.

Meanwhile the mind whispers reasons to the soul which explain why a bad line is a lovely one; how all your strategies have superbly succeeded; why you may march confidently on in cardboard shoes, for no one will notice. My training had stocked me with rationalizations like a pond. I had merely to throw a line in to catch one. The poor phrase, the campy connection, the cheap joke, the trite observation, the cute twist you've contrived, the smart aleck attitude, the infantile ideas and innumerable alliterations, the glib topping you've just poured on a paragraph: these and other 'awfuls' are a part of you; they come from the deepest *cave*; and they must be sent back like a bad bottle no matter what the label says, or the degree of your humiliation.

There is much fright. It settles like a cloud of acid in the stomach. Doctors prescribe milk. They know there is no calcium in kindness. Although unwell, one tries to stick one's words together well; but perhaps, as I write this, the sentences these sentences are supposed to front are melting like icicles, and pointedly passing away; so that, reader, when you turn the final pages of this preface, you will be confronted with a pale, pretentious blank; and if that happens, I know which of us will be the greater fool, for your few cents spent on this book are a little loss from a small mistake; think of me and smile: I misspent a life.

My journal begins to sputter—gutters out. No more little plans, no more recorded glooms or glorious exhortations, and no more practice paragraphs either, like scales run over in the street. For several years before I began 'The Pedersen Kid,' I had practiced them (and single sentences, too, and imaginary words, and sounds I hoped had fallen out of *Alice*); three of which I have put in this preface like odd bits of fruit in a pudding—just a change of texture and a little action for the teeth—and these exercises were another idiocy, because I knew that words were communities made by the repeated crossing of contexts the way tracks formed towns, and that sentences did not swim indifferently through others like schools of fish of another species, but were like lengths of web within a web, despite one's sense of the stitch and knot of design inside them.

Once more right about art and wrong about the world, the Idealist philosophers had argued the same way, Leibniz suggesting that every truth was an analytic one, and that all legitimate predicates would eventually be found (by God) embedded like so many weevils in a single subject there wouldn't be any biscuit; but, then, conversely, was a sentence like that flower in its crannied wall, that speck of sand we might see a world in, and could one observe inside its syntactically small self the shape of a busy populace? would the unity of a well-formed sentence serve as a model for the unity of All or Any? I guess I hoped so.

Hours of insanity and escape . . . hours inventing expressions like 'kiss my teeth,' and then wondering what they meant . . . hours of insanity and escape . . . hours spent looking at objects as if they were women, sketching ashtrays, for instance, and noting of a crystal one

> . . . the eyes, the lines of light, the living luster of the glass—the patterns, the ebb and flow—shadows, streaks—the flowing like water in the quiet streams with the sun on it—the foam and bubble of the glass . . .

and concluding the study grandly (who was I pretending to be? Maupassant tutored by Flaubert?) with this command:

> Never mention an ashtray unless you can swiftly make it the only one of its kind in the world.

A rule I obeyed by never mentioning an ashtray.

As should be obvious from my collection of words about the ashtray, I could not teach myself to see without, at the same time, teaching myself how to write, for the words, and the observation they comprise, coalesce. If one is not alive and lustrous, neither is the other. Here I had made nothing to snuff a smoking end in—a gathering as burnt out and gray as ash.

Thus, obscurely and fortuitously, chance brought these stories forth from nowhere. Icicles once dripped solidly from my eaves, for instance. I thought them remarkable because they seemed to grow as a consequence of their own grief, and I wondered whether my feelings would freeze to me by the time they had traveled my length, and whether each of us wasn't just the size of our consciousness solidified; but these fancies scarcely crept into the story which, like 'Order of Insects,' and everything I've written since, is an exploration of an image. I was impressed not only by their cold, perishable beauty, but by the feeling I had that they were *mine,* and that, though accident had fixed them to my gutters the way it had hung them everywhere, no one had a right to cause their premature destruction. Yet where may the eye fall now its sight is not bruised by vandals and their victims? No matter. The story merely began from this thought, it did not create itself entirely as an icicle should, so that passions warmed elsewhere would cool as they passed along the text until, at the sharp tip, they became themselves text. That would have been ideal. That would have been something!

Hours of insanity and escape . . . collecting names in the hope they'd prove jackpotty, and stories would suddenly shower out like dimes . . .

Horace Bardwell, Ada Hunt Chase, Mary Persis Crofts, Kelsey Flowers, Annie Stilphen, Edna Hoxie, Asher Applegate, Amos Bodge, Enoch Boyce, Jeremiah Bresnan, James G. Burpee, Curtis Chamlet, Decius W. Clark, Revellard Dutcher, Jedediah Felton, Jethro Furber, Pelatiah Hall, George Hatstat, Quartus Graves, Leoammi Kendall, Truxton Orcutt, Plaisted Williams, Francis Plympton, Azariah Shove, Peter Twiss; and in addition the members of the cooking club of Mt. Gilead, Ohio, 1899: Dean Booher, Floy Buxton, Nellie Goorley, Ira Irwin, Bessie Johnson, Clara Kelly, Sadie McCracken, Clara Mozier, Josie Plumb, Sarah Swingle, Maude Smith, Anna, Belle, Deane, and Ivan Talmadge, Roberta Wheeler.

Round, ripe, seedful names like these are seldom found and cannot be invented, though they might be more sweetly arranged. I could not have shaken them from any local tree because I have no locality. I am not a man from Warren. What is it to be from Warren? or weakly half-Protestant, half-Catholic? nondescript in half-wasp white? of German and Scandinavian blood so pale even pure Aryans are disgusted? and with a name made for amusement, and one which, even in German, means 'alley.' Though I am, Gassy was not the worst I was called. I am no one's son, or father, it appears. Not Northern, not American, not a theosophist, not a scholar, not Prufrock, not the Dane. Yet I gathered these

names all the same. From a book . . . books . . .
from the pages that are my streets.

Nature rarely loops. Nature repeats. This spring
is not a former spring rethought, but merely another
one, somewhat the same, somewhat not. However,
in a fiction, ideas, perceptions, feelings, return like
reconsiderations, and the more one sees a piece of
imaginative prose as an adventure of the mind, the
more the linearities of life will be bent and interrupted. Just as revision itself is made of meditative
returns, so the reappearance of any theme consti-
tutes the reseeing of that theme by itself. Otherwise
there is no advance. There is stagnation. The quiet
spiral of the shell, a gyre, even a whirlwind, a tunnel
towering in the air: these are the appropriate forms,
the rightful shapes; yet the reader must not succumb
to the temptations of simple location, but experience
in the rising, turning line the wider view, like a
sailplane circling through a thermal, and sense at
the same time a corkscrewing descent into the subject, a progressive deepening around the reading
eye, a penetration of the particular which is the
partial theme of 'Mrs. Mean'—at once escape and
entry, an inside pulled out and an outside pressed
in, as also is the case with my single *short* story,
'Order of Insects.'

Hours of insanity and escape . . . in which I write
inadequate verse, read, rage . . . record anecdotes
which fade into the page like stains . . . beat time
with my pencil's business end . . . nip at the loose
skin on the side of my hand with my teeth . . . cast
schemes and tropes like horoscopes . . . practice

catachresis as though it were croquet . . . grrrowl
. . . kick wastebaskets into corners . . . realize that
when I picture my methods of construction all the
images are architectural, but when I dream of the
ultimate fiction—that animal entity, the made-up
syllabic self—I am trying to energize old, used-up,
stolen organs like Dr. Frankenstein . . . grrrind
. . . throw wet wads of Kleenex from a spring or
winter cold into the corner where they mainly miss
the basket . . . O . . . Ohio: I hear howling from
both Os . . . play ring agroan the rosie . . . pace
. . . put an angry erection back in my pants . . .
rhyme . . .

Then occasionally perceive beneath me on the
page a few lines which . . . while I was elsewhere
must have . . . yes, a few lines which have . . .
which have *the* sound . . . the true whistle of the
spirit. Wait'll they read that, I say, perhaps even
aloud, over the water running in the kitchen sink,
over the noise of my writing lamp, coffee growing
cold in the cup, the grrowl of my belly. Yet when
I raise my right palm from the paper where, in oath,
I've put it, the whistle in those words is gone, and
only the lamp sings. Till I pull its chain like a john.

Thus the idea of an audience returns like an itch
between the toes, because now we have words
watching words—not surprising: what should Ber-
keley's trees do, hidden in their forest, if they
learned, if they believed, if they knew that unnoticed they were likely to be nothing? encourage
birds? grow eyes and ears and rub remaining leaves
like foreign money?

When Henry James, bruised by his failure in the theater, returned to the novel with *The Awkward Age,* he wrote in the scenery himself; he created his actors and gave them their speeches and gestures. More than that, he filled the spaces around them with sensibility—other observations—the perfect vessel of appreciation—himself, or rather, his roundabout writing. His method has become a model. Now, on the page, though the stage is full, the theater is dark and empty. Red bulbs burn above the exits. And when the theater is empty, and the actors continue to speak into the wings and walk from cupboard to sofa as if in the midst of emotion, to whom are they speaking but to themselves? Suddenly the action is all there is; the made-up words are real; the actors are the parts they play; questions are no longer cues; replies are real replies; there's no more drama; the conditions of rehearsal have become the conditions of reality, and the light which streams like colored paper from the spots is all there'll ever be of day.

1. Continue work . . .
2. Study the masters . . .
3. Do deliberate exercises . . .
4. Regularly enter notes . . . sharpen that peculiar and forgetful eye . . .
5. Take to sketching . . . details . . . exactitude . . .
6. Become steeped in history . . .
7. . . . the better word . . . the better word . . . the better word . . .

8.   Figure it will be five years before any . . .
9.   Wait . . .

A former student, who had reached the lower slopes of a national magazine, charitably wrote to ask if I would do a piece on what it was like to live in the Midwest. Without quite knowing whether my answer would be yes or no, I nevertheless began to gather data on that subject, although it became plain soon enough that the magazine was not interested in the logarithmical disorders of my lyricisms. I had always avoided the autobiographical in my work, reasoning that it was one beginner's trap I'd not fall into (more witless wisdom), and by now I had become suspicious of my own detachment. Could I write close to myself, or would the letter B, which my narrator said he'd sailed to, stand for bathos?

I was living in Brookston, Indiana, then, but I called it B because that's how people and places were sometimes represented in the old days. Pamela is always pulling Mr. B's paw out of her bosom. Turgenev's characters occasionally wait on a low small porch which is fastened like a belt around an inn or posting station, rising like a fresh bump on the road—say—to S, though nothing is in sight yet when we encounter them. Like the reader, they are waiting for the book to begin. (On the other hand, Beckett's roads are letterless, and his figures are waiting for the text to terminate.) Not only has the narrator come to B in a pun (a poor place), with the initial I also wanted to invoke the golden boughs and singing birds of Yeats's Byzantium. Furthermore, I knew that when I'd finished, it wouldn't be Brookston, Indiana, anymore, but a place as full of dream and fabrication as that fabled city itself. Inside my cautious sentences, as against Yeats's monumental poetry, B would become an inverted emblem for man's imagination.

I certainly didn't resort to the letter out of shyness or some belated sense of discretion; but as I got my 'facts' straight (clubs, crops, products, prospects, townshape, bar- and barn-size), I remembered how eagerly I'd come to the community, how much I'd needed to feel my mind—just once—run free and openly in peace, in wholesome and unworried amplitude, the way my legs before in Larimore, N.D., had carried me through streets scaled perfectly for childhood; and I slowly realized, while I drew up my lists (jobs, shops, climate), marking social strata like a kid counts layers in a cake, that I was taking down the town in notes so far from sounding anything significant that they would not even let me find a cow; yet I figured my estimates anyway (population changes, transportation, education, housing, love), and I took my polls (of churches and their clientele, of diets and diseases); I made my guesses about the townspeople's privacy (fun, games, hankie-pankies, high or low finance: pitch or catch, cadge, swap or auction), just as any geographer would, impressed by the seriousness of habit, too, of simple talk or an idle spit or prolonged squat— a reflective shit in a distant field; and as I started to distribute my data gingerly across my manuscript, a steady dissolution of the real began; because the more precisely one walks down a verbal street; indeed, the more precisely trash heap and vagrant shadow, weed stand and wind-feel and walkcrack are rendered; when, in fact, all that can conceivably enter consciousness—like snowlight and horse harness, grain spill and oil odor, hedge and grass growth, the cool tin taste of well-water in a bent tin cup—enters like the member of an orchestra, armed with an instrument (the bee's hum and the fly's death, for instance); the more completely, in short, we observe rather than merely note, contemplate rather than perceive, imagine rather than simply ponder; then the more fully, too, must the reader and writer realize, as their sentences foot the page, that they are now in the graciously menacing presence of the Angel of Inwardness, that radiant guardian of Ideas of whom Plato and Rilke spoke so ardently, and Mallarmé and Valéry invoked; since a sense of resonant universality arises in literature whenever some mute and otherwise trivial, though unique, superfluity is experienced with an intensely passionate exactness: through a ring of likeness which defines for each object its land of unlikeness, too (though who says so aside from Schopenhauer, who was also wrong about the world?); and consequently the heart of the country became the heart of the heart with a suddenness which left me uncomforted, in B and not Byzantium, not Brookston, far from the self I thought I might expose, nowhere near a childhood, and with thoughts I kept in paragraphs like small animals caged.

Hours of insanity and escape . . . tear paper into

thread-thin strips—not easy . . . then to slide lines of words from one side of a page to another, vainly hoping the difference will be agreeable . . . instead of a passionate particularity, to try for a ringing singularity . . . cancel, scratch, XXXXX . . . stop.

The gentle Turgenev (and one of our masters, surely, if we love this arrogantly modest art), writing about *Fathers and Children*—writing about himself—said: 'Only the chosen few are able to transmit to posterity not only the content but also the *form* of their thoughts and views, their personality, which, generally speaking, is of no concern to the masses.' *The form.* That is what the long search is for; because form, as Aristotle has instructed us, is the soul itself, the life in any thing, and of any immortal thing the whole. It is the B in being. *The chosen few* . . . the happy few . . . that little band of brothers . . . Well, the chosen cannot choose themselves, however they connive at it.

And he asked his fellow Russian writers to guard their language. 'Treat this mighty weapon with respect,' he begged, 'in skilled hands it can work miracles.' But miracles cannot be chosen either. And for those of us who have worked none, respect we can still manage. The folly of a hope sustains us: that next time the skill will be there, and the miracle will ensue.

So I am still the obscure man who wrote these words, and if someone were to ask me once again of the circumstances of my birth, I think I should answer finally that I was born somewhere in the middle of my first book; that life, so far, has not

been extensive; that my native state is Anger, a
place nowhere on the continent but rather somewhere at the bottom of my belly; that I presently
dwell in the Sicily of the soul, the Mexico of the
mind, the tower at Duino, the garden house in Rye;
and that I shall be happy to rent, sell, or give away
these stories, which I would have furnished far more
richly if I could have borne the cost, to anyone who
might want to visit them, or—hallelujah—reside.
In lieu of that unlikelihood, however, I am fashion-
ing a reader for these fictions . . . of what kind, you
ask? well, skilled and generous with attention, for
one thing, patient with *longeurs,* forgiving of every
error and the author's self-indulgence, avid for details . . . ah, and a lover of lists, a twiddler of lines.
Shall this reader be given occasionally to mouthing
a word aloud or wanting to read to a companion in
a piercing library whisper? yes; and shall this reader
be one whose heartbeat alters with the tenses of the
verbs? that would be nice; and shall every allusion
be caught like a cold? no, eaten like a fish, whole,
fins and skin; and shall there be a wide brow wrinkled with wonder at the rhetoric? sharp intakes of
breath? and the thoughts found profound and the
sentiments felt to be of the best kind? yes, and the
patterns applauded . . . but we won't need to put
hair or nose upon our reader, or any other opening
or lure . . . not a muscle need be imagined . . . it is
a body quite indifferent to time, to diet . . . it's only
eyes . . . what? oh, it will be a kind of slowpoke on
the page, a sipper of sentences, full of reflective
pauses, thus a finger for holding its place should be

appointed; a mover of lips, then? just so, yes, large soft moist ones, naturally red, naturally supple, but made only for shaping syllables, you understand, for singing . . . singing. And shall this reader, as the book is opened, shadow the page like a palm? yes, perhaps that would be best (mind the strain on the spirit, though, no glasses correct that); and shall this reader sink into the paper? become the print? and blossom on the other side with pleasure and sensation . . . from the touch of mind, and the love that lasts in language? yes. Let's imagine such a being, then. And begin. And then begin.

St. Louis, Missouri
May 26, 1976
January 26, 1981

In the Heart of the Heart of
the Country

The Pedersen Kid

PART ONE

1

Big Hans yelled, so I came out. The barn was dark, but the sun burned on the snow. Hans was carrying something from the crib. I yelled, but Big Hans didn't hear. He was in the house with what he had before I reached the steps.

It was the Pedersen kid. Hans had put the kid on the kitchen table like you would a ham and started the kettle. He wasn't saying anything. I guess he figured one yell from the crib was enough noise. Ma was fumbling with the kid's clothes which were stiff with ice. She made a sound like whew from every breath. The kettle filled and Hans said,

Get some snow and call your pa.

Why?

Get some snow.

I took the big pail from under the sink and the shovel by the stove. I tried not to hurry and nobody said anything. There was a drift over the edge of the porch so I spaded some out of that. When I brought the pail in, Hans said,

There's coal dust in that. Get more.

A little coal won't hurt.

Get more.

Coal's warming.

It's not enough. Shut your mouth and get your pa.

Ma had rolled out some dough on the table where Hans had dropped the Pedersen kid like a filling. Most of the kid's clothes were on the floor where they were going to make a puddle. Hans began rubbing snow on the kid's face. Ma stopped trying to pull his things off and simply stood by the table with her hands held away from her as if they were wet, staring first at Big Hans and then at the kid.

Get.

Why?

I told you.

It's Pa I mean—

I know what you mean.   Get.

I found a cardboard box that condensed milk had come in and I shoveled it full of snow. It was too small as I figured it would be. I found another with rags and an old sponge I threw out.   Campbell's soup.   I filled it too, using the rest of the drift. Snow would melt through the bottom of the boxes but that was all right with me. By now the kid was naked.   I was satisfied mine was bigger.

Looks like a sick shoat.

Shut up and get your pa.

He's asleep.

Yeah.

He don't like to get waked.

I know that. Don't I know that as good as you? Get him.

What good'll he be?

We're going to need his whiskey.

He can fix that need all right. He's good for fixing the crack in his face. If it ain't all gone.

The kettle was whistling.

What are we going to do with these? ma said.

Wait, Hed. Now I want you to get. I'm tired of talking. Get, you hear?

What are we going to do with them? They're all wet, she said.

I went to wake the old man. He didn't like being roused. It was too hard and far to come, the sleep he was in. He didn't give a damn about the Pedersen kid, any more than I did. Pedersen's kid was just a kid. He didn't carry any weight. Not like I did. And the old man would be mad, unable to see, coming that way from where he was asleep. I decided I hated Big Hans, though this was hardly something new for me. I hated Big Hans just then because I was thinking how Pa's eyes would blink at me—as if I were the sun off the snow and burning to blind him. His eyes were old and they'd never seen well, but shone on by whiskey they'd glare at my noise, growing red and raising up his rage. I decided I hated the Pedersen kid too, dying in our kitchen while I was away where I couldn't watch, dying just to pleasure Hans and making me go up snapping steps and down a drafty hall, Pa lumped under the covers at the end like dung covered with snow, snoring and whistling. Oh he'd not care about the Pedersen kid. He'd not care about getting waked so he could give up some of his liquor to a slit of a kid and maybe lose one of his hiding places in the bargain. That would make him mad enough if he was sober. I tried not to hurry though it was cold and the Pedersen kid was in the kitchen.

He was all shoveled up like I thought he'd be. I shoved at his shoulder, calling his name. I think he heard his name. His name stopped the snoring, but he didn't move except to roll a little when I shoved him. The covers slid down his skinny neck so I saw his head, fuzzed like a dandelion gone to seed, but his face was turned to the wall—there was the pale shadow of his nose on the plaster —and I thought: well you don't look much like a pig-drunk bully now. I couldn't be sure he was still asleep. He was a cagey sonofabitch. He'd heard his name. I shook him a little harder and made some noise. Pap-pap-pap-hey, I said.

I was leaning too far over. I knew better. He always slept close to the wall so you had to lean to reach him. Oh he was smart. It put you off. I knew better but I was thinking of the Pedersen kid mother-naked in all that dough. When his arm came up I ducked away but it caught me on the side of the neck, watering my eyes, and I backed off to cough. Pa was on his side, looking at me, his eyes winking, the hand that had hit me a fist in the pillow.

Get the hell out of here.

I didn't say anything—my throat wasn't clear—but I watched him. He was like a mean horse to come at from the rear. It was better, though, he'd hit me. He was bitter when he missed.

Get the hell out of here.

Big Hans sent me. He told me to wake you.

A fat turd to Big Hans. Get out of here.

He found the Pedersen kid by the crib.

Get the hell out.

Pa pulled at the covers. He was tasting his mouth.

The kid's froze like a pump. Hans is rubbing him with snow. He's got him in the kitchen.

Pedersen?

No, Pa. It's the Pedersen kid. The kid.

Nothing to steal from the crib.

Not stealing, Pa. He was just lying there. Hans found him froze. That's where he was when Hans found him.

Pa laughed.

I ain't hid nothing in the crib.

You don't understand, Pa. The Pedersen kid. The kid—

I shittin well understand.

Pa had his head up, glaring, his teeth gnawing at the place where he'd grown a mustache once.

I shittin well understand. You know I don't want to see Pedersen. That cock. Why should I? That fairy farmer. What did he come for, hey? God dammit, get. And don't come back. Find out some shittin something. You're a fool. Both you and Hans. Pedersen. That cock. That fairy farmer. Don't come back. Out. Shit. Out. Out out.

He was shouting and breathing hard and closing his fist on the pillow. He had long black hairs on his wrist. They curled around the cuff of his nightshirt.

Big Hans made me come. Big Hans said—

A fat turd to Big Hans. He's an even bigger turd than you. Fat, too, fool, hey? I taught him, dammit, and I'll teach you. Out. You want me to drop my pot?

He was about to get up so I got out, slamming the door. He was beginning to see he was too mad to sleep. Then he threw things. Once he went after Hans and dumped his pot over the banister. Pa'd been shit-sick in that pot. Hans got an ax. He didn't even bother to wipe himself off and he chopped part of Pa's door down before he stopped. He might not have gone that far if Pa hadn't been locked in laughing fit to shake the house. That pot put Pa in an awful good humor—whenever he thought of it. I always felt the thought was present in both of them, stirring in their chests like a laugh or a growl, as eager as an animal to be out.   I heard Pa cursing all the way downstairs.

Hans had laid steaming towels over the kid's chest and stomach. He was rubbing snow on the kid's legs and feet. Water from the snow and water from the towels had run off the kid to the table where the dough was, and the dough was turning pasty, sticking to the kid's back and behind.

Ain't he going to wake up?

What about your pa?

He was awake when I left.

What'd he say? Did you get the whiskey?

He said a fat turd to Big Hans.

Don't be smart. Did you ask him about the whiskey?

Yeah.

Well?

He said a fat turd to Big Hans.

Don't be smart. What's he going to do?

Go back to sleep most likely.

You'd best get that whiskey.

You go. Take the ax. Pa's scared to hell of axes.

Listen to me, Jorge, I've had enough of your sassing. This kid's froze bad. If I don't get some whiskey down him he might die. You want the kid to die? Do you? Well, get your pa and get that whiskey.

Pa don't care about the kid.

Jorge.

Well he don't. He don't care at all, and I don't care to get my head busted neither. He don't care, and I don't care to have his shit flung on me. He don't care about anybody. All he cares about is his whiskey and that dry crack in his face. Get pig-drunk—that's what he wants. He don't care about nothing else at all. Nothing. Not Pedersen's kid neither. That cock. Not the kid neither.

I'll get the spirits, ma said.

I'd wound Big Hans up tight. I was ready to jump but when ma said she'd get the whiskey it surprised him like it surprised me, and he ran down. Ma never went near the old man when he was sleeping it off. Not any more. Not for years. The first thing every morning when she washed her face she could see the scar on her chin where he'd cut her with a boot cleat, and maybe she saw him heaving it again, the dirty sock popping out as it flew. It should have been nearly as easy for her to remember that as it was for Big Hans to remember going after the ax while he was still spattered with Pa's sour yellow sick insides.

No you won't, Big Hans said.

Yes, Hans, if they're needed, ma said.

Hans shook his head but neither of us tried to stop her. If we had, then one of us would have had to go instead. Hans rubbed the kid with more snow . . . rubbed . . . rubbed.

I'll get more snow, I said.

I took the pail and shovel and went out on the porch. I don't know where ma went. I thought she'd gone upstairs and expected to hear she had. She had surprised Hans like she had surprised me when she said she'd go, and then she surprised him again when she came back so quick like she must have, because when I came in with the snow she was there with a bottle with three white feathers on its label and Hans was holding it angrily by the throat. Oh he was being queer and careful, pawing about in the drawer and holding the bottle like a snake at the length of his arm. He was awful angry because he'd thought ma was going to do something big, something heroic even, especially for her —I know him . . . I know him . . . we felt the same sometimes—while ma wasn't thinking about that at all, not anything like that. There was no way of getting even. It wasn't like getting cheated at the fair. They were always trying, so you got to expect it. Now Hans had given ma something of his—we both had when we thought she was going straight to Pa—something valuable, a piece of better feeling; but since she didn't know we'd given it to her, there was no easy way of getting it back.

Hans cut the foil off finally and unscrewed the cap. He was put out too because there was only one way of understanding what she'd done. Ma had found one of Pa's hiding places. She'd found one and she hadn't said a word while Big Hans and I had hunted and hunted as we always did all winter, every winter since the spring that Hans had come and I had looked in the privy and found the first one. Pa had a knack for hiding. He knew we were looking and he enjoyed it. But now ma. She'd found it by luck most likely but she hadn't said anything and we didn't know how long ago it'd been or how many other ones she'd found, saying nothing. Pa was sure to find out. Sometimes he didn't seem to because he hid them so well he couldn't find them himself or because he looked and didn't find anything and figured he hadn't hid one after all or had drunk it up. But he'd find out about this one because we were using it. A fool could see what was going on. If he found out ma found it—that'd be bad. He took pride in his hiding. It was all the pride he had. I guess fooling Hans and me took doing. But he didn't figure ma for much. He didn't figure her at all. And if he found out—a woman had—then it'd be bad.

Hans poured some in a tumbler.

You going to put more towels on him?

No.

Why not? That's what he needs, something warm to his skin, don't he?

Not where he's froze good. Heat's bad for frostbite. That's why I only put towels on his chest and belly. He's got to thaw slow. You ought to know that.

Colors on the towels had run.

Ma poked her toe in the kid's clothes.

What are we going to do with these?

Big Hans began pouring whiskey in the kid's mouth but the mouth filled without any getting down his throat and in a second it was dripping from his chin.

Here, help me prop him up. I got to hold his mouth open.

I didn't want to touch him and I hoped ma would do it but she kept looking at the kid's clothes piled on the floor and the pool of water by them and didn't make any move to.

Come on, Jorge.

All right.

Lift, don't shove . . . lift.

Okay, I'm lifting.

I took him by the shoulders. His head flopped back. His mouth fell open. The skin on his neck was tight. He was cold all right.

Hold his head up. He'll choke.

His mouth is open.

His throat's shut. He'll choke.

He'll choke anyway.

Hold his head up.

I can't.

Don't hold him like that. Put your arms around him.

Well jesus.

He was cold all right. I put my arm carefully around him. Hans had his fingers in the kid's mouth.

Now he'll choke for sure.

Shut up. Just hold him like I told you.

He was cold all right, and wet. I had my arm behind his back. He sure felt dead.

Tilt his head back a bit . . . not too much.

He felt cold and slimy. He sure was dead. We had a dead body in our kitchen. All the time he'd been dead. When Hans had brought him in, he'd been dead. I couldn't see him breathing. He was awful skinny, sunk between the ribs. We were getting him ready to bake. Hans was basting him. I had my arm around him, holding him up. He was dead and I had hold of him. I could feel my muscles jumping.

Well jesus christ.

He *is* dead. He *is*.

You dropped him.

Dead? ma said.

He's dead. I could feel. He's dead.

Dead?

Ain't you got any sense? You let his head hit the table.

Is he dead? Is he dead? ma said.

Well christ no, not yet, not yet he's not dead. Look what you done, Jorge, there's whiskey all over.

He *is* dead. He *is*.

Right now he ain't. Not yet he ain't. Now stop yelling and hold him up.

He ain't breathing.

Yes he is, he *is* breathing. Hold him up.

I ain't. I ain't holding any dead body. You can hold it if you want. You dribble whiskey on it all you want.

You can do anything you want to. I ain't. I ain't holding any dead body.

If he's dead, ma said, what are we going to do with these?

Jorge, god damn you, come back here—

I went down to the crib where Big Hans had found him. There was still a hollow in the snow and some prints the wind hadn't sifted snow over. The kid must have been out on his feet, they wobbled so. I could see where he had walked smack into a drift and then backed off and lurched up beside the crib, maybe bumping into it before he fell, then lying quiet so the snow had time to curl around him, piling up until in no time it would have covered him completely. Who knows, I thought, the way it's been snowing, we mightn't have found him till spring. Even if he was dead in our kitchen, I was glad Big Hans had found him. I could see myself coming out of the house some morning with the sun high up and strong and the eaves dripping, the snow speckled with drops and the ice on the creek slushing up; coming out and walking down by the crib on the crusts of the drift . . . coming out to play my game with the drifts . . . and I could see myself losing, breaking through the big drift that was always sleeping up against the crib and running a foot right into him, right into the Pedersen kid curled up, getting soft.

That would have been worse than holding to his body in the kitchen. The feeling would have come on quicker, and it would have been worse, happening in the middle of a game. There wouldn't have been any warning, any way of getting ready for it to happen, to know what I'd struck before I bent down, even though Old Man Pedersen would have come over between snows looking for the kid most likely and everybody would have figured that the kid was lying buried somewhere under the snow; that maybe after a high wind someday somebody would find him lying like a black stone uncovered in a field; but probably in the spring somebody would find him in some back pasture thawing out with the mud and have to bring him in and take him over to the Pedersen place and present him to Missus Pedersen. Even so, even with everyone knowing that, and hoping one of the Pedersens would find him first so they wouldn't have to pry him up out of the mud or fetch him out from a thicket and bring him in and give him to Missus Pedersen in soggy season-old clothes—even then, who would expect to stick a foot all of a sudden through the crust losing at the drift game and step on Pedersen's kid lying all crouched together right beside your own crib? It was a good thing Hans had come down this morning and found him, even if he was dead in our kitchen and I had held him up.

When Pedersen came over asking for his kid, maybe hoping that the kid had got to our place all right and stayed, waiting for the blizzard to quit before going home, Pa would meet him and bring him in for a drink and tell him it was his own fault for putting up all those snow fences. If I knew Pa, he'd tell Pedersen to look under the drifts his snow fences had made, and Pedersen would get so mad he'd go for Pa and stomp out calling for the vengeance of God like he was fond of doing. Now though, since Big Hans had found him, and he was dead in our kitchen, Pa might not say much when Pedersen came. He might just offer Pedersen a drink and keep his mouth shut about those snow fences. Pedersen might come yet this morning. That would be best because Pa would be still asleep. If Pa was asleep when Pedersen came he wouldn't have a chance to talk about those snow fences, or offer Pedersen a drink, or call Pedersen a bent prick or a turd machine or a fairy farmer. Pedersen wouldn't have to refuse the drink then, spit his chaw in the snow or call on God, and could take his kid and go home. I hoped Pedersen would certainly come soon. I hoped he would come and take that cold damp body out of our kitchen. The way I felt I didn't think that today I'd be able to eat. I knew every bite I'd see the Pedersen kid in the kitchen being fixed for the table.

The wind had dropped. The sun lay burning on the snow. I got cold just the same. I didn't want to go in but I could feel the cold crawling over me like it must have crawled over him while he was coming. It had slipped over him like a sheet, icy at first, especially around the feet, and he'd likely wiggled his toes in his boots and wanted to wrap his legs around each other like you do when you first come to bed. But then things would begin to warm up some, the sheet feeling warmer all the time until it felt real cozy and you went to sleep. Only when the kid went to sleep by our crib it wasn't like going to sleep in bed because the sheet never really got warm and he never really got warm either. Now he was just as cold in our kitchen with the kettle whistling and ma getting ready to bake as I was out by the crib jigging my feet in our snow.   I had to go in.   I looked but I couldn't see anyone trying to come down where the road was. All I could see was a set of half-filled prints jiggling crazily away into the snow until they sank under a drift. There wasn't anything around. There wasn't anything: a tree or a stick or a rock whipped bare or a bush hugged by snow sticking up to mark the place where those prints came up out of the drift like some-body had come up from underground.

I decided to go around by the front though I wasn't

supposed to track through the parlor. The snow came to my thighs, but I was thinking of where the kid lay on the kitchen table in all that dough, pasty with whiskey and water, like spring had come all at once to our kitchen, and our all the time not knowing he was there, had thawed the top of his grave off and left him for us to find, stretched out cold and stiff and bare; and who was it that was going to have to take him to the Pedersen place and give him to Missus Pedersen, naked, and flour on his bare behind?

2

Just his back.   The green mackinaw. The black stocking cap. The yellow gloves. The gun.

Big Hans kept repeating it. He was letting the meaning have a chance to change. He'd look at me and shake his head and say it over.

"He put them down the cellar so I ran."

Hans filled the tumbler. It was spotted with whiskey and flecks of flour.

"He didn't saying nothing the whole time."

He put the bottle on the table and the bottom sank unevenly in the paste, tilting heavily and queerly to one side —acting crazy, like everything else.

That's all he says he saw, Hans said, staring at the mark of the kid's behind in the dough. Just his back. The green mackinaw. The black stocking cap. The yellow gloves. The gun.

That's all?

He waited and waited.

That's all.

He tossed the whiskey off and peered at the bottom of the glass.

Now why should he remember all them colors?

He leaned over, his legs apart, his elbows on his knees, and held the glass between them with both hands, tilting it to watch the liquor that was left roll back and forth across the bottom.

How does he know? I mean, for sure.

He thinks he knows, Hans said in a tired voice. He thinks he knows.

He picked up the bottle and a hunk of dough was stuck to it.

Christ. That's all. It's how he feels. It's enough, ain't it? Hans said.

What a mess, ma said.

He was raving, Hans said. He couldn't think of anything else. He had to talk. He had to get it out. You should have heard him grunt.

Poor poor Stevie, ma said.

He was raving?

All right, is it something you dream? Hans said.

He must have been dreaming. Look—how could he have got there? Where'd he come from? Fall from the sky?

He came through the storm.

That's just it, Hans, he'd have had to. It was blizzarding all day. It didn't let up—did it?—till late afternoon. He'd have had to. Now what chance is there of that? What?

Enough a chance it happened, Hans said.

But listen. Jesus. He's a stranger. If he's a stranger he's come a ways. He'd never make it in a blizzard, not even knowing the country.

He came through the storm. He came out of the ground like a grub. Hans shrugged. He came.

Hans poured himself a drink, not me.

He came through the storm, he said. He came through

just like the kid came through. The kid had no chance neither, but he came. He's here, ain't he? He's right upstairs, right now. You got to believe that.

It wasn't blizzarding when the kid came.

It was starting.

That ain't the same.

All right. The kid had forty-five minutes, maybe an hour before it started to come on good. That isn't enough. You need the whole time, not a start. In a blizzard you got to be where you're going if you're going to get there.

That's what I mean. See, Hans? See? The kid had a chance. He knew the way. He had a head start. Besides, he was scared. He ain't going to be lazying. And he's lucky. He had a chance to be lucky. Now yellow gloves ain't got that chance. He has to come farther. He has to come through the storm all the way. But he don't know the way, and he ain't scared proper, except maybe by the storm. He hasn't got a chance to be lucky.

The kid was scared, you said. Right. Now why? You tell me that.

Hans kept his eyes on the whiskey that was shining in his glass. He was holding on hard.

And yellow gloves—he ain't scared? he said. How do you know he ain't scared, by something else besides wind and snow and cold and howling, I mean?

All right, I don't know, but it's likely, ain't it? Anyway, the kid, well maybe he ain't scared at all, starting out. Maybe his pa was just looking to tan him and he lit out. Then first thing he knows it's blizzarding again and he's lost, and when he gets to our crib he don't know where he is.

Hans slowly shook his head.

Yes yes, hell Hans, the kid's scared of having run away.

He don't want to say he done a fool stunt like that. So he
makes the whole thing up. He's just a little kid. He made
the whole thing up.

Hans didn't like that. He didn't want to believe the kid
any more than I did, but if he didn't then the kid had
fooled him sure. He didn't want to believe that either.

No, he said. Is it something you make up? Is it something you come to—raving with frostbite and fever and
not knowing who's there or where you are or anything—
and make up?

Yeah.

No it ain't. Green, black, yellow: you don't make up
them colors neither. You don't make up putting your folks
down cellar where they'll freeze. You don't make up his
not saying anything the whole time or only seeing his back
or exactly what he was wearing. It's more than a make-up;
it's more than a dream. It's like something you see once
and it hits you so hard you never forget it even if you want
to; lies, dreams, pass—this *has* you; it's like something that
sticks to you like burrs, burrs you try to brush off while
you're doing something else, but they never brush off,
they just roll a little, and the first thing you know you
ain't doing what you set out to, you're just trying to get
them burrs off.   I know.   I got things stuck to me
like that. Everybody has.   Pretty soon you get tired trying to pick them off. If they was just burrs, it wouldn't
matter, but they ain't. They never is. The kid saw something that hit him hard like that; hit him so hard that
probably all the time he was running over here he didn't
see anything else but what hit him. Not really. It hit him
so hard he couldn't do anything but spit it out raving
when he come to. It hit him. You don't make things like
that up, Jorge.   No.   He came through the storm,

just like the kid. He had no business coming, but he came. I don't know how or why or when exactly, except it must have been during the blizzard yesterday. He got to the Pedersen place just before or just after it stopped snowing. He got there and he shoved them all in the fruit cellar to freeze and I'll bet he had his reasons.

You got dough stuck to the bottom of Pa's bottle.

I couldn't think of anything else to say. What Hans said sounded right. It sounded right but it couldn't be right. It just couldn't be. Whatever was right, the Pedersen kid had run off from his pa's place probably late yesterday afternoon when the storm let up, and had turned up at our crib this morning. I knew he was here. I knew that much. I'd held him. I'd felt him dead in my hands, only I guess he wasn't dead now. Hans had put him to bed upstairs but I could still see him in the kitchen, so skinny naked, two towels steaming on him, whiskey drooling from the corners of his mouth, lines of dirt between his toes, squeezing ma's dough in the shape of his behind.

I reached for the bottle. Hans held it away.

He didn't see him do it though, I said.

Hans shrugged.

Then he ain't sure.

He's sure, I told you. Do you run out in a blizzard unless you're sure?

It wasn't blizzarding.

It was starting.

I don't run out in blizzards.

Crap.

Hans pointed the doughy end of the bottle at me.

Crap.

He shook it.

You come in from the barn—like this morning. As far

as you know there ain't a gun in yellow gloves in a thousand miles. You come in from the barn not thinking anything special. You just get inside—you just get inside when you see a guy you never saw before, the guy that wasn't in a thousand miles, that wasn't in your mind even, he was so far away, and he's wearing them yellow gloves and that green mackinaw, and he's got me and your ma and pa lined up with our hands back of our necks like this—

Hans hung the bottle and the glass behind his head.

He's got me and your ma and your pa lined up with our hands here back of our necks, and he's got a rifle in between them yellow gloves and he's waving the point of it up and down in front of your ma's face real slow and quiet.

Hans got up and waved the bottle violently in ma's face. She shivered and shooed it away. Hans stopped to come to me. He stood over me, his black eyes buttons on his big face, and I tried to look like I wasn't hunching down any in my chair.

What do you do? Hans roared. You drop a little kid's cold head on the table.

Like hell—

Hans had the bottle in front of him again, smack in my face.

Hans Esbyorn, ma said, don't pester the boy.

Like hell—

Jorge.

I wouldn't run, ma.

Ma sighed. I don't know. But don't yell.

Well christ almighty, ma.

Don't swear neither. Please. You been swearing too much—you and Hans both.

But I wouldn't run.

Yes, Jorge, yes. I'm sure you wouldn't run, she said.

Hans went back and sat down and finished his drink and poured another. He could relax now he'd got me all strung up. He was a fancy bastard.

You'd run all right, he said, running his tongue across his lips. Maybe you'd be right to run. Maybe anybody would. With no gun, with nothing to stop him.

Poor child.   Wheweee.   And what are we going to do with these?

Hang them up, Hed, for christ's sake.

Where?

Well, where do you, mostly?

Oh no, she said, I wouldn't feel right doing that.

Then jesus, Hed, I don't know. Jesus.

Please Hans, please. Those words are hard for me to bear.

She stared at the ceiling.

Dear.   The kitchen's such a mess.   I can't bear to see it.   And the baking's not done.

That's all she could think of. That's all she had to say. She didn't care about me. I didn't count. Not like her kitchen. I wouldn't have run.

Stick the baking, I said.

Shut your face.

He could look as mean as he liked, I didn't care. What was his meanness to me? A blister on my heel, another discomfort, a cold bed. Yet when he took his eyes off me to drink, I felt better. I was going to twist his balls.

All right, I said. All right. All right.

He was lost in his glass, thinking it out.

They're awful cold in that cellar, I said.

There was a little liquor burning in the bottom. I was going to twist his balls like the neck of a sack.

What are you going to do about it?

He was putting his mean look back but it lacked enthusiasm. He was seeing things in his glass.

I saved the kid, didn't I? he finally said.

Maybe you did.

You didn't.

No. I didn't.

It's time you did something then, ain't it?

Why should I? I don't think they're freezing. You're the one who thinks that. You're the one who thinks he ran for help. You're the one. You saved him. All right. You didn't let his head hit the table. I did that. You didn't. No. It was you who rubbed him. All right. You saved him. That wasn't the kid's idea though. He came for help. According to you, that is. He didn't come to be saved. You saved him, but what are you going to do now to help him? You've been feeling mighty, ain't you? thinking how you did it. Still feel like a savior, Hans? How's it feel?

You little bastard.

All right. Little or big. Never mind. You did it all. You found him. You raised the rumpus, ordering everybody around. He was as good as dead. I held him and I felt him. Maybe in your way he was alive, but it was a way that don't count. No—but you couldn't leave him alone. Rubbing. Well I felt him . . . cold . . . christ! Ain't you proud? He was dead, right here, dead. And there weren't no yellow gloves. Now, though, there is. That's what comes of rubbing. Rubbing . . . ain't you proud? You can't believe the kid was lying good enough to fool you. So he was dead. But now he ain't. Not for you. He ain't for you.

He's alive for you too. You're crazy. He's alive for everybody.

No he ain't. He ain't alive for me. He never was. I never

seen him except he was dead. Cold . . . I felt him . . .
christ! Ain't you proud? He's in your bed. All right. You
took him up there. It's your bed he's in, Hans. It was you
he babbled to. You believe him too, so he's alive for you
then. Not for me. Not for me he ain't.

You can't say that.

I am saying it though. Hear me saying?   Rubbing
. . . You didn't know what you was bringing to, did you?
Something besides the kid came through the storm, Hans.
I ain't saying yellow gloves did neither. He didn't. He
couldn't. But something else did. While you was rubbing
you didn't think of that.

You little bastard.

Hans, Hans, please, ma said.

Never mind that. Little or big, like I said. I'm asking
what you're going to do. You believe it. You made it. What
are you going to do about it? It'd be funny if right now
while we're sitting here the kid's dying upstairs.

Jorge, ma said, what an awful thing—in Hans's bed.

All right. But suppose. Suppose you didn't rub enough
—not long and hard enough, Hans. And suppose he dies
up there in your bed. He might. He was cold, I know.
That'd be funny because that yellow gloves—he won't die.
It ain't going to be so easy, killing him.

Hans didn't move or say anything.

I ain't no judge. I ain't no hand at saving, like you said.
It don't make no difference to me. But why'd you start rubbing if you was going to stop? Seems like it'd be terrible
if the Pedersen kid was to have come all that way through
the storm, scared and freezing, and you was to have done
all that rubbing and saving so he could come to and tell
you his fancy tale and have you believe it, if you ain't go-

ing to do nothing now but sit and hold hands with that bottle. That ain't a burr so easy picked off.

Still he didn't say anything.

Fruit cellars get mighty cold. Of course they ain't supposed to freeze.

I leaned back easy in my chair. Hans just sat.

They ain't supposed to freeze so it's all right.

The top of the kitchen table looked muddy where it showed. Patches of dough and pools of water were scattered all over it. There were rusty streaks through the paste and the towels had run. Everywhere there were little sandy puddles of whiskey and water. Something, it looked like whiskey, dripped slowly to the floor and with the water trickled to the puddle by the pile of clothes. The boxes sagged. There were thick black tracks around the table and the stove. I thought it was funny the boxes had gone so fast. The bottle and the glass were posts around which Big Hans had his hands.

Ma began picking up the kid's clothes. She picked them up one at a time, delicately, by their ends and corners, lifting a sleeve like you would the flat, burned, crooked leg of a frog dead of summer to toss it from the road. They didn't seem human things, the way her hands pinched together on them, but animal—dead and rotting things out of the ground. She took them away and when she came back I wanted to tell her to bury them—to hide them somehow quick under the snow—but she scared me, the way she came with her arms out, trembling, fingers coming open and closed, moving like a combine between rows.

I heard the dripping clearly, and I heard Hans swallow. I heard the water and the whiskey fall. I heard the frost on the window melt to the sill and drop into the sink. Hans poured whiskey in his glass. I looked past Hans and Pa was watching from the doorway. His nose and eyes were red, his feet in red slippers.

What's this about the Pedersen kid? he said.

Ma stood behind him with a mop.

3

Ever think of a horse? Pa said.

A horse? Where'd he get a horse?

Anywhere—on the way—anyplace.

Could he make it on a horse?

He made it on something.

Not on a horse though.

Not on his feet.

I ain't saying he made it on anything.

Horses can't get lost.

Yes they can.

They got a sense.

That's a lot of manure about horses.

In a blizzard a horse'll go home.

That's so.

You let them go and they go home.

That's so.

If you steal a horse, and let him go, he'll take you to the barn you stole him from.

Couldn't give him his head then.

Must have really rode him then.

And known where he was going.

Yeah, and gone there.

If he had a horse.

Yeah, if he had a horse.

If he stole a horse before the storm and rode it a ways,

then when the snow came, the horse would be too far off and wouldn't know how to head for home.

They got an awful good sense.

Manure.

What difference does it make? He made it. What difference does it make how? Hans said.

I'm considering if he could have, Pa said.

And I'm telling you he did, Hans said.

And I've been telling you he didn't. The kid made the whole thing up, I said.

The horse'd stop. He'd put his head into the wind and stop.

I've seen them put their rears in.

They always put their heads in.

He could jockey him.

If he was gentle and not too scared.

A plower is gentle.

Some are.

Some don't like to be rid.

Some don't like strangers neither.

Some.

What the hell, Hans said.

Pa laughed. I'm just considering, he said. Just considering, Hans, that's all.

Pa'd seen the bottle. Right away. He'd been blinking. But he hadn't missed it. He'd seen it and the glass in Hans's hand. I'd expected him to say something. So had Hans. He'd held on to the glass long enough so no one would get the idea he was afraid to, then he'd set it down casual, like he hadn't any reason to hold it or any reason to put it down, but was putting it down anyway, without thinking. I'd grinned but he hadn't seen me, or else he made out he hadn't. Pa'd kept his mouth shut about the bottle though he'd seen it right away. I guess we had the Pedersen kid to thank for that, though we had him to thank for the bottle too.

It's his own fault for putting out all them snow fences, Pa said. You'd think, being here the time he has, he'd know the forces better.

Pedersen just likes to be ready, Pa, that's all.

Hell he does. He likes to *get* ready, that cock. Get, get, get, get. He's always getting ready, but he ain't never *got* ready. Not yet, he ain't. Last summer, instead of minding his crops, he got ready for hoppers. Christ. Who wants hoppers? Well that's the way to get hoppers—that's the sure way—get ready for hoppers.

Bull.

Bull? You say bull, Hans, hey?

I say bull, yeah.

You're one to get ready, ain't you? Like Pedersen, ain't you? Oh what a wrinkled scrotum you got, with all that thinking. You'd put out poison for a million, hey? You know what you'd get? Two million. Wise, oh these wise men, yeah. Pedersen *asked* for hoppers. He *begged* for hoppers. He went on his knees for hoppers. So me? I got hoppers too. Now he's gone and asked for snow, gone on his knees for snow, wrung his fingers off for snow. Is he ready, tell me? Hey? Snow? For real snow? Anybody ever ready for real snow? Oh jesus, that fool. He should have kept his kid behind them fences. What business—what—what business—to send him here. By god, a man's got to keep his stock up.   Look— Pa pointed out the window. See—see—what did I tell you—snowing . . . always snowing.

You seen a winter it didn't snow?

You were ready, I guess.

It always snows.

You were ready for the Pedersen kid too, I guess. You was just out there waiting for him, cooling your cod.

Pa laughed and Hans got red.

Pedersen's a fool. Wise men can't be taught. Oh no, not old holy Pete. He never learned all the things that can fall out the sky and happen to wheat. His neck's bent all the time too, studying clouds—hah, that shit. He don't even keep an eye on his kid in a blizzard. A man by god's got to keep his stock up. But you'll keep an eye out for him, hey, Hans? You're a bigger fool because you're fatter.

Hans's face was red and swollen like the skin around a splinter. He reached out and picked up the glass. Pa was sitting on a corner of the kitchen table, swinging a leg. The glass was near his knee. Hans reached by Pa and took it. Pa watched and swung his leg, laughing. The bottle was on the counter and Pa watched closely while Hans took it.

Ah, you plan to drink some of my whiskey, Hans?

Yeah.

It'd be polite to ask.

I ain't asking, Hans said, tilting the bottle.

I suppose I'd better make some biscuits, ma said.

Hans looked up at her, keeping the bottle tilted. He didn't pour.

Biscuits, ma? I said.

I ought to have something for Mr. Pedersen and I haven't a thing.

Hans straightened the bottle.

There's a thing to consider, he said, beginning to smile. Why ain't Pedersen here looking for his kid?

Why should he be?

Hans winked at me through his glass. No wink would make me a friend of his.

Why not? We're nearest. If the kid ain't here he can ask us to help him hunt.

Fat chance.

He ain't come through. How do you consider that?

I ain't considering it, Pa said.

Why ain't you? Seems to me like something worth real long and fancy considering.

No it ain't.

Ain't it?

Pedersen's a fool.

So you like to say. I've heard you often enough. All right, maybe he is. How long do you expect he'll wander around looking before he comes over this way?

A long time. A long time maybe.

The kid's been gone a long time.

Pa arranged his nightshirt over his knee. He had on the striped one.

How long's a long time? Hans said.

The kid's been gone.

Oh Pedersen'll be here before too long now, Pa said.

And if he don't?

What do you mean, if he don't? Then he don't. By god, he don't. It ain't no skin off my ass. If he don't he don't. I don't care what he does.

Yeah, Big Hans said. Yeah.

Pa folded his arms, looking like a judge. He swung his leg. Where'd you find the bottle?

Hans jiggled it.

You're pretty good at hiding, ain't you?

I'm asking the questions. Where'd you find it?

Hans was enjoying himself too much.

I didn't.

Jorge, hey. Pa chewed his lip. So you're the nosy bastard.

He didn't look at me and it didn't seem like he was talking to me at all. He said it like I wasn't there and he was thinking out loud. Awake, asleep—it didn't fool me.

It wasn't me, Pa, I said.

I tried to get Hans's attention so he'd shut up but he was enjoying himself.

Little Hans ain't no fool, Big Hans said.

No.

Now Pa wasn't paying attention.

He ain't no kin to you, Pa said.

Why ain't he here then? He'd be looking too. Why ain't he here?

Gracious, I'd forgot all about Little Hans, ma said, quickly taking a bowl from the cupboard.

Hed, what are you up to? Pa said.

Oh, biscuits.

Biscuits? What in hell for? Biscuits. I don't want any biscuits. Make some coffee. All this time you been just standing around.

For Pedersen and little Hans. They'll be coming and they'll want some biscuits and coffee, and I'll put out some elderberry jelly. The coffee needed reminding, Magnus, thank you.

Who found the bottle?

She scooped some flour from the bin.

Pa'd been sitting, swinging. Now he stopped and stood up.

Who found it? Who found it? God dammit, who found it? Which one of them was it?

Ma was trying to measure the flour but her hands shook.
The flour ran off the scoop and fell across the rim of the
cup, and I thought, Yeah, You'd have run, Yeah, Your
hands shake.

Why don't you ask Jorge? Big Hans said.

How I hated him, putting it on me, the coward. And he
had thick arms.

That snivel, Pa said.

Hans laughed so his chest shook.

He couldn't find nothing I hid.

You're right there, Hans said.

I could, I said. I have.

A liar, Hans, hey? You found it.

Pa was somehow pleased and sat on the corner of the
table again. Was it Hans he hated most, or me?

I never said Jorge found it.

I've got a liar working for me. A thief and a liar. Why
should I keep a liar? I'm just soft on him, I guess, and
he's got such a sweet face. But why should I keep a thief
. . . little movey eyes like traveling specks . . . why?

I ain't like you. I don't spend every day drinking just to
sleep the night and then sleep half the day too, fouling
your bed and your room and half the house.

You been doing your share of lying down. Little Hans is
half your size and worth twice. You—you got a small dick.

Pa's words didn't come out clear.

How about Little Hans? Little Hans ain't showed up.
Folks must be getting pretty worried at the Pedersens'.
They'd like some news maybe. But Pedersen don't come.
Little Hans don't come. There's a thousand drifts out there.
The kid might be under any one. If anybody's seen him, we
have, and if we haven't, nobody's going to till spring, or

maybe if the wind shifts, which ain't likely. But nobody comes to ask. That's pretty funny, I'd say.

You're an awful full-up bastard, Pa said.

I'm just considering, that's all.

Where'd you find it?

I forgot. It needed reminding. I was going to have a drink.

Where?

You're pretty good at hiding, Hans said.

I'm asking. Where?

I didn't, I told you, I didn't find it. Jorge didn't find it neither.

You bastard, Hans, I said.

It hatched, Hans said. Like the fellow, you know, who blew in. He hatched. Or maybe the kid found it—had it hid under his coat.

Who? Pa roared, standing up quick.

Oh Hed found it. You don't hide worth a damn and Hed found it easy. She knew right away where to look.

Shut up, Hans, I said.

Hans tilted the bottle.

She must have known where it was a long time now. Maybe she knows where they're all hid. You ain't very smart. Or maybe she's took it up herself, eh? And it ain't yours at all, maybe that.

Big Hans poured himself a drink. Then Pa kicked the glass out of Hans's hand. Pa's slipper flew off and sailed by Hans's head and bounced off the wall. The glass didn't break. It fell by the sink and rolled slow by ma's feet, leaving a thin line. The scoop flew a light white cloud. There was whiskey on Hans's shirt and on the wall and cupboards, and a splash on the floor where the glass had hit.

Ma had her arms wrapped around her chest. She looked faint and she was whewing and moaning.

Okay, Pa said, we'll go. We'll go right now, Hans. I hope to god you get a bullet in your belly. Jorge, go upstairs and see if the little sonofabitch is still alive.

Hans was rubbing the spots on his shirt and licking his lips when I hunched past Pa and went out.

PART TWO

1

There wasn't any wind. The harness creaked, the wood creaked, the runners made a sound like a saw working easy, and everything was white about Horse Simon's feet. Pa had the reins between his knees and he and Hans and I kept ourselves close together. We bent our heads and clenched our feet and wished we could huddle both hands in one pocket. Only Hans was breathing through his nose. We didn't speak. I wished my lips could warm my teeth. The blanket we had wasn't worth a damn. It was just as cold underneath and Pa drank from a bottle by him on the seat.

I tried to hold the feeling I'd had starting out when we'd hitched up Horse Simon when I was warm and decided to risk the North Corn Road to the Pedersen place. It catty-cornered and came up near the grove behind his barn. We figured we could look at things from there. I tried to hold the feeling but it was warm as new bath water and just as hard to hold. It was like I was setting out to do something special and big—like a knight setting out—worth remembering. I dreamed coming in from the barn and finding his back to me in the kitchen and wrestling with him and pulling him down and beating the stocking cap off his head with the barrel of the gun. I dreamed coming in from the barn still blinking with the light and seeing him there and picking the shovel up and taking him on. That had been then, when I was warm, when I was doing something big, heroic even, and well worth remembering. I couldn't put the feeling down in Pedersen's back yard or Pedersen's porch or barn. I couldn't see myself, or him, there. I could only see him back where I wasn't any more—standing quiet in our kitchen with his gun going slowly up and down in ma's face and ma shooing it away and at the same time trying not to move an inch for getting shot.

When I got good and cold the feeling slipped away. I couldn't imagine him with his gun or cap or yellow gloves. I couldn't imagine me coming on to him. We weren't anyplace and I didn't care. Pa drove by staring down the sloping white road and drank from his bottle. Hans rattled his heels on the back of the seat. I just tried to keep my mouth shut and breathe and not think why in the name of the good jesus christ I had to.

It wasn't like a sleigh ride on an early winter evening when the air is still, the earth is warm, and the stars are flakes being born that will not fall. The air was still all right, the sun straight up and cold. Behind us on the trough that marked the road I saw our runners and the holes that Simon tore. Ahead of us it melted into drifts. Pa squinted like he saw where he knew it really went. Horse Simon steamed. Ice hung from his harness. Snow caked his belly. I was afraid the crust might cut his knees and I wanted a drink out of Pa's bottle. Big Hans seemed asleep and shivered in his dreams. My rear was god almighty sore.

We reached a drift across the road and Pa eased Simon round her where he knew there wasn't any fence. Pa figured to go back to the road but after we got round the bank I could see there wasn't any point in that. There were rows of high drifts across it.

They ain't got no reason to do that, Pa said.

It was the first thing Pa'd said since he told me to go upstairs and see if the Pedersen kid was still alive. He hadn't looked alive to me but I'd said I guessed he was. Pa'd gone and got his gun first, without dressing, one foot still bare so he favored it, and took the gun upstairs cradled in his arm, broke, and pointing down. He had a dark speckled spot on the rump of his nightshirt where he'd sat on the table. Hans had his shotgun and the forty-five he'd stolen from the Navy. He made me load it and when I'd stuck it in my belt he'd said it'd likely go off and keep me from ever getting out to stud. The gun felt like a chunk of ice against my belly and the barrel dug.

Ma'd put some sandwiches and a Thermos of coffee in a sack. The coffee'd be cold. My hands would be cold when I ate mine even if I kept my gloves on. Chewing would be painful. The lip of the Thermos would be cold if I drank out of that, and I'd spill some on my chin which would dry to ice; or if I used the cup, the tin would stick to my lip like lousy liquor you didn't want to taste by licking off, and it would burn and then tear my skin coming away.

Simon went into a hole. He couldn't pull out so he panicked and the sleigh skidded. We'd had crust but now the front right runner broke through and we braked in the soft snow underneath. Pa made quiet impatient noises and calmed Simon down.

That was damn fool, Hans said.

He lost his footing. Jesus, I ain't the horse.

I don't know. Simon's a turd binder, Hans said.

Pa took a careful drink.

Go round and lead him out.

Jorge is on the outside.

Go round and lead him out.

You. You go round. You led him in.

Go round and lead him out.

Sometimes the snow seemed as blue as the sky. I don't know which seemed colder.

Oh god I'll go, I said. I'm on the outside.

Your old man's on the outside, Hans said.

I guess I know where I am, Pa said. I guess I know where I'm staying.

Can't you let up, for christ's sake? I'm going, I said.

I threw off the blanket and stood up but I was awful stiff. The snow dazzle struck me and the pain of the space around us. Getting out I rammed my ankle against the sideboard's iron brace. The pain shot up my leg and shook me like an ax handle will when you strike wrong. I cursed, taking my time jumping off. The snow looked as stiff and hard as cement and I could only think of the jar.

You've known where that brace was for ten years, Pa said.

The snow went to my crotch. The gun bit. I waded round the hole trying to keep on tiptoe and the snow away from my crotch but it wasn't any use.

You practicing to be a bird? Hans said.

I got hold of Horse Simon and tried to coax him out. Pa swore at me from his seat. Simon kicked and thrashed and lunged ahead. The front right runner dug in. The sleigh swung around on it and the left side hit Simon's back legs hard behind the knees. Simon reared and kicked a piece out of the side of the sleigh and then pulled straight ahead tangling the reins. The sleigh swung back again and the right runner pulled loose with a jerk. Pa's bottle rolled. From where I sat in the snow I saw him grab for it. Simon went on ahead. The sleigh slid sideways into Simon's hole and the left runner went clear of the snow. Simon pulled up short though Pa had lost the reins and was holding on and yelling about his bottle. I had snow in my eyes and down my neck.

Simon didn't have no call to do that, Hans said, mimicking Pa.

Where's my bottle? Pa said, looking over the side of the sleigh at the torn snow. Jorge, go find my bottle. It fell in the snow here somewheres.

I tried to brush the snow off without getting more in my pockets and up my sleeves and down my neck.

You get out and find it. It's your bottle.

Pa leaned way over.

If you hadn't been so god damn dumb it wouldn't have fell out. Where'd you learn to lead a horse? You never learned that dumb trick from me. Of all the god damn dumb tricks I never seen any dumber.

Pa waved his arm in a circle.

That bottle fell out about here. It couldn't have got far. It was corked, thank god. I won't lose none.

Snow was slipping down the hollow of my back. The forty-five had slipped through my belt. I was afraid it would go off like Big Hans said. I kept my right forearm pressed against it. I didn't want it slipping off down my pants. I didn't like it. Pa shouted directions.

You hid it, I said. You're such a hand at hiding. You find it then. I ain't good at finding. You said so yourself.

Jorge, you know I got to have that bottle.

Then get off your ass and find it.

You know I got to have it.

Then get off.

If I get down off here, it ain't the bottle I'm coming after. I'll hold you under till you drown, you little smart-talking snot.

I started kicking around in the snow.

Hans giggled.

There's a trace broke, he said.

What's so damn funny?

I told you that trace was worn.

I kicked about. Pa followed my feet.

Hell. Not that way. He pointed. You know about everything there is, Hans, I guess, he said, still watching me. First little thing you figure out you tell somebody about. Then somebody else knows. So then they can do what needs to be done, and you don't have to— jesus, not there, *there*. Don't it, Hans? don't it always let you out?   You ain't going deep enough.   I never figured that out. How come somebody else's knowing always lets you out? You're just a pimp for jobs, I guess. You ain't going deep enough, I said.

It ain't my job to fix traces.

Hey, get your hands in it, *your hands*. It's clean. You always was that way about manure. Why ain't it your job? Too busy screwing sheep?   Try over there. You ought to have hit it. No, *there,* not there.

I never fixed traces.

Christ, they never needed fixing while you been here hardly. Jorge, will you stop nursing that fool gun with your cock and use both hands.

I'm cold, Pa.

So'm I. That's why you got to find that bottle.

If I find it do I get a drink?

Ain't you growed up—a man—since yesterday!

I've had a few, Pa.

Ha. Of what, hey? Hear that, Hans? He's had a few. For medicine maybe, like your ma says. The spirits, the spirits, Jorgen Segren . . . ha.   He's had a few he says. He's had a few.

Pa.

He's had a few. He's had a few. He's had a few.

Pa. I'm cold, Pa.

Maybe. Only look, for god's sake, don't just thrash about like a fool chicken.

Well, we're finished anyway, Hans said.

We're finished if we don't find that bottle.

You're finished, maybe. You're the only one who needs that bottle. Jorge and I don't need it, but there you are, old man, eh? Lost in the snow.

My gloves were wet. Snow had jammed under my sleeves. It was working down into my boots. I stopped to pick some out with a finger if I could.

Maybe some of ma's coffee is still hot, I said.

Say.   Yeah.   Maybe.   But that's *my* coffee, boy. I never got none. I ain't even had breakfast. What are you stopping for? Come on. Hell, Jorge, it's cold.

I know that better than you. You're sitting there all nice and dry, bossing; but I'm doing all the work and getting the snow inside me.

Say.   Yeah.   That's right.

Pa leaned back and grinned. He clutched the blanket to him and Hans pulled it back.

It's easier to keep warm moving around, anybody knows

that. Ain't that right, Hans? It's easier to keep warm moving, ain't it?

Yeah, Hans said. If you ain't got a blanket.

See there, Jorge, hey? You just keep good and warm
. . . stirring. It'd be a pity if your pee should freeze. And
moving around good prevents calluses on the bottom.
Don't it, Hans?

Yeah.

Hans here knows. He's nothing but calluses.

You'll wear out your mouth.

I can't find it, Pa. Maybe some of ma's coffee is still
warm.

You damn snivel—you ain't looking. Get tramping
proper like I told you and find it. Find it fast, you hear.
You ain't getting back up on this sleigh until you do.

I started jumping up and down, not too fast, and Pa
blew his nose with his fingers.

Cold makes the snot run, he says, real wise.

If I found the bottle I'd kick it deep under the snow.
I'd kick it and keep kicking it until it sank under a drift.
Pa wouldn't know where it was. I wouldn't come back to
the sleigh either. They weren't going anywhere anyway.
I'd go home though it was a long walk. Looking back I
could see our tracks in the trough of the road. They came
together before I lost them. It would be warm at home and
worth the walk. It was frightening—the endless white
space. I'd have to keep my head down. Winded slopes and
rises all around me. I'd never wanted to go to Pedersen's.
That was Hans's fight, and Pa's. I was just cold . . . cold
. . . and scared and sick of snow. That's what I'd do if I
found it—kick it under a drift. Then later, a lot later in
the spring one day I'd come out here and find the old bottle

sticking out of the rotting snow and stuck in the mud like dough, and I'd hide it back of the barn and have a drink whenever I wanted. I'd get some real cigarettes, maybe a carton, and hide them too. Then someday I'd come in and Pa'd smell whiskey on me and think I'd found one of his hiding places. He'd be mad as hell and not know what to say. It'd be spring and he'd think he'd taken them all in like he always did, harvesting the crop like he said.

I looked to see if there was something to mark the place by but it was all gone under snow. There was only the drifts and the deep holes of snow and the long runnered trough of the road. It might be a mudhole we was stuck in. In the spring cattails might grow up in it and the blackbirds come. Or it might be low and slimy at first and then caked dry and cracked. Pa'd never find out how I came by the bottle. Someday he'd act too big and I'd stick his head under the pump or slap his skinny rump with the backside of a fork full of manure. Hans would act smart and then someday—

Jee-suss, will you move?

I'm cold, Pa.

You're going to be a pig's size colder.

Well, we're finished anyway, Hans said. We ain't going nowhere. The trace is broke.

Pa stopped watching me thrash the snow. He frowned at Horse Simon. Simon was standing quiet with his head down.

Simon's shivering, he said. I should have remembered he'd be heated up. It's so cold I forgot.

Pa yanked the blanket off of Hans like Hans was a bed he was stripping, and jumped down. Hans yelled but Pa didn't pay attention. He threw the blanket over Simon.

We got to get Simon moving. He'll stiffen up.

Pa ran his hand tenderly down Simon's legs.

The sleigh don't seem to have hurt him none.

The trace is broke.

Then Hans stood up. He beat his arms against his body and jigged.

We'll have to walk him home, he said.

Home, hey, Pa said, giving Hans a funny sidewise look.

It's a long walk.

You can ride him then, Hans said.

Pa looked real surprised and even funnier. It wasn't like Hans to say that. It was too cold. It made Hans generous. There was some good in cold.

Why?

Pa waded, patting Simon, but he kept his eye on Hans like it was Hans might kick.

Hans let out a long impatient streamer.

Jesus—the trace.

Hans was being real cautious. Hans was awful cold. His nose was red. Pa's was white but it didn't look froze. It just looked white like it usually did—like it was part of him had died long ago. I wondered what color my nose was. Mine was bigger and sharper at the end. It was ma's nose, ma said. I was bigger all over than Pa. I was taller than Hans too. I pinched my nose but my gloves were wet so I couldn't feel anything except how my nose hurt when I pinched it. It couldn't be too cold. Hans was pointing at the ends of the trace which were trailing in the snow.

Tie a knot in it, Pa was saying.

It won't hold, Hans said, shaking his head.

Tie a good one, it will.

It's too cold to get a good knot. Leather's too stiff.

Hell no, it ain't too stiff.

Well, it's too thick. Can't knot something like that.

You can do it.

She'll pull crooked.

Let her pull crooked.

Simon won't work well pulling her crooked.

He'll have to do the best he can. I ain't going to leave this sleigh out here. Hell, it might snow again before I got back with a new trace.   Or you got back, hey?

When I get home I'm going to stay there and I'm going to eat my breakfast if it's suppertime. I ain't coming back out here trying to beat another blizzard and wind up like the Pedersen kid.

Yeah, Hans said, nodding. Let's get this damn thing out of here and get Simon home before he stiffens. I'll tie the trace.

Hans got down and I stopped kicking. Pa watched Hans real careful from his side of Horse Simon and I could see him smiling like he'd thought of something dirty. I started to get on the sleigh but Pa shouted and made me hunt some more.

Maybe we'll find it when we move the sleigh, I said.

Pa laughed but not at what I said. He opened his mouth wide, looking at Hans, and laughed hard, though his laugh was quiet.

Yeah, maybe we will, he said, and gave Simon an extra hard pat. Maybe we will, hey, at that.

I didn't find the bottle and Big Hans tied the trace. He had to take his gloves off to do it but he did it quick and I had to admire him for it. Pa coaxed Simon while Hans, boosting, heaved. She got clear and suddenly was going— skidding out. I heard a noise like a light bulb busting. A brown stain spread over the sleigh track. Pa peered over his shoulder at the stain, his hands on the halter, his legs wide in the snow.

Oh no, he said.   Oh no.

But Big Hans broke up. He lifted a leg clear of the snow. He hit himself. His shoulders shook. He hugged his belly. He rocked back and forth. Oh—oh—oh, he screamed, and he held his sides. Tears streamed down his cheeks. You— you—you, he howled. Hans's cheeks, his nose, his head was red. Found—found—found, he choked.

Everything about Pa was frozen. The white hair that stuck out from his hat looked hard and sharp and seemed to shine like snow. Big Hans went on laughing. I never saw him so humored. He staggered, weakening—Pa as still as a stake. Hans began to heave and gasp, running down. In a minute he'd be cold again, worn out, and then he'd wish he could drink out of that bottle. Its breaking had made him drunk. The stain had stopped spreading and was fading, the snow bubbling and sagging. We could melt and drink the snow, I thought. I wanted that bottle back bad. I hated Hans. I'd hate Hans forever—as long as there was snow.

Hans was puffing quietly when Pa told me to get in the sleigh. Then Hans climbed awkwardly on. Pa took the blanket off Horse Simon and threw it in the sleigh. Then he got Simon started. I pulled the blanket over me and tried to stop shivering. Our stove, I thought, was black . . . god . . . black . . . lovely sooty black . . . and glowed rich as cherry through its holes. I thought of the kettle steaming on it, the steam alive, hissing white and warm, not like my breath coming slow and cloudy and hanging heavy and dead in the still air.

Hans jumped.

Where we going? he said. Where we going?

Pa didn't say nothing.

This ain't the way, Hans said. Where we going?

The gun was an ache in my stomach. Pa squinted at the snow.

For christ's sake, Hans said. I'm sorry about the bottle. But Pa drove.

2

Barberry had got in the grove and lay about the bottom of the trees and hid in snow. The mossycups went high, their branches put straight out, the trunk bark black and wrinkled. There were spots where I could see the frosted curls of dead grass frozen to the ground and high hard-driven piles of snow the barberry stuck its black barbs from. The wind had thrown some branches in the drifts. The sun made shadows of more branches on their sides and bent them over ridges. The ground rose up behind the grove. The snow rose. Pa and Hans had their shotguns. We followed along the drifts and kept down low. I could hear us breathing and the snow, earth, and our boots squeaking. We went slow and all of us was cold.

Above the snow, through the branches, I could see the peak of Pedersen's house, and nearer by, the roof of Pedersen's barn. We were making for the barn. Once in a while Pa would stop and watch for smoke but there was nothing in the sky. Big Hans bumped into a bush and got a barb through his woolen glove. Pa motioned Hans to hush. I could feel my gun through my glove—heavy and cold. Where we went the ground was driven nearly bare. Mostly I kept my eyes on Big Hans's heels because it hurt my neck so to look up. When I did, for smoke, the faint breeze caught my cheek and drew the skin across the bone. I didn't think of much except how to follow Hans's heels and how, even underneath my cap, my ears burned, and how my lips hurt and how just moving made me ache. Pa followed where a crazy wind had got in among the oaks and blown the snow bare from the ground in flat patches against their trunks. Sometimes we had to break through a small drift or we'd have gone in circles. The roof of Pedersen's house grew above the banks as we went until finally we passed across one corner of it and I saw the chimney very black in the sun stick up from the steep bright pitch like a dead cigar rough-ashed with snow.

I thought: the fire's dead, they must be froze.

Pa stopped and nodded at the chimney.

You see, Hans said unhappily.

Just then I saw a cloud of snow float from the crest of a drift and felt my eyes smart. Pa looked quick at the sky but it was clear. Hans stomped his feet, hung his head, swore in a whisper.

Well, Pa said, it looks like we made this trip for nothing. Nobody's to home.

The Pedersens are all dead, Hans said, still looking down.

Shut up. I saw Pa's lips were chapped . . . a dry dry hole now. A muscle jumped along his jaw.   Shut up, he said.

A faint ribbon of snow suddenly shot from the top of the chimney and disappeared. I stood as still as I could in the tubes of my clothes, the snow shifting strangely in my eyes, alone, frightened by the space that was bowling up inside me, a white blank glittering waste like the waste outside, coldly burning, roughed with waves, and I wanted to curl up, face to my thighs, but I knew my tears would freeze my lashes together. My stomach began to growl.

What's the matter with you, Jorge? Pa said.

Nothing. I giggled. I'm cold, Pa, I guess, I said. I belched.

Jesus, Hans said loudly.

Shut up.

I poked at the snow with the toe of my boot. I wanted to sit down and if there'd been anything to sit on I would have. All I wanted was to go home or sit down. Hans had stopped stomping and was staring back through the trees toward the way we'd come.

Anybody in that house, Pa said, would have a fire.

He sniffed and rubbed his sleeve across his nose.

Anybody—see? He began raising his voice. Anybody who was in that house now would have a fire. The Pedersens is all most likely out hunting that fool kid. They probably tore ass off without minding the furnace. Now it's out. His voice got braver. Anybody who might have come along while they was gone, and gone in, would have started a fire someplace first thing, and we'd see the smoke. It's too damn cold not to.

Pa took the shotgun he'd carried broken over his left arm and turned the barrel over, slow and deliberate. Two shells fell out and he stuffed them in his coat pocket.

That means there ain't anybody to home. There ain't no smoke, he said with emphasis, and that means there ain't *no*body.

Big Hans sighed. Okay, he muttered from a way off. Let's go home.

I wanted to sit down. Here was the sofa, here the bed— mine—white and billowy. And the stairs, cold and snapping. And I had the dry cold toothaching mouth I always had at home, and the cold storm in my belly, and my pinched eyes. There was the print of the kid's rear in the dough. I wanted to sit down. I wanted to go back where we'd tied up Horse Simon and sit numb in the sleigh.

Yes yes yes, let's, I said.

Pa smiled—oh the bastard—the *bastard*—and he didn't know half what I knew now, numb in the heart the way I felt, and with my burned-off ears.

We could at least leave a note saying Big Hans saved their kid. Seems to me like the only neighborly thing to do. And after all the way we come. Don't it you?

What the hell do you know about what's neighborly? Hans shouted.

With a jerk he dumped his shotgun shells into the snow and kicked at them until one skidded into a drift and only the brass showed. The other sank in the snow before it broke. Black powder spilled out under his feet.

Pa laughed.

Come on, Pa, I'm cold, I said. Look, I ain't brave. I ain't. I don't care. All I am is cold.

Quit whimpering, we're all cold. Big Hans here is awful cold.

Sure, ain't you?

Hans was grinding the black grains under.

Yeah, Pa said, grinning. Some.   I'm some. He turned around. Think you can find your way back, Jorge?

I got going and he laughed again, loud and ugly, damn his soul. I hated him. Jesus, how I did. But no more like a father. Like the burning space.

I never did like that bastard Pedersen anyway, he said as we started. Pedersen's one of them that's always asking for trouble. On his knees for it all the time. Let him find out about his kid himself. He knows where we live. It ain't neighborly but I never said I wanted him a neighbor.

Yeah, Hans said. Let the old bastard find out himself.

He should have kept his kid behind them fences. What business did he have, sending his kid to us to take care of? He went and asked for snow. He went on his knees for snow. Was he ready? Hey? Was he? For *snow?* Nobody's ever ready for *snow.*

The old bastard wouldn't have come to tell you if it'd been me who'd been lost, I said, but I wasn't minding my words at all, I was just talking. Neighbor all over him, I said, he has it coming. I was feeling the sleigh moving under me.

Can't tell about holy Pete, Hans said.

I was going fast. I didn't care about keeping low. I had my eyes on the spaces between trees. I was looking for the place where we'd left Simon and the sleigh. I thought I'd see Simon first, maybe his breath above a bank or beside the trunk of a tree. I slipped on a little snow the wind hadn't blown from the path we'd took. I still had the gun in my right hand so I lost my balance. When I put out my left for support, it went into a drift to my elbow and into the barberry thorns. I jerked back and fell hard. Hans and Pa found it funny. But the legs that lay in front of me weren't mine. I'd gone out in the blazing air. It was queer. Out of the snow I'd kicked away with my foot stuck a horse's hoof and I didn't feel the least terror or surprise.

Looks like a hoof, I said.

Hans and Pa were silent. I looked up at them, far away. Nothing now. Three men in the snow. A red scarf and some mittens . . . somebody's ice and coal . . . the picture for January. But behind them on the blank hills? Then it rushed over me and I thought: this is as far as he rid him. I looked at the hoof and the shoe which didn't belong in the picture. No dead horses for January. And on the snowhills there would be wild sled tracks and green

trees and falling toboggans. This is as far. Or a glazed
lake and rowdy skaters. Three men. On his ass: one. Dead
horse and gun. And the question came to me very clearly,
as if out of the calendar a girl had shouted: are you going
to get up and walk on? Maybe it was the Christmas picture. The big log and the warm orange wood I was
sprawled on in my flannel pajamas. I'd just been given a
pistol that shot BBs. And the question was: was I going to
get up and walk on? Hans's shoes, and Pa's, were as steady
as the horse's. Were they hammered on? Their bodies
stolen? Who'd left them standing here? And Christmas
cookies cut in the shape of the kid's dead wet behind . . .
with maybe a cherry to liven the pale dough . . . a coal
from the stove. But I couldn't just say that looks like a
hoof or that looks like a shoe and go right on because Hans
and Pa were waiting behind me in their wool hats and
pounding mittens . . . like a picture for January. Smiling.
I was learning to skate.

Looks like this is as far as he rid him.

Finally Pa said in a flat voice: what are you talking
about?

You said he had a horse, Pa.

What are you talking about?

This here horse.

Ain't you never seen a shoe before?

It's just a horse's hoof, Hans said. Let's get on.

What are you talking about? Pa said again.

The man who scared the Pedersen kid. The man he saw.

Manure, Pa said. It's one of Pedersen's horses. I recognize the shoe.

That's right, Big Hans said.

Pedersen only has one horse.

This here's it, Big Hans said.

This horse's brown, ain't it?

Pedersen's horse has got two brown hind feet. I remember, Big Hans said.

His is black.

It's got two brown hind feet.

I started to brush away some snow. I knew Pedersen's horse was black.

What the hell, Hans said. Come on. It's too cold to stand here and argue about the color of Pedersen's god damn horse.

Pedersen's horse is black, Pa said. He don't have any brown on him at all.

Big Hans turned angrily on Pa. You said you recognized his shoe.

I thought I did.   It ain't.

I kept scraping snow away. Hans leaned down and pushed me. The horse was white where frozen snow clung to his hide.

He's brown, Hans. Pedersen's horse is black. This one's brown.

Hans kept pushing at me. God damn you, he was saying over and over in a funny high voice.

You knew all along it wasn't Pedersen's horse.

It went on like singing. I got up carefully, taking the safety off. Later in the winter maybe somebody would stumble on his shoes sticking out of the snow. Shooting Hans seemed like something I'd done already. I knew where he kept his gun—under those magazines in his drawer—and though I'd really never thought of it before, the whole thing moved before me now so naturally it must have happened that way. Of course I shot them all—Pa in his bed, ma in her kitchen, Hans when he came in from his rounds. They wouldn't look much different dead than alive only they wouldn't be so loud.

Jorge, now—look out with that thing, Jorge.   Jorge.

His shotgun had fallen in the snow. He was holding both hands in front of him. Afterwards I stood alone in every room.

You're yellow, Hans.

He was backing slowly, fending me off—fending—fending—

Jorge . . . Jorge . . . hey now . . . Jorge . . . Like singing.

Afterwards I looked through his magazines, my hand on my pecker, hot from head to foot.

I've shot you, yellow Hans. You can't shout or push no more or goose me in the barn.

Hey now wait, Jorge—listen— What?   Jorge . . . wait . . . Like singing.

Afterwards only the wind and the warm stove. Shivering I rose on my toes. Pa came up and I moved the gun to take him in. I kept it moving back and forth . . . Hans and Pa . . . Pa and Hans. Gone. Snow piling in the window corners. In the spring I'd shit with the door open, watching the blackbirds.

Don't be a damn fool, Jorge, Pa said. I know you're cold. We'll be going home.

. . . yellow yellow yellow yellow . . . Like singing.

Now Jorge, I ain't yellow, Pa said, smiling pleasantly.

I've shot you both with bullets.

Don't be a fool.

The whole house with bullets. You too.

Funny I don't feel it.

They never does, do they? Do rabbits?

He's crazy, jesus, Mag, he's crazy—

I never did want to. I never hid it like you did, I said. I never believed him. I ain't the yellow one but you you made me made me come but you're the yellow yellow ones, you were all along the yellow ones.

You're cold is all.

Cold or crazy—jesus—it's the same.

He's cold is all.

Then Pa took the gun away, putting it in his pocket. He had his shotgun hanging easy over his left arm but he slapped me and I bit my tongue. Pa was spitting. I turned and ran down the path we'd come, putting one arm over my face to ease the stinging.

You little shit, Big Hans called after me.

3

Pa came back to the sleigh where I was sitting hunched up under the blanket and got a shovel out of the back.

Feeling better?

Some.

Why don't you drink some of that coffee?

It's cold by now. I don't want to anyhow.

How about them sandwiches?

I ain't hungry. I don't want anything.

Pa started back with the shovel.

What are you going to do with that? I said.

Dig a tunnel, he said, and he went around a drift out of sight, the sun flashing from the blade.

I almost called him back but I remembered the grin in his face so I didn't. Simon stamped. I pulled the blanket closer. I didn't believe him. Just for a second, when he said it, I had. It was a joke. Well I was too cold for jokes.

What did he want a shovel for? There'd be no point in digging for the horse. They could see it wasn't Pedersen's.
Poor Simon. He was better than they were. They'd left us
in the cold.

Pa'd forgot about the shovel in the sleigh. I could have
used it hunting for his bottle. That had been a joke too.
Pa'd sat there thinking how funny Jorge is out there beating away at the snow, I'll just wait and see if he remembers
about that shovel. It'd be funny if Jorge forgot, he'd
thought, sitting there in the blanket and bobbing his head
here and there like a chicken. I'd hear about it when we
got home till I was sick. I put my head down and closed
my eyes. All right. I didn't care. I'd put up with it to be
warm. But that couldn't be right. Pa must have forgot the
same as me. He wanted that bottle too bad. Now it was all
gone. It was colder with my eyes closed. I tried to think
about all that underwear and the girls in the pictures. I had
a crick in my neck.

Whose horse was it then?

I decided to keep my eyes closed a while longer, to see
if I could do it. Then I decided not to. There was a stream
of light in my eyes. It was brighter than snow, and as white.
I opened them and straightened up. Keeping my head down
made me dizzy. Everything was blurry. There were a lot
of blue lines that moved.

Did they know the horse even so? Maybe it was Carlson's horse, or even Schmidt's. Maybe he was Carlson in
yellow gloves, or Schmidt, and the kid, because he came in
sudden from the barn and didn't know Carlson had come,
saw him in the kitchen holding a gun like he might of if
it'd been Schmidt, and the kid got scared and run, because
he didn't understand and it'd been snowing lots, and how
did Schmidt get there, or Carlson get there, if it was one of

them, so the kid got scared and run and came to our crib
where the snow grew around him and then in the morning
Hans found him.

And we'd been god damn fools. Especially Hans. I shivered. The cold had settled in my belly. The sun had bent
around to the west. Near it the sky was hazy. The troughs
of some of the drifts were turning blue.

He wouldn't have been that scared. Why'd Carlson or
Schmidt be out in a storm like that? If somebody was sick,
they were closer to town than either the Pedersens or us. It
was a long way for them in this weather. They wouldn't get
caught out. But if the horse was stole, who was there but
Carlson and Schmidt or maybe Hansen to steal it from?

He goes to the barn before the snow, most likely in the
night, and knows horses. Oats or hay lead it out. He's running away. The blizzard sets down. He drives himself and
the horse hard, bending in the wind, leaning over far to see
fences, any marks, a road. He makes the grove. He might
not know it. The horse runs into the barberry, rears, goes
to its knees; or a low branch of a mossycup he doesn't see
knocks him into a drift; or he slides off when the horse
rears as the barbs go in. The horse wanders a little way,
not far. Then it stops—finished. And he—he's stunned,
windburned, worn like a stone in a stream. He's frozen and
tired, for snow's cold water. The wind's howling. He's
blind. He's hungry, frozen, and scared. The snow is stinging his face, wearing him smooth. Standing still, all alone,
it blows by him. Then the snow hides him. The wind blows
a crust over him. Only a shovel poking in the drifts or a
warm rain will find him lying by the horse.

I threw off the blanket and jumped down and ran up
the path we'd made between the drifts and trees, slipping,
cutting sharply back and forth, working against my stiff-

ness, but all the time keeping my head up, looking out carefully ahead.

They weren't by the horse. A hoof and part of the leg I'd uncovered lay by the path like nothing more went with them. Seeing them like that, like they might have blown down from one of the trees in a good wind, gave me a fright. Now there was a slight breeze and I discovered my tongue was sore. Hans's and Pa's tracks went farther on— toward Pedersen's barn. I wasn't excited any more. I remembered I'd left the blanket on the seat instead of putting it on Simon. I thought about going back. Pa'd said a tunnel. That had to be a joke. But what were they doing with the shovel? Maybe they'd found him by the barn. What if it really was Schmidt or Carlson? I thought about which I wanted it to be. I went more slowly in Pa's tracks. Now I kept down. The roof of Pedersen's barn got bigger; the sky was hazier; here and there little clouds of snow leaped up from the top of a drift like they'd been pinched off, and sailed swiftly away.

They *were* digging a tunnel. They didn't hear me come up. They were really digging a tunnel.

Hans was digging in the great drift. It ran from the grove in a high curve against the barn. It met the roof where it went lowest and flowed onto it like there wasn't a barn underneath. It seemed like the whole snow of winter was gathered there. If the drift hadn't ended in the grove it would have been swell for sledding. You could put a ladder on the edge of the roof and go off from there. The crust looked hard enough.

Hans and Pa had put about a ten-foot hole in the bank. Hans dug and Pa put what Hans dug in small piles behind him. I figured it was near a hundred feet to the barn. If we'd been home and not so cold, it would have been fun.

But it would take all day. They were great damn fools.

I been thinking, I started out, and Hans stopped in the tunnel with a shovel of snow in the air.

Pa didn't turn around or stop.

You can help dig, he said.

I been thinking, I said, and Hans dropped the shovel, spilling the snow, and came out. I been thinking, I said, that you're digging in the wrong place.

Hans pointed to the shovel. Get digging.

We need something to carry snow with, Pa said. It's getting too damn far.

Pa kicked at the snow and flailed with his arms. He was sweating and so was Hans. It was terrible foolish.

I said you was digging in the wrong place.

Tell Hans. It's his idea. He's the hot digger.

You thought it was a good idea, Hans said.

I never did.

Well, I said, it ain't likely you'll find him clear in there.

Pa chuckled. He ain't going to find us neither.

He ain't going to find anybody if he's where I think.

Oh yeah—*think*. Hans moved nearer. Where?

As far as he got. It really didn't make much difference to me what Hans did. He could come as close as he liked. In the snow near that horse.

Hans started but Pa chewed on his lip and shook his head.

Probably Schmidt or Carlson, I said.

Probably Schmidt or Carlson, shit, Pa said.

Of course, Hans shouted.

Hans scooped up the shovel, furious, and carried it by me like an ax.

Hans has been working like a thrasher, Pa said.

You'll never finish it.

No.

It's higher than it needs to be.

Sure.

Why are you digging it then?

Hans.   Hans wants to.

Why, for christ's sake?

So we can get to the barn without being seen.

Why not cross behind the drift?

Hans.   Hans says no.   Hans says that from an upstairs window he could see over the bank.

What the hell.

He's got a rifle.

But who knows he's upstairs?

Nobody. We don't know he's even there. But that horse
is.

He's back where I said.

No he ain't. You only wish he was. So does Hans, hey?
But he ain't. What did the kid see if he is—his ghost?

I walked into the tunnel to the end. Everything seemed
blue. The air was dead and wet. It could have been fun,
snow over me, hard and grainy, the excitement of a tunnel, the games. The face of a mine, everything muffled, the
marks of the blade in the snow. Well I knew how Hans
felt. It would have been wonderful to burrow down, disappear under the snow, sleep out of the wind in soft sheets,
safe. I backed out. We went to get Hans and go home. Pa
gave me the gun with a smile.

We heard the shovel cutting the crust and Hans puffing.
He was using the shovel like a fork. He'd cut up the snow
in clods around the horse. He grunted when he drove the
shovel in. Next he began to beat the shovel against the

snow, packing it down, then ripping the crust with the side of the blade.

Hans.   It ain't no use, Pa said.

But Hans went right on pounding with the shovel, spearing and pounding, striking out here and there like he was trying to kill a snake.

You're just wasting your time. It ain't no use, Hans. Jorge was wrong. He ain't by the horse.

But Hans went right on, faster and faster.

Hans. Pa had to make his voice hard and loud.

The shovel speared through the snow. It struck a stone and rang. Hans went to his knees and pawed at the snow with his hands. When he saw the stone he stopped. On his knees in the snow he simply stared at it.

Hans.

The bastard.   I'd have killed him.

He ain't here, Hans. How could he be? The kid didn't see him here, he saw him in the kitchen.

Hans didn't seem to be listening.

Jorge was wrong. He ain't here at all. He sure ain't here. He couldn't be.

Hans grabbed up the shovel like he was going to swing it and jumped up. He looked at me so awful I forgot how indifferent I was.

We got to think of what to do, Pa said. The tunnel won't work.

Hans didn't look at Pa. He would only look at me.

We can go home, Pa said. We can go home or we can chance crossing behind the bank.

Hans slowly put the shovel down. He started dragging up the narrow track to the barn.

Let's go home, Hans, I said. Come on, let's go home.

I can't go home, he said in a low flat voice as he passed us.

Pa sighed and I felt like I was dead.

―――――――

PART THREE

1

Pedersen's horse was in the barn. Pa kept her quiet. He rubbed his hand along her flank. He laid his head upon her neck and whispered in her ear. She shook herself and nickered. Big Hans opened the door a crack and peeked out. He motioned to Pa to hush the horse but Pa was in the stall. I asked Hans if he saw anything and Hans shook his head. I warned Pa about the bucket. He had the horse settled down. There was something that looked like sponges in the bucket. If they was sponges, they was hard. Hans turned from the door to rub his eyes. He leaned back against the wall.

Then Pa came and looked out the crack.

Don't look like anybody's to home.

Big Hans had the hiccups. Under his breath he swore and hiccuped.

Pa grunted.

Now the horse was quiet and we were breathing careful and if the wind had picked up we couldn't hear it or any snow it drove. It was warmer in the barn and the little light there was was soft on hay and wood. We were safe from the sun and it felt good to use the eyes on quiet tools and leather. I leaned like Hans against the wall and put my gun in my belt. It felt good to have emptied that hand. My face burned and I was very drowsy.   I could dig a hole in the hay. Even if there were rats, I would sleep with them in it.   Everything was still in the barn. Tools and harness hung from the walls, and pails and bags and burlap rested on the floor. Nothing shifted in the straw or moved in hay. The horse stood easy. And Hans and I rested up against the wall, Hans sucking in his breath and holding it, and we waited for Pa, who didn't make a sound. Only the line of sun that snuck under him and lay along the floor and came up white and dangerous to the pail seemed a living thing.

Don't look like it, Pa said finally. Never can tell.

Now who will go, I thought.   It isn't far.   Then it'll be over.   It's just across the yard.   It isn't any farther than the walk behind the drift.   There's only windows watching.   If he's been, he's gone, and nothing's there to hurt.

He's gone.

Maybe, Jorge. But if he came on that brown horse you stumbled on, why didn't he take this mare of Pedersen's when he left?

Jesus, Hans whispered. He's here.

Could be in the barn, we'd never see him.

Hans hiccuped. Pa laughed softly.

Damn you, said Big Hans.

Thought I'd rid you of them hics.

Let me look, I said.

He must be gone, I thought. It's such a little way. He must be gone.   He never came.   It isn't far but who will go across?   I saw the house by squinting hard. The nearer part, the dining room, came toward us. The porch was on the left and farther off. You could cross to the nearer wall and under the windows edge around. He might see you from the porch window. But he'd gone. Yet I didn't want to go across that little winded space of snow to find it out.

I wished Big Hans would stop. I was counting the spaces. It was comfortable behind my back except for that. There was a long silence while he held his breath and afterwards we waited.

The wind was rising by the snowman. There were long blue shadows by the snowman now. The eastern sky was clear. Snow sifted slowly to the porch past the snowman. An icicle hung from the nose of the pump. There were no tracks anywhere. I asked did they see the snowman and I heard Pa grunt. Snow went waist-high to the snowman. The wind had blown from his face his eyes. A silent chimney was an empty house.

There ain't nobody there, I said.

Hans had hiccups again so I ran out.

I ran to the dining room wall and put my back flat against it, pushing hard. Now I saw clouds in the western sky. The wind was rising. It was okay for Hans and Pa to come. I would walk around the corner. I would walk around the wall. The porch was there. The snowman was alone beside it.

All clear, I shouted, walking easily away.

Pa came carefully from the barn with his arms around his gun. He walked slow to be brave but I was standing in the open and I smiled.

Pa sat hugging his knees as I heard the gun, and Hans screamed. Pa's gun stood up. I backed against the house. My god, I thought, he's real.

I want a drink.

I held the house. The snow'd been driven up against it. I want a drink. He motioned with his hand to me. Shut up. Shut up.   I shook my head.   Shut up. Shut up and die, I thought.

I want a drink, I'm dry, Pa said.

Pa bumped when I heard the gun again. He seemed to point his hand at me. My fingers slipped along the boards. I tried to dig them in but my back slipped down. Hopelessly I closed my eyes. I knew I'd hear the gun again though rabbits don't. Silently he'd come.   My back slipped.   Rabbits, though, are hard to hit the way they jump around. But prairie dogs, like pa, they sit.   I felt snowflakes against my face, crumbling as they struck. He'd shoot me, by god.   Was pa's head tipped? Don't look.   I felt snowflakes falling softly against my face, breaking. The glare was painful, closing the slit in my eyes. That crack in pa's face must be awful dry. Don't look. Yes . . . the wind was rising . . . faster flakes.

2

When I was so cold I didn't care I crawled to the south side of the house and broke a casement window with the gun I had forgot I had and climbed down into the basement ripping my jacket on the glass. My ankles hurt so I huddled there in the dark corner places and in the cold moldy places by boxes. Immediately I went to sleep.

I thought it was right away I woke though the light through the window was red. He put them down the cellar, I remembered. But I stayed where I was, so cold I seemed apart from myself, and wondered if everything had been working to get me in this cellar as a trade for the kid he'd missed. Well, he was sudden. The Pedersen kid—maybe he'd been a message of some sort. No, I liked better the idea that we'd been prisoners exchanged. I was back in my own country. No, it was more like I'd been given a country. A new blank land. More and more, while we'd been coming, I'd been slipping out of myself, pushed out by the cold maybe. Anyway I had a queer head, sear-eyed and bleary, everywhere ribboned. Well, he was quick and quiet. The rabbit simply stumbled. Tomatoes were unfeeling when they froze. I thought of the softness of the tunnel, the mark of the blade in the snow. Suppose the snow was a hundred feet deep. Down and down. A blue-white cave, the blue darkening. Then tunnels off of it like the branches of trees. And fine rooms. Was it February by now? I remembered a movie where the months had blown from the calendar like leaves. Girls in red peek-a-boo BVDs were skiing out of sight. Silence of the tunnel. In and in. Stairs. Wide tall stairs. And balconies. Windows of ice and sweet green light. Ah. There would still be snow in February. Here I go off of the barn, the runners hissing. I am tilting dangerously but I coast on anyway. Now to the trough, the swift snow trough, and the Pedersen kid floating chest down. They were all drowned in the snow now, weren't they? Well more or less, weren't they? The kid for killing his family. But what about me? Must freeze. But I would leave ahead of that, that was the nice thing, I was already going. Yes. Funny. I was something to run my hands over, feeling for its hurts, like there were worn places in leather, rust and rot in screws and boards I had to find, and the places were hard to reach and the fingers in my gloves were stiff and their ends were sore. My nose was running. Mostly interesting. Funny. There was a cramp in my leg that must have made me wake. Distantly I felt the soft points of my shoulders in my jacket, the heavy line of my cap around my forehead, and on the hard floor my harder feet, and to my chest my hugged-tight knees. I felt them but I felt them differently . . . like the pressure of a bolt through steel or the cinch of leather harness or the squeeze of wood by wood in floors . . . like the twist and pinch, the painful yield of tender tight together wheels, and swollen bars, and in deep winter springs.

I couldn't see the furnace but it was dead. Its coals were cold, I knew. The broken window held a rainbow and put a colored pattern on the floor. Once the wind ran through it and a snowflake turned. The stairs went into darkness. If a crack of light came down the steps, I guessed I had to shoot. I fumbled for my gun. Then I noticed the fruit cellar and the closed door where the Pedersens were.

Would they be dead already? Sure they'd be. Everybody was but me. More or less. Big Hans, of course, wasn't really, unless the fellow had caught up with him, howling and running. But Big Hans had gone away a coward. I knew that. It was almost better he was alive and the snow had him. I didn't have his magazines but I remembered how they looked, puffed in their bras.

The door was wood with a wooden bar. I slipped the bar off easily but the door itself was stuck. It shouldn't have stuck but it *was* stuck—stuck at the top. I tried to see the top by standing on tiptoe, but I couldn't bend my toes well and kept toppling to the side. Got no business sticking, I thought. There's no reason for that. I pulled again, very hard. A chip fell as it shuddered open. Wedged. Why? It had a bar.　　It was even darker in the fruit cellar and the air had a musty earthen smell.

Maybe they were curled up like the kid was when he dropped. Maybe they had frost on their clothes, and stiff hair. What color would their noses be? Would I dare to tweak them? Say. If the old lady was dead I'd peek at her crotch.   I wasn't any Hans to rub them. Big Hans had run. The snow had him. There wasn't any kettle, any stove, down here.   Before you did a thing like that, you'd want to be sure. I thought of how the sponges in the bucket had got hard.

I went back behind the boxes and hid and watched the stairs. The chip was orange in the pattern of light. He'd heard me when I broke the glass or when the door shook free or when the wedge fell down. He was waiting behind the door at the top of the stairs. All I had to do was come up. He was waiting. All this time. He waited while we stood in the barn. He waited for pa with his arms full of gun to come out. He took no chances and he waited.

I knew I couldn't wait. I knew I'd have to try to get back out. There he'd be waiting too. I'd sit slowly in the snow like pa. That'd be a shame, a special shame after all I'd gone through, because I was on the edge of something wonderful, I felt it trembling in me strangely, in the part of me that flew high and calmly looked down on my stiff heap of clothing. Oh what pa'd forgot. We could have used the shovel. I'd have found the bottle with it. With it we'd have gone on home. By the stove I'd come to myself again. By it I'd be warm again. But as I thought about it, it didn't appeal to me any more. I didn't want to come to myself that way again. No. I was glad he'd forgot the shovel.
But he was . . . he was waiting.   Pa always said that he could wait; that Pedersen never could. But pa and me, we couldn't—only Hans stayed back while we came out, while all the time the real waiter waited. He knew I couldn't wait. He knew I'd freeze.

Maybe the Pedersens were just asleep.   Have to be sure the old man wasn't watching. What a thing. Pa pretended sleep. Could he pretend death too? She wasn't much. Fat. Gray. But a crotch is a crotch. The light in the window paled. The sky I could see was smoky. The bits of broken glass had glimmered out. I heard the wind. Snow by the window rose. From a beam a cobweb swung stiffly like a net of wire. Flakes followed one another in and disappeared. I counted desperately three, eleven, twenty-five. One lit beside me.   Maybe the Pedersens *were* just asleep. I went to the door again and looked in. Little rows of lights lay on the glasses and the jars. I felt the floor with my foot. I thought suddenly of snakes. I pushed my feet along. I got to every corner but the floor was empty. Really it was a relief. I went back and hid behind the boxes. The wind was coming now, with snow, the glass glinting in unexpected places. The dead tops of roofing nails in an open keg glowed white. Oh for the love of god.   Above me in the house I heard a door slam sharply. He was finished with waiting.

The kid for killing his family must freeze.

The stair was railless and steep. It seemed to stagger in the air. Thank god the treads were tight, and didn't creak. Darkness swept under me. Terror of height. But I was only climbing with my sled under my arm. In a minute I'd shoot from the roof edge and rush down the steep drift, snow smoke behind me. I clung to the stair, stretched out. Fallen into space I'd float around a dark star. Not the calendar for March. Maybe they would find me in the spring, hanging from this stairway like a wintering cocoon.

I crawled up slowly and pushed the door open. The kitchen wallpaper had flowerpots on it, green and very big. Out of every one a great red flower grew. I began laughing. I liked the wallpaper. I loved it; it was mine; I felt the green pots and traced the huge flower that stuck out of it, laughing. To the left of the door at the head of the stair was a window that looked out on the back porch. I saw the wind hurrying snow off toward the snowman. Down the length of it the sky and all its light was lead and all the snow was ashy. Across the porch were footprints, deep and precise.

I was on the edge of celebration but I remembered in time and scooted in a closet, hunkering down between brooms, throwing my arms across my eyes. Down a long green hill there was a line of sheep. It had been my favorite picture in a book I'd had when I was eight. There were no people in it.

I'd been mad and pa had laughed. I'd had it since my birthday in the spring. Then he'd hid it. It was when we had the privy in the back. God, it was cold in there, dark beneath. I found it in the privy torn apart and on the freezing soggy floor in leaves. And down the hole I saw floating curly sheep. There was even ice. I'd been seized, and was rolling and kicking. Pa had struck himself and laughed. I only saved a red-cheeked fat-faced boy in blue I didn't like. The cow was torn. Ma'd said I'd get another one someday. For a while, every day, even though the snow was piled and the sky dead and the winter wind was blowing, I watched for my aunt to come again and bring me a book like my ma'd said she would. She never came.

And I almost had Hans's magazines.

But he might come again. Yet he'd not chase me home, not now, no.   By god, the calendar was clean, the lines sharp and clear, the colors bright and gay, and there were eights on the ice and red mouths singing and the snow belonged to me and the high sky too, burningly handsome, fiercely blue.   But he might. He was quick.

If it was warmer I couldn't tell but it wasn't as damp as

by the boxes and I could smell soap. There was light in the kitchen. It came through the crack I'd left in the closet door to comfort me. But the light was fading. Through the crack I could see the sink, now milky. Flakes began to slide out of the sky and rub their corners off on the pane before they were caught by the wind again and blown away. In the gray I couldn't see them. Then they would come—suddenly—from it, like chaff from grain, and brush the window while the wind eddied. Something black was bobbing. It was deep in the gray where the snow was. It bounced queerly and then it went. The black stocking cap, I thought.

I kicked a pail coming out and when I ran to the window my left leg gave way, banging me against the sink. The light was going. The snow was coming. It was coming almost even with the ground, my snow. Puffs were rising. Then, in a lull when the snow sank and it was light enough to see the snowbank shadows growing, I saw his back upon a horse. I saw the tail flick. And the snow came back. Great sheets flapped. He was gone.

3

Once, when dust rolled up from the road and the fields were high with heavy-handled wheat and the leaves of every tree were gray and curled up and hung head down, I went in the meadow with an old broom like a gun, where the dandelions had begun to seed and the low ground was cracked, and I flushed grasshoppers from the goldenrod in whirring clouds like quail and shot them down. I smelled wheat in the warm wind and every weed. I tasted dust in my mouth, and the house and barn and all the pails burned my eyes to look at. I rode the broom over the brown rocks. I hunted Horse Simon in the shade of a tree. I rode the broom over the brown meadow grass and with a fist like pistol butt and trigger shot the Indian on Horse Simon down. I rode across the dry plain. I rode into the dry creek. Dust rose up behind me. I went fast and shouted. The tractor was bright orange. It shimmered. Dust rolled behind it. I hid in the creek and followed as it came. I waited as its path curved toward me. I watched and waited. My eyes were tiny. I sprang out with a whoop and rode across the dry plain. My horse had a golden tail. Dust rolled up behind me. Pa was on the tractor in a broad-brimmed hat. With a fist like a pistol butt and trigger, going fast, I shot him down.

Pa would stop the tractor and get off and we'd walk across the creek to the little tree Simon stood his bowed head under. We'd sit by the tree and pa would pull a water bottle out from between its roots and drink. He'd swish it around in his mouth good before he swallowed. He'd wipe off the top and offer it to me. I'd take a pull like it was fiery and hand it back. Pa'd take another drink and sigh and get on up. Then he'd say: you feed the chickens like I told you? and I'd say I had, and then he'd say: how's the hunting? and I'd say pretty good. He'd nod like he agreed and clap Simon on the behind and go on off, but he'd always say I'd best not play in the sun too long. I'd watch him go over the creek, waving his hat before his face before he put it on. Then I'd take a secret drink out of the bottle and wipe my lips and the lip of it. After that I'd go and let the ragweed brush against my knees, and then, sometimes, go home.

The fire had begun to feel warm. I rubbed my hands. I ate a stale biscuit.

Pa had taken the wagon to town. The sun was shining.

Pa had gone to meet Big Hans at the station. There was snow around but mud was flowing and the fields had green in them again. Mud rode up on the wagon wheels. There was sweet air sometimes and the creek had water with the winter going. Through a crack in the privy door I saw him take the wagon to the train. I'd a habit, when I was twelve, of looking down. Something sparkled on the water. It was then I found the first one. The sun was shining. Mud was climbing the wagon wheels and pa was going to the train and down the tight creek snow was flowing. He had a ledge beneath the seat. You could reach right down. Already he had a knack for hiding. So I found it and poured it out in the hole. That was the last year we had the privy because when Big Hans came we tore it down.

I ate an apple I'd found. The skin was shriveled but the meat was sweet.

Big Hans was stronger than Simon, I thought. He let me help him with his chores, and we talked, and later he showed me some of the pictures in his magazines. See anything like that around here? he'd say, shaking his head. Only teats like that round here is on a cow. And he would tease, laughing while he spun the pages, giving me only a glimpse. Or he would come up and spank me on the rump. We tore the privy down together. Big Hans hated it. He said it was a dirty job fit only for soldiers. But I helped him a lot, he said. He told me that Jap girls had their slice on sideways and no hair. He promised to show me a picture of one of them and though I badgered him, he never did. We burned the boards in a big pile back of the barn and the flames were a deep orange like the sun going down and the smoke rolled darkly. It's piss wet, Hans said. We stood by the fire and talked until it sank down and the stars were out and the coals glowed and he told me about the war in whispers and the firing of big guns.

Pa liked the summer. He wished it was summer all year long. He said once whiskey made it summer for him. But Hans liked the spring like me, though I liked summer too. Hans talked and showed me this and that. He measured his pecker once when he had a hard one. We watched how the larks ran across the weeds and winked with their tails taking off. We watched the brown spring water foam by the rocks in the creek, and heard Horse Simon blow and the pump squeak.

Then pa took a dislike to Hans and said I shouldn't go with Hans so much. And then in the winter Hans took a dislike to pa as he almost had to, and Hans said fierce things to ma about pa's drinking, and one day pa heard him. Pa was furious and terrible to ma all day. It was a night like this one. The wind was blowing hard and the snow was coming hard and I'd built a fire and was sitting by it, dreaming. Ma came and sat near me, and then pa came, burning inside himself, while Hans stayed in the kitchen. All I heard was the fire, and in the fire I saw ma's sad quiet face the whole evening without turning, and I heard pa drinking, and nobody not even me said anything the whole long long evening. The next morning Hans went to wake pa and pa threw the pot and Hans got the ax and pa laughed fit to shake the house. It wasn't long before Hans and I took to hating one another and hunting pa's bottles alone.

The fire was burning down. There was some blue but mostly it was orange. For all Pedersen's preparing like pa said he always did, he hadn't got much wood in the house. It was good to be warm but I didn't feel so set against the

weather as I had been. I thought I'd like winter pretty well
from now on. I sat as close as I could and stretched and
yawned.   Even if his cock was thicker . . . I was here
and he was in the snow.   I was satisfied.

He was in the wind now and in the cold now and sleepy
now like me. His head was bent down low like the horse's
head must be and he was rocking in the saddle very tired
of holding on and only rocking sleepy with his eyes shut
and with snow on his heavy lids and on his lashes and
snow in his hair and up his sleeves and down inside his
collar and his boots. It was good I was glad he was there it
wasn't me was there sticking up bare in the wind on a
horse like a stick with the horse most likely stopped by this
time with his bowed head bent into the storm, and I
wouldn't like lying all by myself out there in the cold white
dark, dying all alone out there, being buried out there while
I was still trying to breathe, knowing I'd only come slowly
to the surface in the spring and would soon be soft in the
new sun and worried by curious dogs.

The horse must have stopped though he made the other
one go on. Maybe he'd manage to drive this one too until
it dropped, or he fell off, or something broke. He might
make the next place. He just might. Carlson's or Schmidt's.
He had once before though he never had a right or any
chance to. Still he had. He was in the thick snow now.
More was coming. More was blowing down. He was in it
now and he could go on and he could come through it
because he had before. Maybe he belonged in the snow.
Maybe he lived there, like a fish does in a lake. Spring
didn't have anything like him. I surprised myself when I
laughed the house was so empty and the wind so steady
it didn't count for noise.

I saw him coming up beside our crib, the horse going

down to its knees in the drift there. I saw him going to the
kitchen and coming in unheard because of all the wind. I
saw Hans sitting in the kitchen. He was drinking like pa
drank—lifting the bottle. Ma was there, her hands like a
trap on the table. The Pedersen kid was there too, naked in
the flour, towels lapping his middle, whiskey and water
steadily dripping. Hans was watching, watching the kid's
dirty toes, watching him like he watched me with his pin-
black eyes and his tongue sliding in his mouth. Then he'd
see the cap, the mackinaw, the gloves wrapped thick
around the gun, and it would be the same as when pa
kicked the glass from Big Hans's hand, only the bottle
this time would roll on the floor, squirting. Ma would
worry about her kitchen getting tracked and get up and
mix biscuits with a shaky spoon and put the coffee on.

They'd disappear like the Pedersens had. He'd put them
away somewhere out of sight for at least as long as the
winter. But he'd leave the kid, for we'd been exchanged,
and we were both in our own new lands. Then why did he
stand there so pale I could see through? Shoot. Go on.
Hurry up. Shoot.

The horse had circled round in it. He hadn't known the
way. He hadn't known the horse had circled round. His
hands were loose upon the reins and so the horse had
circled round. Everything was black and white and everything the same. There wasn't any road to go. There wasn't
any track. The horse had circled round in it. He hadn't
known the way. There was only snow to the horse's thighs.
There was only cold to the bone and driving snow in his
eyes. He hadn't known. How could he know the horse had
circled round in it? How could he really ride and urge the
horse with his heels when there wasn't anyplace to go and
everything was black and white and all the same? Of

course the horse had circled round, of course he'd come around in it. Horses have a sense. That's all manure about horses. No it ain't, pa, no it ain't. They do. Hans said. They do. Hans knows. He's right. He was right about the wheat that time. He said the rust was in it and it was. He was right about the rats, they do eat shoes, they eat anything, so the horse has circled round in it. That was a long time ago. Yes, pa, but Hans was right even though that was a long time ago, and how would you know anyway, you was always drinking . . . not in summer . . . no, pa . . . not in spring or fall either . . . no, pa, but in the winter, and it's winter now and you're in bed where you belong—don't speak to me, be quiet. The bottle made it spring for me just like that fellow's made it warm for you.   Shut up.   Shut up.   I wanted a cat or a dog awful bad since I was a little kid.   You know those pictures of Hans's, the girls with big brown nipples like bottle ends . . .   Shut up.   Shut up.   I'm not going to grieve. You're no man now. Your bottle's broken in the snow. The sled rode over it, remember? I'm not going to grieve. You were always after killing me, yourself, pa, oh yes you were. I was cold in your house always, pa.   Jorge—so was I.   No. I was. I was the one wrapped in the snow. Even in the summer I'd shiver sometimes in the shade of a tree. And pa—I didn't touch you, remember—there's no point in haunting me. *He* did. He's even come round maybe.   Oh no jesus please.
Round.   He wakes. He sees the horse has stopped. He sits and rocks and thinks the horse is going on and then he sees it's not. He tries his heels but the horse has finally stopped. He gets off and leads him on smack into the barn, and there it is, the barn, the barn he took the horse from.

Then in the barn he begins to see better and he makes out
something solid in the yard where he knows the house is
and there are certain to be little letups in the storm and
through one of them he sees a flicker of something almost
orange, a flicker of the fire and a sign of me by it all
stretched out my head on my arm and near asleep.   If
they'd given me a dog, I'd have called him Shep.

I jumped up and ran to the kitchen only stopping and
going back for the gun and then running to the closet for
the pail which I dropped with a terrible clatter. The tap
gasped. The dipper in the pail beneath the sink rattled. So
I ran to the fire and began to poke at it, the logs tumbling,
and then I beat the logs with the poker so that sparks flew
in my hair.

I crouched down behind a big chair in a corner away
from the fire. Then I remembered I'd left the gun in the
kitchen. My feet were sore and bare. The room was full of
orange light and blackened shadows, moving. The wind
whooped and the house creaked like steps do. I was alone
with all that could happen. I began to wonder if the Pedersens had a dog, if the Pedersen kid had a dog or cat maybe
and where it was if they did and if I'd known its name and
whether it'd come if I called. I tried to think of its name as
if it was something I'd forgot. I knew I was all muddled
up and scared and crazy and I tried to think god damn
over and over or what the hell or jesus christ, instead, but
it didn't work. All that could happen was alone with me
and I was alone with it.

The wagon had a great big wheel.   Papa had a paper
sack.   Mama held my hand.   High horse waved his
tail.   Papa had a paper sack. We both ran to hide.
Mama held my hand.   The wagon had a great big

wheel.　　High horse waved his tail. We both ran to hide.
　　Papa had a paper sack.　　The wagon had a great
big wheel.　　Mama held my hand.　　Papa had a paper
sack.　　High horse waved his tail.　　The wagon had
a great big wheel. We both ran to hide.　　High horse
waved his tail.　　Mama held my hand. We both ran to
hide.　　The wagon had a great big wheel.　　Papa had
a paper sack.　　Mama held my hand.　　High horse
waved his tail.　　Papa had a paper sack. We both ran to
hide.　　Papa had a paper sack. We both ran to hide.
　　The wind was still. The snow was still. The sun burned
on the snow. The fireplace was cold and all the logs were
ashy. I law stiffly on the floor, my legs drawn up, my arms
around me. The fire had gone steadily into gray while I
slept, and the night away, and I saw the dust float and
glitter and settle down. The walls, the rug, the furniture,
all that I could see from my elbow looked pale and tired
and drawn up tight and cramped with cold. I felt I'd never
seen these things before. I'd never seen a wasted morning,
the sick drawn look of a winter dawn or how things were
in a room where things were stored away and no one ever
came, and how the dust came gently down.
　　I put my socks on. I didn't remember at all coming from
behind the chair, but I must have. I got some matches from
the kitchen and some paper twists out of a box beside the
fireplace and I put them down, raking the ashes aside.
Then I put some light kindling on top. Pieces of orange
crate I think they were. And then a log. I lit the paper and
it flared up and flakes of the kindling curled and got red
and black and dropped off and finally the kindling caught
when I blew on it. It didn't warm my hands any, though
I kept them close, so I rubbed my arms and legs and jigged,

but my feet still hurt. Then the fire growled. Another log.   I found I couldn't whistle.   I warmed my back some.   Outside snow.   Steep. There were long hard shadows in the hollows of the drifts but the eastern crests were bright.   After I'd warmed up a little I walked about the house in my stocking feet, and snagged my socks on the stairs. I looked under all the beds and in all the closets and behind most of the furniture. I remembered the pipes were froze. I got the pail from under the sink and opened the door to the back porch against a drift and scooped snow in the pail with a dipper. Snow had risen to the shoulders of the snowman. The pump was banked. There were no tracks anywhere.

I started the stove and put snow in a kettle. It always took so much snow to make a little water. The stove was black as char. I went back to the fireplace and put more logs on. It was beginning to roar and the room was turn-ing cheerful, but it always took so much fire. I wriggled into my boots. Somehow I had a hunch I'd see a horse.

The front door was unlocked. All the doors were, likely. He could have walked right in. I'd forgot about that. But now I knew he wasn't meant to. I laughed to see how a laugh would sound.   Again.   Good.

The road was gone. Fences, bushes, old machinery: what there might be in any yard was all gone under snow. All I could see was the steep snow and the long shadow lines and the hard bright crest about to break but not quite breaking and the hazy sun rising, throwing down slats of orange like a snow fence had fallen down. He'd gone off this way yet there was nothing now to show he'd gone; nothing like a bump of black in a trough or an arm or leg sticking out of the side of a bank like a branch had

blown down or a horse's head uncovered like a rock; nowhere Pedersen's fences had kept bare he might be lying
huddled with the horse on its haunches by him; nothing
even in the shadows shrinking while I watched to take for
something hard and not of snow and once alive.

I saw the window I'd broke. The door of the barn hung
ajar, banked steeply with snow. The house threw a narrow
shadow clear to one end of the barn where it ran into the
high drift that Hans had tunneled in. Higher now. Later
I'd cut a path out to it. Make the tunnel deeper maybe.
Hollow the whole bank like a hollow tree. There was time.
I saw the oaks too, blown clean, their twigs about their
branches stiff as quills. The path I'd taken from the barn to
the house was filled and the sun was burning brightly on
it. The wind had curled in and driven a steep slope of
snow against the house where I'd stood. As I turned my
head the sun flashed from the barrel of pa's gun. The snow
had risen steeply around him. Only the top of the barrel
was clear to take the sun and it flashed squarely in my eye
when I turned my head just right. There was nothing to do
about that till spring. Another snowman, he'd melt. I
picked my way back to the front of the house, a dark spot
dancing in the snow ahead of me. Today there was a fine
large sky.

It was pleasant not to have to stamp the snow off my
boots, and the fire was speaking pleasantly and the kettle
was sounding softly. There was no need for me to grieve. I
had been the brave one and now I was free. The snow
would keep me. I would bury pa and the Pedersens and
Hans and even ma if I wanted to bother. I hadn't wanted
to come but now I didn't mind. The kid and me, we'd done
brave things well worth remembering. The way that fellow
had come so mysteriously through the snow and done us

such a glorious turn—well it made me think how I was told to feel in church. The winter time had finally got them all, and I really did hope that the kid was as warm as I was now, warm inside and out, burning up, inside and out, with joy.

Mrs. Mean

1

I call her Mrs. Mean. I see her, as I see her husband and each of her four children, from my porch, or sometimes when I look up from my puttering, or part my upstairs window curtains. I can only surmise what her life is like inside her little house; but on humid Sunday afternoons, while I try my porch for breeze, I see her hobbling on her careful lawn in the hot sun, stick in hand to beat her scattered children, and I wonder a lot about it.

I don't know her name. The one I've made to mark her and her doings in my head is far too abstract. It suggests the glassy essence, the grotesquerie of Type; yet it's honestly come by, and in a way it's flattering to her, as if she belonged on Congreve's stage. She could be mean there without the least particularity, with the formality and grandeur of Being, while still protected from the sour and acrid community of her effect, from the full sound and common feel of life; all of which retain her, for me, on her burning lawn, as palpable and loud and bitter as her sting-ing switch.

I may have once said something to her—a triviality—and perhaps once more than that, while strolling, I may have nodded to her or I may have smiled . . . though not together. I have forgotten.

When I bought my house I wished, more than anything, to be idle, idle in the supremely idle way of nature; for I felt then that nature produced without effort, in the manner of digestion and breathing. The street is quiet. My house is high and old, as most of the others are, and spreading trees shade my lawn and arch the pavement. Darkness is early here at any time of year. The old are living their old age out, shawled in shadows, cold before fires. A block away they are building stores. One feels the warmth that is the movement of decay. I see the commercial agent. He wears gold rings. His hand partitions. Lamps will grow in these unlucky windows. Wash will hang from new external stairs. No one has his home here but myself; for I have chosen to be idle, as I said, to surround myself with scenes and pictures; to conjecture, to rest my life upon a web of theory—as ready as the spider is to mend or suck dry in-truders. While the street is quiet, the houses whole, their windows shaded; while the aged sit their porches and swap descriptions of their health; the Means, upon the oppor-tunity of death, have seized the one small house the neigh-borhood affords. Treeless and meager, it stands in the sum-mer in a pool of sun and in the winter in a blast of air.

My house has porches fore and aft and holds a corner. I spy with care and patience on my neighbors but I seldom speak. They watch me too, of course, and so I count our evils even, though I guard my conscience with a claim to scientific coldness they cannot possess. For them no idleness is real. They see it, certainly. I sit with my feet on the rail. My wife rocks by me. The hours pass. We talk. I dream. I sail my boats on their seas. I rest my stories on their backs. They cannot feel them. Phantoms of idleness never burden. If I were old or sick or idiotic, if I shook in my chair or withered in a southern window, they would understand my inactivity, and approve; but even the wobblers make their faithful rounds. They rake their leaves. They mow and shovel. They clip their unkempt hedges and their flowers. Their lives are filled by this. I do no more.

Mrs. Mean, for instance: what could she think? She is never idle. She crowds each moment with endeavor.

When I had my cottage I used to see, on Sabbaths, a wire-haired lady drive her family to the beach. She rented everything. Her family dressed in the car, the windows draped with blankets, while the lady in her jacket rapped on the hood for speed, then rushed them to the surf. She always gestured grandly at the sea and swung a watch by its strap. "So much money, so much time, let us amuse," she always said, and sat on a piece of driftwood and shelled peas. The children dabbled at the water with their fingers. Her husband, a shriveled, mournful soul, hung at the water's edge and slowly patted his wrists with ocean. Inertia enraged her. She thrust her pods away, pouring her lap in a jar. "Begin, begin," she would shout then, jumping up, displaying the watch. The children would squat in the sand until foam marked their bottoms, staring in their pails. Papa would drip water to his elbows and upper arm while Mama receded to her log. The children fought then. It began invisibly. It continued silently, without emotion. They kicked and bit and stabbed with their shovels. When she found them fighting she would empty her lap and start up, shaking the watch and shouting, but the children fought on bitterly, each one alone, throwing sand and swinging their pails, rolling over and over on the beach and in and out of the moving ocean. She ran toward them but the sea slid up the sand and drove her off, squealing on tiptoe, scuffing and denting the smooth sand. The children plunged into the surf and broke apart. "Don't lose your shovels!" The waves washed the children in. They huddled on dark patches of beach. At last their mother would run among them, quickly, between breaths of ocean, and with her hands on her hips, her legs apart, she would throw her head back in the mimic of gargantuan guffaws, soundless and shaking. "Laugh," she would say then, "there is only an hour."

The people by me primitively guess that I am enemy and hate me: not alone for being different, or disdaining work, or worse, not doing any; but for something that would seem, if spoken for them, words of magic; for I take their souls away—I know it—and I play with them; I puppet them up to something; I march them through strange crowds and passions; I snuffle at their roots.

From the first they saw me watching. I can't disguise my interest. They expected, I suppose, that I would soon be round with stories. I would tell Miss Matthew of Mr. Wallace, and Mr. Wallace of Mrs. Turk, and Miss Matthew and Mr. Wallace and Mrs. Turk would take the opportunity to tell me all they knew of one another, all they knew about diseases, all they thought worthy of themselves and could remember of their relatives, and the complete details of their many associations with violent forms of death. But when I communicated nothing to them; when I had nothing, in confidence, to say to anyone; then they began to treat my eyes like marbles and to parade their lives indifferently before me, as if I were, upon my porch, a motionless, graven idol, not of their religion, in my niche; yet I somehow retained my mystery, my potency, so that the indifference was finally superficial and I fancy they felt a compulsion to be observed—*watched* in all they did. I should say they dread me as they dread the supernatural. How Mr. Wallace dreads it, dead as he nearly is, twisted on his cane. Every morning, when he can, he comes down the block past my porch, his left arm hung like a shawl from his shoulder, shuffling his numb feet, poking cracks. "I'll have to go back." His voice is hoarse and loud. "I used to walk to the end of the street." He mops his face and dries his running eyes. "Hot," he shouts, propped against his cane. "Last summer I went to the end." The cane comes out of his belly. He sways. Will he die like this? palsy seize him? sweat break before that final clip of pain and his surprise? The cane will gouge cement. His hat will float into my privet hedge and the walk drive blood from his nose.

He turns at last and I relax. His eyes are anxious for a friend to cry at, to bellow to a stop. He squints up the street, and if, by any chance, someone appears, Mr. Wallace grins and howls hello. He inches forward, pounds the walk, roars reports of weather for the middle of the night. "Know what it was at one? Eighty-seven. June, not hell we're in, but eighty-seven. I ain't even eighty-seven. There was a cloud across the moon at two. It rained alongside five but nothing cooled." And the dawn was gray as soapy water. Fog lay between garages. A star, almost hidden by the morning light, fell past the Atlas stack and died near Gemini. The friend is fixed and Mr. Wallace closes, his face inflamed, his eyeballs rolling. He describes the contours of his aches, the duration, strength, and quality of

every twinge, the subtle nuances of vague internal hurts.
He distinguishes blunt pains from sharp, pale ones from
bright, wiry from watery, morning, night. His brown teeth
grin. Is it better, he discourses, to suffer when it's hot or
when it's cold, while standing or sitting, reading or walking, young or old?

"I say it's better to be cold. You'll say not. I know what
you'll say. You'll say, 'The knuckle, now, if rapped when
cold, will ring.' I know. A cold shin on the sharp, hard
edge of something—that's a real one. I know. Never mind.
Hurts are all fires. Keep you warm. Know those fellows like
that fellow in a book I read about? His name was Scott.
You know him? Froze. Scott. If I'd been with him, freezing, I'd of pounded on me some great sore so when I hit
it I would burn all over. Keep you warm. Say, they didn't
think of that, did they? Froze. I read about it. I read a lot,
except for seeing, or I would. Half an hour. I used to, all
the time. My eyes burn though. Your eyes burn sometimes?
Scott. Froze. Hey, you know freezing's quiet. Ha! You
know—it's warm!"

Mr. Wallace wavers on his stick and spits. The whole
street echoes with him. His friend dwindles.

Portents are next. They follow pain as pain the weather.
Anyone is a friend of Mr. Wallace who will stay.

The starfall past the Atlas stack—a cruel sign. They are
all bad, the signs are. Evil is above us. "Evil's in the air
we breathe or we would live forever." Mr. Wallace draws
the great word out as he's doubtless heard his preacher.
The cane rises with difficulty. The tip waves above the
treetops. "There," bellows Mr. Wallace, his jowls shaking.
"There!" And he hurls the cane like a spear. "Smoke,
sonny, comes out and hides the sky and poisons everything.
I've got a cough." His hand is tender on his chest. He taps

with it. He hacks, and stumbles. Spit bubbles on the walk and spreads. The friend or friendly stranger bobs and smiles and flees while Mr. Wallace waits, expecting the return of his cane. "I can't bend," he almost whispers, peering at the disappearing back. His smile stays, but the corners of his mouth twitch. Wearily his eyes cross.

"Cane cane cane," Mr. Wallace calls. His wife hurries. "Cane cane," Mr. Wallace calls. She waves her hanky. "Cane," he continues until it's handed back. "Hot." Mrs. Wallace nods and mops his brow. She settles his hat and smooths his sleeve. "You threw your cane again," she says. Mr. Wallace grows solemn. "I tried to kill a squirrel, pumpkin." Mrs. Wallace leads him home, her face in tears.

What a noise he makes! I thought I couldn't stand it when I came. His puffed face frightened me. His eyes were holes I fell in. I dodged his shadow lest it cover me, and felt a fool. He's not so old, sixty perhaps; but his eyes run, his ears ring, his teeth rot. His nose clogs. His lips pale and bleed. His knees, his hips, his neck and arms, are stiff. His feet are sore, the ankles swollen. His back, head and legs ache. His throat is raw, his chest constricted, and all his inner organs—heart, liver, kidneys, lungs, and bowels—are weak. Hands shake. His hair is falling. His flesh lies slack. His cock I vision shriveled to a string, and each breath of life he draws dies as it enters his nose and crosses his tongue. But Mr. Wallace has a strong belly. It is taut and smooth and round, like a baby's, and anything that Mr. Wallace chooses to put into it mashes up speedily, for Mr. Wallace, although he seeps and oozes and excretes, has never thrown up in his life.

I could hear him walking. That was worst. When I raked the yard I faced in his direction and went in when I saw him coming. With all my precautions his voice would sometimes boom behind me and I would jump, afraid and furious. His moist mouth gaped. His tongue curled over his bent brown teeth. I knew what Jonah felt before the whale's jaws latched. Mr. Wallace has no notion of the feelings he creates. I swear he stinks of fish on such occasions. I feel the oil. It's a tactile nightmare, an olfactory dream—as if my smell and touch divided from my hearing, taste, and vision, and while I watched his mouth and listened to its greeting, fell before whales in Galilee, brine stung and bruised while the fish smell grew as it must grow in the mouth of a whale, and the heat of an exceptionally hardy belly rose around.

More and more I knew my budding world was ruined if he were free in it. As a specimen Mr. Wallace might be my pride. Glory to him in a jar. But free! Better to release the sweet moving tiger or the delicate snake, the monumental elephant. I was just a castaway to be devoured. It was bad luck and I rocked and I cursed it. Mr. Wallace spouted and I paced the porch with Ahab's anger and his hate. Mrs. Mean wanted my attention. She passed across my vision, brilliant with energy, like the glow of a beacon. Each time my stomach churned. Her children tumbled like balls on the street, like balls escaping gloves and bats; and on the day the boy Toll raced in front of Mr. Wallace like a bolting cat and swung around a sapling like a rock at the end of a string, deadly as little David, then I saw how. Well, that's all over now. Mr. Wallace dreads me as the others do. He inches by. He looks away. He mumbles and searches the earth with his cane. When Mr. Wallace completes his death they will wind crape around his cane and stick it in his grave. Mrs. Wallace will stand by to screech and I shall send—what shall I send?—I shall send begonias with my card. I say Good Morning, Mr. Wallace,

how did you pass the night? and Mr. Wallace's throat puffs
with silence. I cannot estimate how much this pleases me.
I feel I have succeeded to the idleness of God.

Except in the case of Mrs. Mean. I am no representative
of preternatural power. I am no image, on my porch—no
symbol. I don't exist. However I try, I cannot, like the
earth, throw out invisible lines to trap her instincts; turn
her north or south; fertilize or not her busy womb; cause
her to exhibit the tenderness, even, of ruthless wild things
for her wild and ruthless brood. And so she burns and
burns before me. She revolves her backside carefully
against a tree.

2

Mrs. Mean is hearty. She works outside a good bit, as
she is doing now. Her pace is furious, and the heat does
not deter her. She weeds and clips her immaculate yard,
waging endless war against the heels and tricycles of her
children. She rolls and rakes. She plants and feeds. Does
she ever fall inside her house, a sprung hulk, and lap at
the dark? The supposition is absurd. Observation mocks
the thought. But how I'd enjoy to dream it.

I'd dream a day both warm and humid, though not
alarming. Leaves would be brisk about and the puff clouds
quick. This, to disarm her. She'd be clipping the hedge;
firmly bent, sturdily moving, executing stems; and then the
pressure of her blood would mount, mount slowly as each
twig fell; and a cramp would grow as softly as a bud in
the blood of her back, in the bend of her legs, the crook-
snap of her arms, tightening and winding about her back
and legs and arms like a wet towel that knots when wrung.

Now the blood lies slack in her but the pressure mounts,

mounts slowly. The shears snip and smack. She straightens like a wire. She strides on the house, tossing her lank hair high from her face. She will fetch a rake; perhaps a glass of water. Strange. She feels a dryness. She sniffs the air and eyes a sailing cloud. In the first shadow of the door she's stunned and staggered. There's a blaze like the blaze of God in her eye, and the world is round. Scald air catches in her throat and her belly convulses to throw it out. There's a bend to her knee. The sky is black and comets burst ahead of her. Her hands thrust ahead, hard in the sill of the door. Cramp grasp her. Shrivel like a rubber motor in a balsa toy her veins. Does her husband waddle toward her, awag from stern to stem with consternation? Oh if the force of ancient malediction could be mine, I'd strike him too!

. . . the vainest dream, for Mrs. Mean is hearty, and Mr. Mean is unpuncturable jelly.

Mr. Wallace can bellow and Mrs. Wallace can screech, but Mrs. Mean can be an alarm of fire and war, falling on every ear like an aching wind.

Among the many periodicals to which I subscribe is the very amusing *Digest of the Soviet Press* and I remember an article there which described the unhappiness of one neighborhood in a provincial Russian city over the frightfully lewd, blasphemous, and scatological shouts a young woman named Tanya was fond of emitting. She would lean from the second-story window of her apartment, the report said, and curse the countryside. Nothing moved her. No one approached without blushing to the ears. Her neighbors threatened her with the city officials. The city officials came—were roundly damned. They accused her of drunkenness, flushed, and threatened her with the party officials. The party officials came—were thoroughly execrated. They said she was a dirty woman, a disgrace to Russia—an abomination in the sight of the Lord, they would have said, I'm sure, if the name of the Lord had been available to them. Unfortunately it was available only to Tanya, who made use of it. The party officials advised the city officials and the city officials put Tanya in jail. Useless. She cursed between bars and disturbed the sleep of prisoners. Nor was it well for prisoners to hear, continually, such things. They transferred her to another district. She cursed from a different window. They put her in the street, but this was recognized at once as a terrible error and her room was restored. The report breathed outrage and bafflement. What to do with this monster? In their confusion they failed to isolate her. They couldn't think to shoot her. They might have torn out her tongue. Abstractly, I'd favor that. All the vast resources of civilization lay unused, I gathered, while Tanya leaned obscenely from her sill, verbally shitting on the world.

Mrs. Mean, too, dumbfounds her opposition. There have been complaints, I understand. Mrs. Mean, herself, has been addressed. The authorities, more than once, have been notified. Nothing has come of it. Well, this is wisdom. Far better to do nothing than act ineptly. Mrs. Mean could out-Christ Pius.

Thus the trumpet sounds. The children scatter. They run to the neighbors, pursued by her stick and her tongue, so she can mow and tamp and water her crop of grass that it may achieve the quiet dignity of lawn. At the distance of oceans and continents, I admire Tanya. I picture her moving lips. I roll the words on my own tongue—the lovely words, so suitable for addressing the world—but they roll silently there, as chaste as any conjunction; whereas Mrs. Mean's voice utters them with all the sharp, yet exagger-

ated enunciation of an old Shakespearean. They are vol-
umed by rage and come sudden and strident as panic. Mrs.
Mean, moreover, is almost next door and not oceans and
continents and languages away.

"Ames. You little snot. Nancy. Witch. Here now. Look
where you are now. Look now, will you? God almighty.
Move. Get. Oh jesus why do I trouble myself. It'll die now,
little you care. Squashed. That grass ain't ants. Toll, I warn
you. God, god, how did you do that? Why, why, tell me
that. Toll, what's that now? Toll, I warn you now. Pike.
Shit. Get. What am I going to do with you? Step on you
like that? Squash. Like that? Why try to make it nice?
Why? Ames. Damn. Oh damn. You little snot. Wait'll I
get hold of you. Tim. You are so little, Tim. You are so
snotty, so dirty snotty, so nasty dirty snotty. Where did you
get that? What *is* that? What's it now? Drop that. Don't
bring it here. Put it back. Nancy. Witch. Oh jesus, jesus,
sweet, sweet jesus. Get. Did you piss in the flowers?
Timmy? Timmy, Timmy, Timmy, did you? By god, I'll
beat your bottom flat. Come here. You're so sweet, so
sweet, so nice, so dear. Yes. Come here. All of you. Nancy.
Toll. Ames. Tim. Get in here. Now, now I say. Now. Get.
I'll whale you all."

It is, however, an old play and Mrs. Mean is an old, old
player. The recitation, loud as it is, emphatic, fearsome as
it is, everyone has heard before. The children almost wholly
ignore it. When her voice begins they widen away and
start to circle, still at their little vicious games. Mrs. Mean
threatens and cajoles but she does not break the rhythm
of her weeding. Toll digs with his shovel. "Don't dig, don't
dig," Mrs. Mean chants, and Toll digs. "Don't dig, Toll,
don't dig," and Toll digs harder. "Didn't you hear me?
didn't you? Stop now. Don't dig." Toll comes red with

effort. "I'll take that shovel. Don't dig. Toll, you little creeping bastard, did you hear me? I'll take that shovel. Toll!" The earth is pierced and the turf heaved. Mrs. Mean drops her trowel, rushes upon Nancy, who is nearest, and slams her violently to the ground. Nancy begins screaming. Toll runs. Ames and Timmy widen out and watch. Mrs. Mean cries: "Ah, you little stink—eating mud!" Nancy stops crying and sticks out her muddy tongue; and perhaps this time she learns, although she isn't very bright, that Mrs. Mean always moves on her real victim silently and prefers, whenever possible, surprise.

Toll and Ames are hard to catch. They keep an eye out. If Mrs. Mean leans on her rake and yells pleasantries at Mrs. Cramm—unfortunate Mrs. Cramm—Toll and Ames push each other from their wagons; but they keep an eye out. The sudden leap of Mrs. Mean across the tulip bed deceives only tiny Tim, his finger in his nose. Mrs. Cramm pales and shrinks and endures it like a slave.

Once I went to a lavish dinner party given by a most particular and most obstinate lady. The maid forgot to serve the beans and my most particular dear friend, rapt in a recollection of her youth that lasted seven courses, overlooked them. I did not nor did the other guests. We were furtive, catching eyes, but we were careful. Was it asparagus or broccoli or brussels sprouts or beans? Was she covering up the maid's mistake like the coolest actress, as if to make the tipped table and the broken vase a part of every evening's business? She enjoyed the glory of the long hours of her beauty. The final fork of cake was in her mouth when her jaws snapped. I would have given any sum, then, performed any knavery, to know what it was that led her from gay love and light youth to French-cut green beans and the irrevocable breach of order. She had just said: "We were dancing. I was wearing my most daring gown and I was cold." She went on a word or two before turning grim and silent. By what Proustian process was the thing accomplished? I suppose it was something matter-of-fact. She shivered—and there in her mind were the missing beans. She rose at once and served them herself, cold, in silver, before the coffee. The hollandaise had doubtless separated so we were spared that. But only that. We ate those beans without a word, though some of us were, on most occasions, loquacious, outspoken, ragging types. Our hostess neglected her own portion and rushed sternly back to glory. Of her sins that evening I never forgave the last.

Mrs. Mean bounds over the tulip bed, her rake falling from her, her great breasts swinging like bells, her string hair rising and whirling, while Mrs. Cramm pretends that Mrs. Mean is calm against the end of her implement and finishes her quiet sentence in her quiet voice and looks straight ahead where her neighbor was as if she were, as good manners demanded, still respectably there. Mrs. Mean roars oaths and passes the time of day. She fails even a gesture of interruption. So Toll and Ames, the older and the wiser ones, keep a good lookout and keep in motion. Mrs. Cramm, however, remains as if staked while Mrs. Mean genially hammers her deeper with rough platitudes and smooth obscenity.

Mrs. Cramm is a frail widow whose shoes are laced. Her misfortune is to live by Mrs. Mean and to be kind. She bestows upon the children, as they flee, the gentlest, tenderest glances. Compassion clothes her, and docility. She flinches for boxed ears. She grimaces at the sight of Mrs. Mean's stick, but unobtrusively, so much against her will to show the slightest sign that Mrs. Mean, who reads

in the world only small words written high, misses it all—
the tight hands and nervous mouth and melting eyes. Too
stupid to understand, too stupid, therefore, to hate, Mrs.
Mean nevertheless plays the tyrant so naturally that her
ill will could hardly prove more disagreeable to Mrs.
Cramm than her good.

It would almost seem that Mrs. Mean is worse for wit-
nesses. She grows particular. What passed unnoticed before is noted and condemned. The wrestling that was
merely damned is suddenly broken by violence. The shrill
commands rise to shouts and change to threats. It is as if
she wished to impress her company with the depth of her
concern, the height of her standards. I knew a girl in college who spent her time, while visiting with you, cleaning
herself or the room, if it were hers: lifting lint from her
skirt or the hairs of her Persian cat from sofas and chairs;
pinching invisible flecks of dirt off the floor, sleeving dust
from tables, fingering it from the top edge of mirrors; and
it never mattered in the least as far as I could discover
whether you came unexpectedly or gave her a week of
warning or met her at a play or on the street, she tidied
eternally, brushing her blouse with the flickering tips of her
fingers, sweeping the surrounding air with a wave of her
hand.

It's early. I'm waiting for the bus when Mrs. Cramm
scuttles anxiously from her house carrying a string bag. I
prepare to tip my hat and to be gracious for I've had little
commerce with Mrs. Cramm, and what knowledge that
frail lady must possess! Mrs. Mean is then in her doorway
crying: "Cramm! It's a peach of a day, Mrs. Cramm, isn't
it? Come over here!" And Mrs. Cramm, most hesitantly,
leaves me. "A peach. Grass is a little thin in back. It's been
too hot for green things. God damn you, Toll, don't you

move. Don't you move a shitting inch! Here. Scrubbed the kitchen floor. You can't be too particular. Kids pick up things. Nancy. Be careful. Cut her finger on Dad's razor. Nancy! Bring your finger. Show Mrs. Cramm your sore-sore. There. Like to scare us to death." Mrs. Cramm is murmuring, bending, the wounded finger thrust at her nose. "Bled too," says Mrs. Mean. "Got on her dress, damn her. How's your sore-sore now, Nennie? The hell it needs more medicine. Kids, kids. Barely broke the skin. Run and play, go on." Mrs. Mean pushes the child off. I avert my eyes and turn my back. She stares at me—I feel her face—and her voice drops for an instant. When it rises again it is to curse and to command. "Keep your brother off that floor, my god!" The bus comes into view and I lose all talk in its noise. Mrs. Cramm does not board with me. She takes the next bus, or none, I can only presume.

Thus they flee: Ames, Nancy, Toll, and Tim. They pick the flowers next door to me. They tramp the garden down the street. They run through Mr. Wallace's hedge, and while Mr. Wallace bellows like a burnt blind Polyphemus, they laugh like frightened crystal. I've had no trouble myself. Maybe she's warned them. No. She wouldn't. I don't exist. And out of her reach a warning is laughter. They are a curse to Miss Matthew, to Dumb Perkins, Wallace, Turk, yet not to me. So she may cry them out of Christendom if she likes, as she would if she were put in garden charge of all the Christian grass.

Ames, Nancy, Toll, and Tim: they go. Wires are strung on little sticks and strips of cloth are bowed upon the wires. Orders are promulgated. Threats are rung over the neighborhood, and Mrs. Mean takes her turn in the famished grass, spinning like a wind-turned scarecrow, stubbornly and personally plump with her ambition.

It's no use. Her children pour repeatedly, end on end, across it. They find the natural path. They scuff the grass. They chafe it. They stamp and jump and drive it. They scream it down. The wires sag. The bows drag in the mud. The sticks finally snap or pull out. Nancy wraps her foot in a loop of wire and is hauled up briskly like a hare, howling; and Mr. Mean appears, sullenly rolls the wire around the sticks, over the bows, signaling his wife's surrender. The children stand in a line while Mrs. Mean watches from between her kitchen curtains.

The surrender is far from unconditional. Mrs. Mean vents her hate upon the dandelions. She scours them out of the earth. She packs their bodies in a basket and they are dried and burned. She patrols with an anxious eye the bordering territory where the prevailing winds blow the soft heads from the plants of her negligent neighbor—not, of course, Mrs. Cramm, who has a hired boy, but the two young worshipers of flesh who live on her right and who never appear except to hang out towels or to speed in and out of the late afternoon in their car. Their hands are for each other. They allow the weeds all liberty. There the dandelions gloriously flourish. From their first growth across her line, she regards them with enmity. Their blooming fills her with fury and the instant the young couple drive off in their convertible, Mrs. Mean is among the bright flowers, snapping their heads until her fingers are yellow; flinging the remains, like an insult, to the ground where no one but the impervious pair could fail to feel the shame of their beheaded and shattered condition. With a grand and open gesture, unmistakable from where my wife and I boldly sit and enjoy it, and meant for the world, Mrs. Mean lifts her soiled hands above her head and shakes them rapidly.

There are too many dandelions of course. The young couple does not go out often; and while Mrs. Mean dares, during the time of the dandelions' cottoning, to pace the property line, glaring, her arms in scorn upon her hips, her face livid with furiously staged resignation, watching helplessly the light bolls rise and float above her peonies, hover near her roses, fall like kisses upon her grass, indecently rub seed against her earth; she would not consider —honor would not permit—stepping one foot across the borders if the young couple might observe it, or speaking to them, even most tactfully, about the civic duties of householders; and indeed, she is right this once at any rate; for if those two could not see what we saw so easily, and if they were not shamed or outraged into action by Mrs. Mean's publicly demonstrated anger against them, she might plow and salt the whole of the land their castle grows on and expect no more effect than the present indifferent silence and neglect.

So there are too many dandelions and they go speedily to seed. The seeds rise like a storm and cross in clouds against her empty threats and puny beatings of the air. Mrs. Mean, then, as with all else, sets her children to it. They chase the white chaff. It dances from their rush. Mrs. Mean screams incoherent instructions. The children run faster. They leap higher. They whirl more rapidly. They beat back the invasion. But inevitably the seeds bob beyond them and float on. Mrs. Mean is herself adept. She snatches the cotton as it passes. She crushes it; drops it in a paper bag. Her eye never misses a swatch of the white web against the grass, and after every considerable wind, she carefully rakes the ground. The children, however, soon make a game of it. They gambol brightly and my heart goes out to them, dancing there, as it goes out seldom: gay as they are within the ridiculous, happy inside the insane.

The children hesitate to destroy their favorites. Instead they begin to cheer them on, calculating distance and drift, imagining balloons on tortured courses. Who would want to bring such ships prematurely down or interfere with their naturally appointed, wind-given paths?

Mrs. Mean.

She waits, motionless. The clusters come, one drifting near. Her arm flies out. Her fingers snap. The boll disappears in the beak of her hand. The prize is stuffed in her sack. Mrs. Mean is motionless again though the sack shakes. I am reminded of lizards on rocks, my wife of meat-eating plants. Mrs. Mean's patience here is inexhaustible, her skill astonishing, her devotion absolute. The children are gone. Their shouts make no impression on her. Mrs. Mean is caught up. She waits. She fills her sack. But at last the furious fingers close on air, the arm jerks back an empty hand, and Mrs. Mean lowers her head to her failure. Alive, she whirls. Her wide skirt lifts. It is a crude ballet, a savage pantomime; for Mrs. Mean, unlike the other mothers of my street, does not shout her most desperate and determined wishes at her children. She forewarns with a trumpet but if her warnings are not heeded, she is silent as a snake. Her head jerks, and I know, reading the signs, that Mrs. Mean is seeking a weapon. The children are now the errant chaff, the undisciplined bolls, and although they are quite small children, Mrs. Mean always augments her power with a stick or a strap and dedicates to their capture and chastisement the same energy and stubborn singleness of purpose she has given to the destruction of weeds.

No jungle hunt's been quieter. She discovers a fallen branch, the leaves still green. She shakes it. The twigs whip and the leaves rustle. She catches sight of her oldest boy beside the barn, rigid with the wildest suspense. His boll is floundering in a current of air. It hurtles toward a hole in the barn where cats crawl. His mother hobbles on him, her branch high, stiff, noiseless, as if it were now part of the punishment that he be taken unaware, his joy snuffed with fright as much as by the indignity of being beaten about the ears with leaves.

I think she does not call them to their idiotic tasks because they might obey. Her anger is too great to stand obedience. The offense must be fed, fattened to fit the feeling, otherwise it might snap at nothing and be foolish. So it must seem that all her children have slunk quietly and cunningly away. It must seem that they have mocked her and have mocked her hate. They must, therefore, be quietly and cunningly pursued, beaten to their home, driven like the dogs: bunched on all fours, covering their behinds, protecting the backs of their bare legs from the sting of the switch and their ears with their hands; contorted like cripples, rolling and scrabbling away from the smart of the strap in jerks, wild with their arms as though shooing flies; all the while silent, engrossed, as dumb as the dumbest beasts; as if they knew no outcry could help them; refusing, like the captive, to give satisfaction to his enemy—though the youngest child is only two—and this silence as they flee from her is more terrible to me than had they screamed to curdle blood and chill the bone.

3

Mrs. Mean seizes Ames's arm, twists it behind him, rains blows upon his head and neck. He pulls away and runs. It's to her purpose. She permits his flight. Now the words come and I understand that the silence has been a dam. Her arm points accusingly at his eyeless back. She curses him. She pronounces judgment upon him. She cannot understand his laziness, his uselessness, his disobedience, his stupidity, his slovenliness, his dirtiness, his ugliness; and Mrs. Mean launches into her list, not only of those faults she finds in his present conduct, but all she can remember having found since he first dangled from the doctor's fist and was too slow to cry or cried too faintly or was too red or too wizened or too small or was born with eczema on his chest—a terrible mortification to his mother. He has been nothing but a shame since, a shame in all his days and all his doings. The ultimate word is hurled after him as he slams the door: Shame! He is given to understand by shouts directed toward the upstairs windows that there will be more to come, that she is not done with him, the shameful, disrespectful boy, the shameful, discourteous child; and now and then, though not this time, if the boy's spirits are unusually high, if he is filled more than ordinarily with rebellion, he will thrust his head from the window of what I take to be his room, for that is where he has been sent, and make a horrible face at his mother, and a horrible bracking noise; whereupon Mrs. Mean will stop as though struck, suck in her breath, pause dreadfully to scream "What!" at the affront; and then explode derisively, contemptuously, "You! you! you!" until she sputters out. She rounds up the other children if they remain to be rounded up and some minutes later howls of pain and grief can be heard over the whole block.

It is on these occasions, I think, that the children are really hurt. The cuffs, the slaps, the switches they receive are painful, doubtless, but they are brief. They are also, in a sense, routine. The blows remind me of the repertoire of the schoolyard bully: the pinch, the shove, the hair-pull, the sudden blow on the muscle of the arm, the swift kick to the shin, elbow in the groin. Evil that is everyday is lost in life, goes shrewdly into it; becomes a part of habitual blood. First it is a convenient receptacle for blame. It holds all hate. We fasten to it—the permanent and always good excuse. If it were not for it, ah then, we say, we would improve, we would succeed, we would go on. And then one day it is necessary, as if there's been a pain to breathing for so long that when the pain at last subsides, out of fright, we suffocate. So they grow up in it. At any rate, they get larger. They know the rules by heart for it's like a game, a game there is no fun in playing and no profit. Ames retreats into the house with Mrs. Mean's damnations at his back while the others, warned now, ready, circle widely out in alleys and around garages and old carriage barns, between the nearby houses, as Mrs. Mean cautiously seeks them, carefully guarding her rear, swiveling often, doubling back, peering craftily around corners until she finds one and the distance has been closed, when she makes a sudden, silent rush with her switch extended, beating before her the empty air, whipping the heels of the child as it runs for home. I don't know all the rules or I don't fully understand them but I gather that when Mr. Mean's at work the front door is always locked, for the children never try to sneak in that way; and I guess the house must be home base, must be sanctuary except in the gravest cases. If they are not let out again, they are at least not beaten. They don't have to dance after dandelion seeds in the hot yard.

My wife and I find it strange that they should all run home. It seems perverse, unnaturally sacrificial: the self leading itself, as in a great propelling crowd, blind over

cliffs, stupidly to the sea. We'd run away, we affirm in our
adulthood to one another, knowing, as we make the affirmation, that even old as we are, adult as we claim to be,
we would return to the poisonous nest as they return, children still largely on turned-out feet, the girl unbreasted, the
boys inadequate and bare for manhood. We would chew
on our hurt and feel the pain again of our beginnings. We
would languish for the glory of complaint in the old ties.
The eldest Mean child may someday say, confronted by a
meanness that's his own, by his own mean soul, that he was
beaten as a boy; and he may take a certain solace from the
fact; he may shift at least a portion of his blame to the
ages. "This shit's not mine." *"Mann ist was er isst."* "Alas
for the present time!"

We wish they *would* run off, certainly, as we wanted to
run off, for had we run away, had we had the courage we
so easily wish for them and the necessary resource, we feel
we'd be as much as moral now, clear of the need to dis-
claim our dirt, round, holding our tail between our teeth.
For that, we must exaggerate the past. We inflate it with
our wrongs. Fortunately for us then, unfortunately for us
now, it was really not so bad. We were not pursued and
beaten. We were not beggared in our own yard. We were
not flayed within the hearing of the world. Our surprise is
symbolic. It is a gesture of speech. It expresses a wish of
our own; and if we really felt the indignation and disappointment we put into words when we see the Mean children flying to their hive, my wife and I; if we ever borrowed to apply to them any anger from our feelings for
Mrs. Mean, it would be an injustice on our part almost as
great as in our power as mere observers to do them; although I am not above injustice and must confess, despite
my knowledge of the dreadful circumstances of his life,

a dislike of Ames, the eldest Mean child, especially upon his bike, as deep as my dislike for his cow-chested, horse-necked, sow-faced mother. "It may have been put in him, but he *is* nasty, unnaturally nasty," I'm afraid I often say. "He can't help it," my wife replies, and I glare at the children too, as Mrs. Mean flushes them one by one and they run or toddle to the house, because I know my wife is right. I exclaim at their stupidity, their lack of character, their lack of fight—I have my list as Mrs. Mean has hers—for I am, in these remote engagements, as fearsome, as bold and blustering as a shy and timorous man can be.

But after all there must be corners in that little house for each of them, corners that are personal and familiar where the walls come together like the crook of a soft, warm arm and some hour has been passed in quiet love with a private treasure. There must be some sight, some touch, that is a comfort and can draw them to the trap. We haven't been suckled, thank god, by Mrs. Mean, or bathed or clothed or put to bed or nursed when we've been ill. Perhaps her touch is sometimes tender and her tone is sweet. My wife is hopeful.

Really I am not. Their house is chocolate. The paint is peeling badly. It has a tin roof. The front porch is narrow. The house is narrow. The windows are low and small. The gutters need repair. There are rust stains on the side of the house. There are cracks in the foundation. The chimney tilts. I cannot think of it as sanctuary for very long. I try. I see the children orbiting. They vanish within and I try to think they could, like Quasimodo, cry their safety. But is there any reason for us to suppose that life inside is any better than the life outside we see? My wife wishes to believe it—for the children—but I cannot imagine the deep shadows of that little house full of anything warm except perhaps the rolled, damp fat of Mr. Mean, squatting like a toad in his underwear, his bright, hard eyes pinned like beads to his face, his tongue licking the corners of his mouth, his fingers rubbing softly up and down his other fingers, his legs gliding against themselves, his pale skin bluish in the bad light.

But then my wife is subject to failures of the imagination. I have tried to carry her but her sentiments are too readily aroused. Her eyes stay at the skin. Only her heart, only her tenderest feelings, go in. I, on the other hand, cut surgically by all outward growths, all manifestations, merely, of disease and reach the ill within. I conceive the light, for instance, as always bad, of insufficient strength and a poor color, as having had to travel through too much dust and too much muslin, as having had to dwell too long in the company of dark rugs and mohair chairs and satin-shaded lamps. The air, I feel, is bad too. The windows never open. The back door bangs but the breeze is metaphorical. All things in their little house that hang, hang motionless and straight. Nothing is dirty, but nothing feels clean. Their writing paper sticks to the hand. Their toilet sweats. The halls are cool. The walls are damp.

I was playing with toy cars and digging roads around the supports of the family porch when I accidentally placed my hand upon a cold wet pipe which rose out of the ground there and saw near the end of my nose, moist on the ridge of a post, four fat white slugs. I think of that when I think of the Means' house and of pale fat Mr. Mean, and the urge to scream as I did then rises strongly in me. I bumped my head, I remember, scrambling out. I was afraid to tell my father why I'd yelled. He was very angry. Even yet I have a distaste for the odor of earth.

My wife maintains that Mrs. Mean is an immaculate

housekeeper and that her home is always cool and dry and airy. She's very likely correct as far as mere appearance goes but my description is emotionally right, metaphysically appropriate. My wife would strike up friendships, too, and so, as she says, find out; but that must be blocked. It would destroy my transcendence. It would entangle me mortally in illusion.

Yes. The inside of the Mean house is clear and horrible in my mind like a nightmare no one willingly would want to enter. It may be five rooms. It can't be more. And into these five rooms, at best, the six Means are squeezed with the machinery to keep them alive, with the gewgaws she buys, the bright blue china horses which trot in the windows, and some of the children's toys, for they do not lack for toys, at least the kind you ride. They have a scooter, a small tricycle, a large tricycle, one that has a wagon welded to its rear, and a sidewalk bike with which the eldest Mean child rides down flowers, people, cats and dogs. I must salute their taste this once. They haven't bought their children cycles shaped by great outriding fenders of tin and paint like rockets, airplanes, horses, swans or submarines. They have an eye for the practical, the durable, in such things. I remember with fondness my own tricycle, capable of tremendous speed or so it seemed then, and because it was not fangled up by paid imaginations, it could be Pegasus, if I liked, and it was.

There is no Pegasus—imaginary—real—in the house of the Means. There is father floating among the couches, white as animals long in caves, quiet as a weed, his round mouth working, his eyes twitching, his fat fingers twisting a button on his sleeve.

Purple bath towels hang in the bathroom. I have seen them on the line. They have some colored sheets—one lavender, one rose, one wine—and some brightly yarned doilies you can buy in the living room of a house, a block away, where articles of religion are sold among candies and cozies and pickles in mason jars. The two ladies who make them are also immensely fat and immensely pious. They furthermore sell signs which gloomily, but with a touch, I fancy, of spiteful triumph, herald the Coming of the Lord and the Eventual Destruction of the World. There is a fine one I have noticed in their dining room window which says in scarlet letters simply, Armageddon, like an historical marker. The expectation is tastefully surrounded by a dark border of crosses and small skulls. Mr. Mean bore one of their placards home and tacked it up on the door of the small barn where he keeps his car. In silver script that glitters from the black card it warns of Eternity Tomorrow, and it must have cost him a dollar and a half. At least I take it as a warning. My wife says it reminds him to drive carefully. You see how easily and dangerously she is deceived. However, perhaps for the Means it is not a warning but a hope, a promise of reward; and it no doubt speaks plainly and poorly for my destination that I regard its message so pessimistically.

The Means are Calvinists, I'm certain. They may be unsure of heaven but hell is real. They must feel its warmth at their feet and the land tremble. Their meanness must proceed from that great sense of guilt which so readily becomes a sense for the sin of others, and poisons everything. There is no pleasure. There is only the biological propriety of the penis. In another, more forthright age, they would have read to their children from *Slovenly Peter,* the picture story book of the righteous, where the reward of moral weakness, of which it was an illustrated catalogue, was a severed limb, the loss of teeth and vision, the promise of a bloody and crippling accident, a painful and malignant disease, or fits of madness—all of these disasters tailored by a wise and benevolent Providence to fit the crime. I remember very well, too, a poem of our Puritan ancestors, in rather strenuous iambics, about a child called Harry, perverse to the heart, who went fishing against his father's wishes, doubtless on the Lord's day too, and with the devil's pleasure.

> Many a little fish he caught,
> And pleased was he to look,
> To see them writhe in agony,
> And struggle on the hook.
>
> At last when having caught enough,
> And also tired himself,
> He hastened home intending there
> To put them on the shelf.
>
> But as he jumped to reach a dish,
> To put his fishes in,
> A large meat hook, that hung close by,
> Did catch him by the chin.
>
> Poor Harry kicked and call'd aloud,
> And screamed and cried and roared,
> While from his wounds the crimson blood
> In dreadful torrents poured.

The pattern of punishment here is based on the principle of a comparable eye for a comparable eye but I feel sure that while the Mean children might dread their moral transmigration into ants (a steamroller mash them flat) or butterflies (their arms fall off), all ants and butterflies would dread as much their total intersection. A butterfly, I think,

would prefer to die of burned-off wings, with some im-
mediacy, possessing beauty, than to be rubbed, pinched,
and buffeted about, losing, before the power of flight, the
desire, and before the desire, the eloquence of its design.

I should like to see Providence take the side of the dandelion. A tooth for a tooth would suit me fine.

But of course all the Means have suffered metamorpho-
sis. They are fly-beleaguered bears in a poor zoo with nothing to claw but each other and a dead trunk and no one
to hate but themselves, their flies, and the bare, hot, pea-
nut-spotted ground.

4

Mr. Wallace has displayed a certain strength. I had
thought him shorn but he has joined the Means. They
gather now on cooler evenings on the Means' front porch,
the misters and the missuses, heads together. Shouts and
wails of laughter, snorts and bellows as from steers rise
out of the porch's shadows as out of shadowing trees by a
wallow bank. It is a juncture, I must confess, that had not
occurred to me although I sometimes fancy I am master of
the outside chance. It was a part of *her* that I let slip. Following her gyrations in the grass, her rush and whirl and
roaring curse, I forgot her geologic depth, the vein of
meanness deep within her earth. Against the mechanical
flutter of appearance I failed to put the glacial movement
of reality.

I drove them together . . . an unpleasant end for so
pleasant a beginning.

Mr. Wallace was before at large, as I have said; gigantic
in the landscape, swallowing life. There was, in him, no
respect for my mysteries, only for his own: signs, omens,

portents, signatures and symbolings whose meaning he alone was privy to. Mr. Wallace was the paramour of prophecy, yet it came to me when the boy Toll catted across his path that day that it was a stone symbolic more than real that struck the light from Goliath's eyes. It was for prophecy that Jonah fled the Lord. For Jonah's flight the tempest rose, and for the tempest was Jonah flung between the whale's jaws. To be properly swallowed, then, was the secret; to cause, in going down, the oils to flow that would convulse the membranes of the stomach. What must that whale have felt, his moist cavernous maw reverberating prayers and pledges! Would Mr. Wallace be a dog and eat his vomit? I judged that I should soon be cast on dry land. Thenceforth the mystery would be mine, as it was Jonah's. To be the bait, to carry the harpoon down and in that round and previously unshaken belly stick it, then escape—that would be the trick. And prophecy would do it.

How I was enamored of the notion! All day I lightly walked. Mr. Wallace obliged me by appearing almost at once to record his aches, to dilate upon the midnight's weather, and to wallow surely, by absolutely predictable thrashes, toward the topic. I was on a vast dry plain. Red rock rose out of its distances. Behind me and before me there were multitudes embannered—murmuring. The sun's light struck from shields and spears. I squinted at the giant. His figure wavered. I sensed the wet and dry together. Perhaps the ancient Greek philosophers were right about the wedding of these opposites. Dust clouded my shuffling feet. Spume flew to the giant's face. It is amazing how the feelings of the universal fables sometimes focus in a single burning vision. Of course that singleness of sight has always been my special genius.

I waited. The ankles were painful. I said I had a mole that itched. A bad sign, Mr. Wallace said, and I saw the thought of cancer fly in his ear. Moles are special marks, he said. I was aware, I said, of how they were, but the places of my own were fortunate and I divined from them a long life. Moles go deep, I said. They tunnel to the heart. Mr. Wallace grinned and wished me well and with great effort turned away. It was a good start. Wonder and fear began in him and twitched his face. When again he came he thought aloud of moles and I discoursed upon them: causes, underflesh connections, cosmic parallels, relations to divinity. There was a fever in him, dew on his lip, brightness in his eye. Moles. Every day. At last there was no art in how he brought the subject up. I spoke of the mark of Cain. I mentioned the deformities of the devil. I talked of toads and warts. I discussed the placing of blemishes and the ordering of stars. Stigmata. The world of air is like the skin and signs without are only symbols of the world within. I referred to the moles of beauty, to those of avarice, cunning, gluttony and lust, to those which, when touched, made the eyes water, the ears itch, or caused the prick to stand and the shyest maid to flower. My fancy soared. I related moles and maps, moles and mountains, moles and the elements of interior earth. Oh it was wondrous done! How he shook and warmed his lips like an old roué and trembled and put anxiety in every place! I was everywhere specific and detailed. *This* may correspond to *that*. The region of the spine is like unto the polar axis. But I was at all times indeterminate and vague as well. A certain horn-shaped mole upon a certain place may signify a certain spiritual malignity. I informed him of everything and yet of nothing. I moved his sight from heaven to hell and drew from him the most naïve response of bliss, followed first by a childlike disappointment as our viewpoint fell, then a childlike fright. His cane quivered against the pavement. He was in the grip. To be so near, continually, to dying; to feel within yourself the chemistry of death; to see in the glass, day by day, your skull emerging; to rot while walking and to fear the sun; to pick over the folds of your loosening flesh like infested clothing; to know, not merely by the logician's definition or the statistician's count that men are mortal, but through the limpsting of your own blood—to know so surely so directly so immediately this, I thought, would be a burden needing, if a man were to bear up under it, a staff of self-deceiving hope as sturdy and leveling as the truth was not: an unquenchable, blasphemous, magical hope that the last gasp when it came would last forever, death's rattle an eternity.

There were moles upon that body I was certain. And he would want to know their meaning. It wouldn't matter if he had, before me, given sense and order to their being; these things despair of guarantee. He would want to know. He would have to know. And he would fear to know. What if I said: This is the mole of death most painful? Yet what if I said: This is the mole of everlasting mortal life? What if a miracle should happen? What if?

I waited. Again and again he came, nibbling. Excitement, worry, anticipation, profoundest thought passed and repassed like winds across him. Finally I broached the deadly topic. Mr. Wallace showed his teeth and his eyes hunted in the trees. His cane chattered. He admitted his wife had a mole or two. Ah, I said, where are they? Mr. Wallace blew his nose and bade farewell. Not yet. The rogue would offer up his wife. He wanted a safe bite, a free taste of the news. Well I should freely give it. I worried only that the shriveled witch had moles upon her privates

—this shame silencing speech. Such a sign, if I could pronounce upon it, I would deed the whole of fortune to.

Again and again he came until I grew so sick of the smell of oil and the sound of water that I thrust the question boldly toward him. Each time, in silence, he refused it. Again and again he came. I had no heart any more. I feared his coming. I hesitated to enter my yard. And then he said that there were moles upon her body, on her thigh. The thigh, I exclaimed, the home of beauty. The right side or the left? The left. The left! Momentous conditions are being satisfied. Are they low upon it? high? Near the hip. The hip! Glorious! Were there two? Two. Two! And the color: brown? red? black? Yellow. Yellow! What a marvel! And the hair that grew there? the color of the hair that grew there? Surely there was hair. There must be. My friend, you must look again. Look again. Again. Determine it precisely.

So he sounded with the bait. He was hooked through his throat to the tail.

Even now I dare not let my mind look upon the picture of that pair peering beneath her lifted skirts. How infernally lewd! How majestically revolting! She would ask him if he saw any. He would hesitate, realizing more than she how important it was to say yes, and yet not clearly, not surely finding grounds for an affirmation. He moistens his finger and applies it to the spot. Perhaps a brighter light. Perhaps if she removed her dress. In worry she watches him. What does it all mean? Can they say for certain that hair grows there; that it does not? She is persuaded to pronounce the negative but he holds her back. There is a doubt. There must be a doubt.

Or he has kept the substance of our conversations from

her. He spies out her moles, creeps upon her dressing, at her bath, or he remembers lovelier days when he was whole and she was smooth and clean and there was flesh to glory in. Then those moles were yellow on her hip perhaps like beads inviting kisses. No. I see the moistened finger, the hiked skirt, the inquiring frown. I see it clearly, bright with color, dimensional with shadow. There is somehow a bond between them greater than comfort. She is a nurse. She is a wife. But what else really? Was there a time when that same finger touched her thigh with love? I consider it and shudder. The mind plays strange games. No. No youth for them. They were always old. Does that finger touch her now with any tenderness or is it, as I rather fancy, like the touch of a dry stick?

There was a time when my hand, too, held heat and when its touch left a burn beneath the skin and I sought beauty like the bee his queen; but it was a high flight for an old tyrant, and not worth wings. Doubtless there were sweet and brave and foolish times between them. There may be sweet times now. Such times lie beyond my conjuring. I only know that thorough evil is as bright as perfect good and seems as fair; for animals that live in caves are bleached by darkness and so shine in their surroundings as the good soul does in its, albino as the stars. But beauty or any of its brilliant semblances is foreign to Mr. Wallace and his wife and to the Means. Real wickedness is rare. Certainly it does not rest in the tawdry murder of millions, even Jews. It rests rather on the pale brow of every saviour who to save us all from death first kills. Nevertheless, it is the Jewish fleshsmoke that one smells, the burning cords of bodies, and it is hard to see the soul through that stiff irreverent wood, I suppose, just as it is hard for me to light a bright bulb in the house of the Means, or place between the boards of husband Wallace and his wife a lover's need and pleasure.

Although, as it turned out, I was unable to capture Mr. Wallace, who clung tenaciously to his secrets, my triumph was complete. I broke the weaker vessel. I heard his cane rap on the front door and I rushed from my study to prevent his entrance. However, my wife forestalled me and Mr. Wallace was already in the living room when I arrived, sinking on the piano bench, his face alarmingly red and his eyes blinking at shadows. He filled the room with his hoarse hospitalities. I was brusque with my wife. I had hoped to hold him to the porch. I had read of saints who kissed the suppurating sores of beggars and I had always doubted the spiritual merit of it, but in front of Mr. Wallace I could only marvel that the act had been performed. At last I turned my wife away and Mr. Wallace pulled at the brim of his straw hat and stuttered at a shout his puzzlement. He shook, poor fellow, with anxiety. I laughed. I made light of everything. Moles are of course, I said, the accidents of birth. There's no more to be seen in their position than in the order of the stars. The ancient Greek philosophers, for the most part, have spoken clearly on the subject. Perhaps Pythagoras was not as plain as one would wish, while Socrates had in him from his birth a warning voice and Plato was given on occasion to behavior which was, well, scarcely consistent with his love of mathematics; yet Aristotle remained firm and did not generally recognize the power of premonition. The Christian Church, to be frank, regards such things as satanic, although there have been happenings which do appear upon their face to be . . . of a nature nearer to—what shall I say?—the epiphany of an occult world: nail holes on the feet and hands of even little boys, visions of the virgin, voices, seizures, transports, ecstasies, then the miracles worked by sainted bones, the wood of the true cross, cloth of the holy cape, blood, excrement, and so on . . . wounds in the side from which cool water flows as pure as the purest spring. Still . . . still . . . the church is stern. The Jews, too, are a hardheaded lot. There is of course the Cabala, the magical book. Nevertheless Yaweh is forthright. And so we know the leaves of tea arrange themselves for our amusement while the warm insides of fowl permit only the primitive to divine. Was it not before Philippi that the ghost of Julius Caesar . . . ? However . . . all omens are imaginings. We should laugh when we read disaster. In medieval days the story went about of a stream of spring-fresh water so sweet and pure that on the tongue it made the spirit eloquent and the head giddy with thanksgiving. Yet when men followed its turnings to its source they found it sprang from the decaying jaws of a dead dog. Thence the faithful spoke of how it was that from a foul, corrupt, and wicked world the clean and whole and good would one day flow. Mr. Wallace thanked me and tried to rise. He beckoned me and I went close and a powerful hand gripped my upper arm and pulled. The monster rose and his mouth broke open bitterly. Good-bye.

At last. But Mr. Wallace cannot whisper. The walls rang with him. What did she think when she heard? Will she cringe again? She came with tea some minutes later and pretended surprise at finding him gone. I had to stare at her until her cup shook. Then I went upstairs to my room.

When all was well begun and seemed well ended, the Wallaces joined the Means. Perhaps the Means read moles better than I do. Better: perhaps they do not know what moles may mean.

The houses here are served by alleys. Garages face them. Trash spills over the cinders and oil flavors the earth. The Wallaces have helped themselves up the Means' porch steps and day is falling when I begin my walk through the alleys by the backsides of the houses. The house of love is first. The shades are drawn. Who knows when passion may choose to spring from its clothes? I hear the Wallaces moving on the porch—the scrape of a chair. Eternity Tomorrow. It is tacked on the inside of the door. The letters swallow at the light. Their car is parked elsewhere but I resist the temptation to go in. Cracks in the walls net the floor. Beer cans glow. A wagon hangs precariously by its handle to the wall. I am at the entrance and frightened by it as a child is frightened by the cold air that drifts from a cave to damp the excitement of its discovery. Not since I was very young have I felt the foreignness of places used by others. I had forgotten that sensation and its power—electric to the nerve ends. The oiled ash, the cool air, the violet light, the wracked and splintered wood, the letters of the prophecy—they all urge me strangely. Mrs. Wallace hoots. I move on. The lane looks empty of all life like a road in a painting of a dream. I am a necromancer carrying a lantern. The lamp is lit but it gives no light. My steps are unnaturally loud and I tell myself I have fallen into the circle of my own spell. Tin briefly fires. Then I hear the voice of Mrs. Cramm. Her virtuous shoes show beneath the partly opened door of her garage. She stores things there for she has no car. By her shoes are another pair— a child's. The child giggles and is shushed. I have been loud in the lane yet they have not heard me. Now stock still, I fear to move. The door swings and I back in panic. I jump into the Means' garage. The door does not close and Mrs. Cramm remains hidden behind it with the child, convers-

ing in low tones. Finally the feet begin to move and I
duck deeply into the darkness of the Means. I feel a fool.
Steps are coming quickly. Light steps. What a fool. They
turn in. The child is in the door, a boy I think—Tim or
Ames. I crouch in the dark by a tire, hiding my eyes as if
he might see me with them. Fool. Why? Why have I done
this? Why am I hiding here like a thief? The child's feet
pass me and I hear a loud clink. Then he comes from the
rear of the barn and goes out and his feet disappear onto
grass. My courage returns and I follow what my ears have
remembered back into the barn but I fail to find what it
was he has deposited there. I bark my shin on a cycle. In
the lane I put my hands in my pockets. The alley is empty.
The light is nearly gone. I realize that I have breached the
the fortress, yet in doing so I lost all feeling for the Means
and sensed only myself, fearful, hiding from a child. A cat
fires from a crack in Mrs. Cramm's garage and passes
silently into the darkness. My stomach burns. I walk forward until I reach the turf and stand by redbud and by
dogwood trees. I see her then, utterly gray and unshaped
and unaccompanied, a thin gray mist by a tree trunk, and
I stand dumbly too while the dusk deepens. Indeed I am
not myself. This is not the world. I have gone too far. It
is the way fairy tales begin—with a sudden slip over the
rim of reality. The streetlights flare on Mrs. Cramm. Her
arms are clenched around her. She is watching the Means'
front porch from which I hear a whinny. Unaccountably
I think of Hänsel and Gretel. They were real and they went
for a walk in a real forest but they walked too far in the
forest and suddenly the forest was a forest of story with the
loveliest little cottage of gingerbread in it. There is a flash
in the ribboned darkness. From the corner of my eye I
think I see the back door of the Means' house close. Mrs.

Cramm is fixed—gray and grotesque as primitive stone.
I back away. The ribbons of light entangle me. I crawl between garages. My feet slip on cans. Fool fool fool. I try
to think what I'm doing. One day Jack went to town to
buy a cow and came home with a handful of beans. I slip.
There is a roar of ocean like a roaring mob. Have I gone
down before the giant? Mrs. Cramm is suddenly gone and
I slink home.

It was an experience from which I have not yet recov-
ered. I go back each evening just when dusk is falling and
stand by the redbud tree at the back of Mrs. Cramm's
yard. I never see her, yet I know that on the evenings when
the Wallaces visit with the Means, she talks to the children.
I have lain like fog between the garages and only heard
whispers—vague, tantalizing murmurs. Every evening I
hope the streetlights will surprise her again. I know where
every streak will be. I think I have seen her in the back
seat of the Means' car when it is parked in the barn sometimes—a blank patch of stone gray. Is it Ames who slips
out to meet her? Recently, while I've been loitering at the
end of the alley, taking my last look around, I've felt I've
mixed up all my starts and endings, that the future is over
and the past has just begun. I await each evening with
growing excitement. My stomach turns and turns. I am terribly and recklessly impelled to force an entrance to their
lives, the lives of all of them; even, although this is absurd,
to go into the fabric of their days, to mote their air with
my eyes and move with their pulse and share their feeling;
to be the clothes that lie against their skins, to shift with
them, absorb their smells. Oh I know the thought is awful,
yet I do not care. To have her anger bite and burn inside
me, to have his brute lust rise in me at the sight of her sagging, tumbling breasts, to meet her flesh and his in mine or

have the sores of Mr. Wallace break my skin or the raw hoot of his wife crawl out my throat . . . I do not care . . . I do not care. The desire is as strong as any I have ever had: to see, to feel, to know, and to possess! Shut in my room as I so often am now with my wife's eyes fastened to the other side of the door like blemishes in the wood, I try to analyze my feelings. I lay them out one by one like fortune's cards or clothes for journeying and when I see them clearly then I know the time is only days before I shall squeeze through the back screen of the Means' house and be inside.

Icicles

1

It had snowed heavily during the night, but by morning the sky had cleared, deepening the frost. The sun when it rose was dazzling, and at once it began to melt the roofs and window edges, power lines and limbs of trees. Icicles formed rapidly. At first they were thick and opaque like frozen slush, but later, lengthening, they cleared and began to glitter brilliantly like pieces of heavy glass. When Fender left his house he had to duck, sweeping a number away with his arm, they were that long already, and there were more when he returned at five—a row had formed above his picture window. Multiply like weeds, he thought, kicking fragments from his stoop with the side of his foot. Later he sat in his living room eating a pot pie from a tray in his lap and chewing crackers, his gaze passing idly along the streets in the wheel ruts and leaping the disorderly heaps of shoveling. He was vaguely aware of the ice that had curtained a quarter of his window, and of the light from the streetlamps reflected by it, but he was thinking how difficult it was to sell property so suspiciously hidden. This time of year the wind blew over the porches of the houses he was showing. His prospects were invariably shivering before he got them in. He'd say it was no day to trade caves, or some such thing, and they'd nod in a determined way that made him realize they meant it. A faint smile might drift to their faces. Inside there were boots and rubbers and the mess of snow and papers, sellers like shabby furniture, their wan and solemn children staring large-eyed at the strangers, while in-laws, made fat, no doubt, by their wisdom, held their arms like bundles to their chests and stopped up the doorways. There was always frost on the windows, darkening the rooms, and the attics and basements and enclosed porches were cold and grim, and his prospects had stiff, inhuman faces.

Prospects: a pickly word, a sour betrayer. It was supposed to fill your thoughts with gold, or with clear air and great and lovely distances. Well, the metal came quickly enough to mind, but beards followed shortly, dirt and the deceptions of the desert, biscuits like powdered pumice, tin spoons, stinking mules, clattering cups, stinking water, deceiving air.

You've got to watch their eyes, Glick. Watch their eyes. Then at the first sign (here Fender would bang his hands together) close in. Greed. (He'd hug himself.) Greed's what you want to see—all the worst, Glick—envy, that possessive eye. Bang! That eagerness. That need.

But he had a list of numbers to call. He'd better get at it.

He hated winter. The same gray sky lay on the ground, day after day, gray as industrial smoke, and in the sky the ground floated like a street that's been salted, and his closets were cold, holes wore through his pockets, and he was lonely, indoors and out, with a loneliness like the loneliness of overshoes or someone else's cough. At the office you seldom got out; your hours weren't your own; you figured insurance and read the ads in the papers and called when people were home. At the other desk, stacking brochures that advertised lots in Florida and sucking on his fountain pen, rearranging flowers that were dead and dialing numbers without lifting the receiver, was Glick— Glick, the wiseman, Glick, the joker—green all winter like a pine . . . all winter. There was no one else to talk to but Isabelle, and of course Isabelle . . .

Glick, why do you do that? I mean, why do you dial like that, with the receiver on the hook? Glick leans over his desk, placing both hands on the phone like a healer. I rehearse the number I'm going to call. He's very serious, very intense. I rehearse everything. He says it proudly. Preparation is the secret of success.

Advice. From the start. Very wise. And Glick was the younger man. Glick. A pickle. A pickly fellow. Fender's fork poked through the crust of his pie, releasing steam, and he squinted at the crawling, winking snow. No friend of his. Who knew what shape the lawns were in?

Fender allowed his first bite to fall back. Still staring aimlessly, he rinsed his mouth with air and sent it coasting against the pane. Another advantage of living alone. No embarrassment. Only sensible. He stirred the pie with his fork. If he touched his tongue to the window—that would be cooling. Undeniably another advantage. Who would dare to . . . publicly? Even alone he felt constraint. As if Pearson might be passing and would see him apply such a kiss to the glass. To Pearson it would look strange and Pearson would hold the strangeness against him.

Again there was no beef to speak of. Deftly he exposed a piece. Lights pierced the pie as about them the gravy darkly oozed and bubbled. The pies were best when the company was still trying to make a good impression. There would be lots of meat then, and the crust would be tender. Pies, he thought, pies . . .

He wondered whether he ought to try another kind, maybe the kind with the cow on the label. He believed the cow was smiling and he tried to imagine its face and its figure clearly but shards of ice in the drifts disturbed him. There were sales, times of year the price subsided, others again when it rose; there was a rhythm in the market as regular as though it were moved by the moon. He was supposed to keep his ear to the ground and hear the new supermarket opening or the branch bank or the store, the block of offices going up, the factory closing. . . .

Fortunate if you had a freezer.

Pearson, this morning, had once again whacked Fender's desk with his newspaper. Suddenly: whackwhack. Keep your ears to the ground, Fender. Listen. Listen with all you've got, with the whole business—hard—with your eyes, with your nose—with the soul, Fender—yes, that's what I mean, that's it—the soul. So keep those ears down. That's how we get on in this business. That's how, I should say, *you* get on, hay, fair friend? But look—I mean Isabelle, Glick—look: there Fender sits. He sits. Where's your spirit, Fender, your sporting spirit? Merry up. Oh . . . sad. He's a sad old dog, Glick. Sad old dog. Try to match me, Fender. Here—take on a real master. Get your blood up. Ah, but look: he sits. Poor pooch. I say, Isabelle—poor pooch. Come on, Fender, try to top the old pro just once and really *harken*, fair friend, hay?—really listen in. Think if you heard as much as I do. A din! Now then, are you ready, wound and set? Okay—okay—what's happening—here's a nice one for you—what's happening at sixteen thirty-two, oh let's make it, um, ah—Balinese? What say? . . . fair enough? . . . okay?

Pearson is listening. He wrinkles his nose. The newspaper, folded to real estate, comes down. The image of his heavy gold ring passes across the desk. Years ago he'd explained the ring to Fender, holding his hand to the light. I love this business, Fender, he'd said. I have this funny feeling about it. I love it. That's what this ring has always meant. The first time I slipped it on, it struck me—love! Pearson twisted the ring but Fender never saw it clearly, he was looking away at his shoes, and he still had no idea what the emblem on it represented. Fender, you know, it's like—you aren't Catholic, Fender, are you?—well, it's like being married to the church. Like nuns or monks are. Aren't they? That's it. That's fine. Like monks or nuns.

Pearson is listening . . . listening . . . and it seems unlikely that Fender will be able to surpass him, he's so alert. But Pearson coaxes. Try. It's possible. It's barely possible, Fender. Try. Anyway—that's all. Just keep up. Keep up.

Fender now imagines that he's shrugged disdainfully, displaying his palms. He fires off a clever retort. In this weather, Mr. Pearson, he decides he's saying, smiling wisely, all I'll get is an earful of ice. The remark falls short of his hopes, somehow.

Fender resumed his chewing. Suppose he had though? He blew softly, feeling the warmth of the fork in his fingers. When they cut their prices like that, they were unloading all their old stock, clearing their warehouses of what would otherwise spoil, no doubt of it. How long would such things keep, frozen like bricks of ice? Antarctic explorers had . . . what? Lethargic bacteria. The beef would spoil first, or the gravy would. Then salt was a factor. Of course they salted the pies. Didn't salt hasten . . . ? He remembered it did. Ham and bacon poorest. Perhaps some preservative was added. Yes, a good question: how long would they last? Funny that such a figure should control the fluctuation. He thought how Pearson would sway to the music of the market like a dancer. Keep your fingers on the pulse. Measure the flow. Calculate the rate.

When Fender had first entered the business, Pearson had taken him in hand and taught him what he could, so there was little point in his standing before Fender's desk like a startled stag, as if every sale of real estate set up vibrations in the air to which his sensitive organs immediately responded, for Fender knew he gathered his information in a more prosaic way. He read the papers mainly, devoting the largest portion of his day and nearly the whole of his energy to them. He read each line on every page, proceeding patiently from front to rear, therefore including even overseas and national news, the comics and the columns of opinion—those parts of the paper which presumed to paint what Pearson, peering beneath his palm like an Indian, called "the wider prospect," since it was his fiercely held conviction that events which seemed of world importance were, when you thought about them deeply, but weak misleading echoes of a sound made strongly only once and then in some close place of no real size. Do you realize, Fender, he was fond of saying, that all news is kitchen gossip at the first—is merely nearby, local, neighbor news—and that nothing happens—anywhere—that doesn't happen on a piece of property? And once when Fender had suggested air and ocean, Pearson, angry, had replied: you're a water-strider, are you? you regularly fly by flapping? Triumphantly he'd shouted: what's the airplane, if you please? *Elizabeth?* what's *Mary? Leonardo? Flandre? France?* And he went on with a dizzying list of ships and planes.

In order that no such happening should escape him (at least this seemed to Fender to be the reason), Pearson ran a broad-nibbed pen behind the path of his eye to cancel what he'd read and frequently to decorate the margins with perfectly symmetrical stars he then carefully colored in, so that the paper, when he finished, was a bewildering splay and run of bright blue ink from one end to the other—soaked through with lines, blots, finger smears and stars. Because he read on slowly, cautiously, and artfully, because of his devotion, his passion, his love, because—it was really impossible, Fender thought, to be absolutely certain why, the effect so dwarfed the causes—still, whatever the reason, he remembered everything: births, deaths, divorces, auctions, wills, proceedings of the city council and the courts, all the endless activities of the fraternal orders whose officers and properties he knew (they were the Masons, Moose, Odd Fellows, Elks, Knights Templar, Pythias and Columbus, the Eagles and the Eastern Star), as well as the countless civic programs and charitable resolves of the Chamber of Commerce and the service clubs which he sometimes read aloud in solemn priestly tones while circling the office (these were the Optimists, Rotary, Lions, Kiwanis and Golden Rule), nor did he overlook the movements of the VFW, DAR, AmVets and Legion either, or the apparently infinite interests of every church and synagogue (indeed he had a quip about that), and he seemed to have overcome whatever handicap in age and sex he might have had to keep warmly on the trail of the women's groups, the young people's fellowships too, the children's even (the Future Farmers, for example, the Sunshine Girls, Boy Scouts, Brownies, Rainbows, Hi-Ys and 4-H), also he greedily received the news of the sporting leagues (kittyball, softball, hardball, basketball, bowling, dartball, handball, tennis, ping-pong, volleyball, golf), as well as those dreary items from the clubs of the lonely (fish, stamps, chess, photography, birds) for which his memory was complete, just as it seemed to be for everything . . . for everything . . . for all the advertisements . . . particularly those . . . while at the same time he was passionately interested in political side-taking, the choice of queens, awards of trophies, conventions of salesmen and dentists, all testimonials, fund luncheons, gift announcements, threats of epidemic sickness, sales, transfers, removals, celebrations, weddings, accidents, elections, thefts, and with the let of bids, permits for new construction, licenses and notes of condolence, mergers, promotions, bankruptcies, foreclosures, hearings, fires, suits, settlements, raids, arrests; if there was an address—anywhere— it caught his eye, for an address was the name of a property, and it was important (it was everything!) to know properties—how they fared—because properties were like people, they had characters; they suffered from vicissitudes, as he'd told Fender often, and fell upon evil times like the best of us did, only to rise up again and be renewed as it also happened sometimes; and the consequence of all this continuous, close, and fanatical concern was that Pearson could, when he drove a street, pass judgment on it, read its future, as he'd done so many times in those early days, in the lawns and porches of its houses, in their lamps or curtains or their paint and chimneys, but largely in the lines from the papers that sprang into his mind at the sight of their numbers: three fifty-two, for instance, has diabetes, Fender, he'd say—serious—I wouldn't give her long . . . then three sixty-four is eighty-seven, very feeble, needs a cane to breathe . . . and there was a golden wedding across the street not long ago . . . ah, here— three more in a row—not a one under seventy, living in these great big houses all alone, in these worn old trees, can't even crawl the stairs—the same as empty: say! what would you hear if you were a mouse in the basement or a wasp in the attic? not a noise, eh? not a sound, nothing— just the whole house running—running down . . . well, well, we're being watched, someone wonders why I've stopped, she's peeping between her curtains, see her?— suppose she knew, Fender, hah! suppose she knew . . . this street's about to move, that's the fact to remember, it's a street of old ladies—now are we going to take command or not? . . . you've got to be creative, Fender, you've got to *see* . . . here, look at five one oh, that two-steepled business with the porte cochere—all right, what are the possibilities there? that was a coach house once, in back . . . oh come on, come on, it's easy—friend, it's easy— you spot the house and instantly—like that!—it fills your mind: name, slogans, programs, the whole package, everything! . . . let's see—Twin Steeples—no, Twin Pinnacles Funeral Home—*Twin Pinnacles!* ah! superb!—you haven't been in the business long enough to know how good that name is, Fender, so don't make a face . . . no sir—bravo, Pearson, fine friend, bravo!—not Smerz, Block, Nicolay— names of people—no, a *place,* a lofty position, perfect for final rest—peaks—deserved—sure, a little paint is all, some facing stone, enlarge that window, lots of space for the hearse in back, big basement likely, if it isn't damp, a few spots hid by shrubbery at the corners of the lot to light it up . . . Twin Pinnacles . . . perfect, perfect . . . paint the turrets gold—with the sun glinting from them, a little suggestion of the Great Gate Above—can't you see it? a flood lamp at night—ideas! ideas! that's what this job is, it's creative . . . you've got to consider how the undertaking business is, who needs to move, who might, all that —facts . . . how's this street to go? that's what you've got to think—will they be lodge halls? offices? or are there too many cheap apartments in this neighborhood already? —there's one, for instance, with two outside stairs—no good—his driver's license up a year, he drinks and rust is in his eaves—see those stains? . . . you've got to know how far it is to the center of town, what other businesses there are around, what the general direction of the traffic is—north-south, west-east? consider, see? . . . this is your person, Fender—these streets, these buildings, this town— the body of your beloved—yes, yes, yum—and you've got to *know* it . . . think, perceive, consider and create . . . who were those biddies with the string? yeah, fates—well that's our function, Fender, we're the fates . . . so maybe dentists, doctors—you've got to think—how far is it from the hospital? happen to know? . . . six-tenths of a mile from this corner—not bad, considering . . . see what I mean? here she is, Fender, feel her up, eh? hah! yum . . . oh say, figure, Fender, figure—beauticians? barbers? chapter of the Red Cross? or realtors even! maybe me! hay, maybe Pearson! . . . you've got to have everything at the tip—the tip . . . Fender, the thing is: it's moving, and the thing to ask yourself is: am I going to create, control, direct, manage, *make* that move, or is it going to manage and move and make me? see? . . . they talk about subdivisions—out in the country—weed fields and drainage ditches—that's child's play, sandbox stuff—slides! swings! —but look what's here, right here! we can subdivide this street, that's what it comes to, it's in our hands! . . . responsibility! . . . ah, it's terrific, this business, Fender, terrific.

Terrific. Years ago. When he seemed a prophet, sometimes a god. At the tip, he'd exclaim, raising his ink-stained fingers. A thrill would shoot through Fender, and he'd repeat the words to himself, considering again the wisdom of his teacher. Everything is property. Pearson's face would glow, his hair shake. Everything is property. Think of it. Some sort of property. Then he'd rush through the office naming objects, lifting them up. This, and this, and this . . . This ear, he says triumphantly, fingering the lobe, this ear belongs to Isabelle. . . .

Buy at the bottom. Fill your freezer. Fortunate . . . to take advantage of the time . . .

People pass on. In the midst of life, you know, Fender . . . well . . . but property, property endures. Sure, sure, cars go to junk before the people in them do sometimes, but there's all sorts of property, that's all, and a house will outlast its builder usually. Lots of things outlast us, Fender. Lots of things. Lots do. Hah hah. Well. That's it. Land's damn near immortal. Land lasts forever. That's why it's called real, see? oh it makes sense, Fender, old fellow and friend, it makes sense!

A rhythm in the market . . . up and down . . . your fortune . . . if . . .

People are property. Does that seem like a hard saying, people are property? not even real? Oh let me tell you, Fender, we've got it all wrong, most of us . . . backwards . . . most of us. People own property—that's what we say—that's what we think. Oh sure. Sure. A howler—that one. Listen: *property owns people.* Everything's property, and the property that lasts longest—it owns what lasts least. Stands to reason. Fender, Fender, wait'll you die, you'll see! So the property that lives, Fender, that lasts and lives and goes right on, Fender, and then goes on again, that overlives us, Fender, that *overlives . . .* well, that's the property that's real, and *it—it owns the rest—* lock, stock, and barrel—*right?* Makes sense.

Fundless Fender, freezerless Fender . . .

It made sense, yes. It still made sense. But now it did seem a hard saying . . . hard to bear. His little house possessed him, it was true. He'd been cut to fit its walls. He saw what it permitted. He did not reach beyond the rooms. Up the steps of a glowering, blind-eyed house, how many times had he led them, like pets in search of owners? Pearson was right. The question his buyers should have asked—do I want to belong to this house?—they never asked. What will these floors and corners, these views, these halls and closets, do with my life? Pearson was right. Prop-purr-tee, he'd cry, a lovely sound. And Fender was bothered; he was worried. His car owned him and his shirts and shoes owned him, his socks and ties, even his towels and toothbrush were tyrannical. He moved uneasily in his clothes, staring at his suit. Imagine—there were faint stripes in the trousers he'd never noticed before. They gave him a fright, lurking in the cloth. What else might be? Body too—Pearson would lean over the desk and whisper —your body owns you . . . another house, isn't it? Up front steps—how many times? He'd scrape the key in the lock and wave them in, the fools, he'd wave them in. *Run,* he ought to scream, and ring an alarm.

Pearson has entered, beaming, flourishing a magazine.

An emperor in here, he says, twisting the magazine into a roll and aiming it at Fender, an emperor—and a man doesn't get to be an emperor by sitting on his ass—excuse me, Isabelle—but just the same, his ass! anyway—this emperor says the secret is, ah, *to live in harmony with nature.* That's what I mean, Fender. That's what I've been telling you all these years. Here it is. Whack. With the flow, Fender, with the flow. Times change—you change. Business, money, people—if they move, Fender, you move. Ride with the punch. Absorb the blow. See? It's so clear. It's so easy. It's so clean. An emperor. Whack. Imagine. Whack. Lived way back there, you know. It's true. Anyway —a great magazine, Fender. Great. Whack. They weren't so dumb in those days, were they? Read it. Clear as a bell. Whack. Slick as a whistle. Whack. Neat as a pin, hay? Clean. Whack. And remember what you read. Okay? Whackwhackwhackwhackwhack . . .

The cow stood squarely in a clump of daisies. At least it was some white-petaled flower with an orange or yellow eye. Smiling. He'd cut his finger on a blade of paper. Now he felt it stinging pleasantly, and his shoulders were aching. Then there the peas were finally, huddled together.

Glick, why do you do that? I mean, what are you tearing up all that paper for? Glick carefully folds a sheet and sharpens the crease with his thumbnail. This paper's a piece of property. He smiles indulgently. You've got to have imagination, Fender. I'm subdividing. Numbering lots, figuring sizes, you know, drainage, easements, everything. He pulls at the corners. The land parts cleanly. . . .

Peas. In one pie there might be anywhere from nine to eighteen peas. Eighteen was quite a few. He'd counted peas but never bits of beef or carrot. Now he wondered why. Peas cried out to be counted, they were so green and discrete, nevertheless it was the beef that determined the quality of the product. Automatically he began phrasing the letter. *As you are perfectly aware, it is the meat that chiefly determines* . . . Pig in a poke, that's what. He chewed cautiously. *Doubtless it never occurred to you that someone would actually trouble to number* . . . The world out the window shifted. Houselights streaked the snow. Like the urine of dogs by trees. Though it didn't seem corrosive but lay lightly on top like something transparent—a diaphanous robe. *However it happens that I have been counting the pieces of beef in your pies for some*—how long should he say? what would make for the greatest effect? everything took such time—well say for some years, that would put the fear of the public properly back in them. *Therefore my data is quite complete and my conclusions well nigh indisputable* . . . yes . . . well nigh, that was nice. . . .

Fender was weary—weary of winter. The little energy he had was ebbing. The cloth of his suit was scraping his knees. The scraping seemed dangerous, his skin felt so thin. Miserable business. Drops of water were wavering at the points of the icicles and he decided there must be a breeze. Then too, the hull of a pea had fastened itself to a molar. He crushed his tongue against it. There ought to be a guarantee but he'd never examined the package. Had he thrown the wrapper away? It was no use, his interest was waning, though he tried to revive it by thinking of the consternation his letter might cause if it reached the right people. Threat of exposure—the Food and Drug Administration, the Federal Trade Commission. Just for a moment he was pleased and the fluid of the pie seemed thick and rich, but his pleasure was quickly gone and he felt himself empty like one of his houses, staring out at the wind and snow, at the undulating lanes of light and shadow, waiting for someone . . . anyone . . . to enter. There would be patches of ice in the streets in the morning, and then the city's trucks would spread sand and salt about so that by afternoon each automobile would be spraying slush in its wake, and this would collect and freeze in rough gray blocks behind the wheels until, incontinent, the machine let them fall into the street.

Halting in front of Glick, Pearson says somberly: do you know what's the matter with you, Glick? do you? have you any idea? any real notion, the least comprehension of it? Pearson waits for Glick to surface his troubled, obsequious face. Pearson's autumnal joke is coming. It is always painful. You spend too much time raking leaflets, he says, passing swiftly through the door to his office where after a moment—always the same—they hear him whoop and roar, then roar again. Fender stares into the mess in his drawer, aimlessly shifting sheets of paper and turning over clips and pins and rubberbands. He scarcely thinks that once all this was in radiant order, each thing bespeaking its place through its nature. Another advantage of living alone—you couldn't very well say: excuse me, don't interrupt, I'm counting the peas in this pie; or: I'm composing a letter to those pot pie people; or— No, he was finished for the evening; he was bored by his own voice; yawns stretched his jaws and filled his eyes with tears. The phone calls would have to wait. The snowlight, though soft now, had made his eyes burn, he decided, and he put down his fork to press them tenderly and wipe the moisture from their corners. He resolved, though weakly, to draw the drapes, but as he shifted in his chair the long row of icicles blazed and his breath went out of him. For an instant Fender sat quite still, as someone wounded may who does not know what pain he'll bring himself or blood he'll spill, but his eyes were drawn into the string and held while the light from the living room lay burning in them. The purity of the ice was astonishing, the tips were like needles, and they ran together at their source like fingers into palms. Snow was no longer melting and the icicles had a hard dry gleam. He set aside his tray and stood. Fish in a bowl—he felt that conspicuous. He was conscious, too, of the soft warmth of the room. It was shining out to them, but the light that entered was slowly cooled and added to the ice. He tugged at the pull and dragged the curtains across the pane. No sense everyone seeing in. Better to live like a mole out of eyeshot. He'd look at a magazine, he decided, and go to bed early. Indeed he was tired. Always, even as a child, he'd needed his sleep.

2

The following morning the icicles were still there. Every eave had them. They hung in clusters from poles and from the elbows of trees. Where the snow had melted from the faces of the traffic signs, the icicles were spindly, but they emerged from spouts like muscular arms and clung to the gutters in dense strings. The sky was clear again, the cold continuing, and the snow remained deep on the roofs. Good growing weather, Fender thought, letting his breath seep from his mouth. It was simply a question of how much weight their stems would hold. Or had they stems? Parsnips, he remembered, were white. Under a faucet a cone. It put him in mind of caves. From floor to ceiling. Like sets of teeth. And there was scarcely a breeze. The impulse to see if his own string had survived the night was very strong when he awoke. His concern surprised him and he thought there was something wrong with the feeling, something silly, childish almost—yes, childish, that was right; moreover he blamed the icicles for his having slept badly and for the struggle he'd had to prevent himself from drawing the curtains first thing like a fool. The impulse had come on before he was slippered even, had grown while he used the bathroom, become clamorous while he dressed and had his juice, so that he took no pleasure in anything, but thought of the icicles and whether they were safe and whether he was picturing their lengths correctly, except that occasionally, as if there was some connection, he would remember the list in his pocket and all the tasks he'd failed to do, the endless number of things put off: bills, letters, papers, phone calls, errands, odd jobs— god, he was showing a house to a couple at when? ten? eleven—a regular dog's house—Ringley—empty all winter—fine, damn fine—in bad shape now—dark, cold, walrus-jawed Ringley . . . who was it hunted caves? some funny name . . . gah, to crawl through holes in the earth like worms, who knew what you'd come on? water dripping somewhere and the white pouches of spiders—adventure, they called it . . . nothing like the fire of the mountain, at least as he saw it, the glittering air, distance sloping brilliantly away. . . . Then a vision of an immense snowfield triumphed briefly in Fender, blinding him pleasantly, and he stretched to tiptoe, meaning to look, it was stupid to fight oneself over such a thing, Ringley, three floors of basement, a park for bats . . . and the appointment would run through lunch most likely. . . . He ought to catch up on the figures but what was the use, no one wanted a place like that. This pair, these people: who were they? they wouldn't want it—a trap. . . . Pearson should tell Clara to sell it herself, he wasn't a wizard, for heaven's sake. Look, Pearson, I'm no magician and that place is a

pumpkin; it's full of rats, well anyway mice, they leave
their droppings on the kitchen counters—not a chance.
. . . So he'd hear Pearson preach the power of imagination: Fender! think what you're selling! happiness is our
commodity! you want to dream for them—dream! But
Fender remembered how a Baby Ruth wrapper had ruined
a sale, it had gone through their dreams like a brick. . . .
He ought to have made those calls, Pearson would ask
him about them. No dice, Mr. Pearson, nothing doing
there, he'd have to say, while Glick grinned greenishly—
soaked in dill. . . . He could use his tape and if they
were still there, he could measure them, that would be interesting—to know how large.

Then another thing I do is I always draw a picture of
the house, a simple floor plan. Take this away with you, I
say, it'll help you remember; and let me tell you, they're
grateful. And another thing I always do is I always . . .
but Glick is not listening, he is looking away—the newer,
the younger man, he has his sharp eyes stuck in something.
Glick? I hope you don't think Pearson's taught me all I
know about this business. Not by a long shot. I always try
to think of a way they can save, trim, cut some corner—a
fifth one—so they'll believe they can safely spend their
money on the four I'm selling; it gives them the right feeling; they've got to have the right feeling—it's an art—it
takes years. Well . . . Ah . . . Glick? I've picked up a few
things myself, you know, yes sir. Pearson can't tell you
everything. But Glick was not listening to Pearson either,
even when Pearson spoke directly to him and Glick looked
serious and nodded and the muscle in his jaw jumped. He
never listened; even when Pearson told his joke and Glick
surfaced his troubled, obsequious face like a fish to receive
it, his ears were full. Well you'll want to know *what* things,

I suppose, a fellow just starting out like you are, learning the ropes, getting the feel, you'll want to cotton on to what you can, the accumulated wisdom, as they say, well that's what civilization is, I guess, knowledge handed on, isn't it? experience of the years; elders, betters, eh? . . . Glick? For instance, sizes. Damn, he was deaf as his flowers. Fender had wanted to take him under his wing. How foolish that was. He was a bramble, a burr. Awf—sharp, he never scratched himself except in pleasure. Sizes of rooms, Glick—think. You want to have them right here, see, on the tip of your tongue—living room: twenty-four by fifteen; master bedroom: thirteen and a half by eleven and a fourth; kitchen: nine by five; bath: six by four, and so on . . . sizes. The dining room is a spacious square, an elegant and useful twelve. Make it sound professional. Smooth. That siding, see? that's one-by-four t-and-g re-sawn redwood, my good friend, there's no better. Your clients are thin with the worms of worry, skinny from the scares inside them. Fatten them on certainty. They want to believe. This closet? It's twenty-two deep—that's standard. You say that—you say it's standard—even if it isn't. Next the missus'll want to know whether she can get her what-not in that corner. Quick—the facts! the figures! you rattle off the sizes. Twelve hundred square feet of living space. You're buying a house, here, Mr. Ramsay, you say, laughing, at only nine bucks a yard. Yes sir, sizes. Gives them confidence. They see your concern. I tell you they're worn; they're wires; worry is crawling through them, breeding; they want to believe. So: height of the ceilings. Width of the windows. Here's a fellow who knows, they think, some-one really familiar with his property, someone who has the facts at the tip of his tongue, someone who's been around and understands the market, someone we can trust. It works, Glick. It has quite an effect. Try it out. One try'll convince. You feed them facts as sharp as needles. You surprise them. See this piece of pipe, Mr. Ramsay, it's six feet long. You know how important that sort of thing is— I mean how far your water travels. It flabbergasts them, Glick. Yes sir, it sets them on their ears.

But Glick was not listening . . . awash in his barrel, sunning himself in brine.

Fender had triumphed over himself, he had managed not to look, so that now, while the engine of his car was warming, he was able to enjoy the icicles thoroughly, and he thought it was perhaps this righteousness that had driven out the sense, always present and dominant before, that icicles were, after all, well, icicles; yet he could not help noticing that his were longer than any of his neighbors'—they were grander in every way—and since the weather had been considerate enough to remain fine, they would certainly continue growing, they might even double themselves during the day—it was purely a question of how much weight their stems would bear. He tried to remember when he'd last paid icicles any mind—in his childhood sometime, surely—but his memory failed him, he was left with a blank. There was a house, doubtless, somewhere, he'd lived in, but he'd lost the address. Even now his life slid swiftly by and was soon out of sight like a stick on a river. It vanished so completely, in fact, that at a party once, when he was asked as a part of a game to compose his autobiography, he'd had to answer that he couldn't tell the story of his life because he couldn't in the least remember it. At this confession everyone laughed strenuously, warming him with shame and pleasure, but it was not a joke, the remark was true, even if he'd recognized its truth himself only at the moment he was making it, and the idea frightened him a bit, though he forgot about it finally along with everything else: the party, his unmeant wit, its small surprise, the anxiety that was a consequence of it, and his smoothly disappearing life. He did remember that at first he'd had the same fear of the icicles he'd had from time to time of sharpened pencils—that one might pierce his eye. There was no discomfort in his gaze now, however, only pride, and when he felt the cool mass of the tape measure against his thigh, he had to triumph over himself again. What would people think if they saw him . . . anyone passing . . . Pearson conceivably? He wished his icicles were growing on the other side —within—where he might measure them in private, examine them in any way he liked. But if one broke off . . . The thought was dismaying. Really—good heavens—look here, he exclaimed quite aloud, ducking into his car, you're not right, Fender, old fellow and friend, one of these days they'll be taking you away . . . and he backed in reckless bursts out the snowy drive.

Glick was holding a ballpoint pen between his teeth like a pirate. It was a green pen and it made Fender think: pickle. Glick nodded briefly at Fender who was feeling his way now through an office unnaturally dark and full of lurking obstacles. Goodness but it's bright outside, he said, his voice false as a wig, which both surprised and annoyed him, since it was a small thing to have said, and he'd certainly meant it. The typewriter was repeating a letter—likely *x*. Glick nodded again and sucked noisily on his saliva. Fender, in his turn, blinked hard to unmuddy his eyes. Prospects. They made him think dirt. They made him think rags, snakes, picks, and the murder of companions. With difficulty he wriggled out of his coat, found he was angry, and began impatiently stuffing his scarf in a sleeve.

Glick's flowers were rustling like ghosts behind him. The coat hanger swayed and clinked. The typewriter continued to drum and rattle. Isabelle . . . Ah, Isabelle—but unfortunately . . .

At his desk he opened drawers. Glick was saluting him, wasn't he? with a flower. These are new, Glick said, removing the pickle to speak. New, Fender wondered, how, new? I just brought them in this morning, a change, Glick said, and time for it too, the others were dusty. Fender grew watchful. It was a joke perhaps. And he realized he'd given voice to his thoughts. But . . . I mean . . . why, he finally said, why these . . . well . . . these old dead flowers? *Dried,* they're *dried,* Glick said, it's a hobby of mine, strawflowers are easy—*Helichrysum, Helichrysum monstrosum;* then there's *Statice,* sea lavender, *Statice sinuata;* and Angel's Breath, of course, *Gypsophila; Xeranthemum; Rhodanthe,* Swan River . . . Why was Glick going on like this just now? He'd been in the office over a year and there'd never been any occasion for—any need to mention—to go into that strange foolishness of his. Fender squeezed his head in the corner of his arm and thought of his icicles growing in long carroty lines. Ah, they should be careful. . . . Slowly the room began to sort itself. Glick had a heap of leaves and other withered things on a newspaper. He kept thrusting stems in a vase, then yanking their heads. Grasses, he was saying. Pampas grass grows anywhere from ten to twenty feet high. Grasses, said Fender blankly. Hare's-tail grass and foxtail millet, that's *Setaria italica.* Quaking grass, which is *Briza maxima.* Fender's anger suddenly flared. He bent and rummaged through his file drawer. That ass, that ass, he thought, just like him too—ten to twenty feet indeed, what a liar—just think, how could he compare . . . I saw a good many icicles this morning, he said, his tongue thick. He hated that foreign language. Glick was standing back, tipping his head from side to side, winking absurdly. They're all over, he said. All over? Well, I suppose they are. All over, eh? Everywhere, Glick said, like weeds; you should have seen the bunch I kicked off my car. I can bet, said Fender, hardly able to speak. His head was filled to bursting. When I think of you, Glick, he said to himself, I think: pickle! Have you ever really looked at an icicle, Glick? really looked? Sure, Glick said, straightening, sure I have, why? But Glick wasn't listening and there was no need for Fender to reply. He slid back deeply in himself, into the threatening heat, his heart and the typewriter thumping, while fear for his icicles passed like a cloud across his stomach. I've a fever, Fender decided, shivering as though to verify the diagnosis. So Glick had a hobby. Think of that. Where were the figures on the Ringley house? A hobby. Imagine. No, his mind drew back, he couldn't picture it. Where was that colored card? He always put those figures on a colored card. Glick was folding and removing the newspaper from his desk whose surface, gleaming, seemed to leap beneath it. He'd put it—he'd put it somewhere—where? . . . oh he was in a fury, a fury. He glared at Glick to be rude. Blue suit this morning, by george. Desk rubbed. Tightly knotted dark tie lit by metallic threads. What was the reason? And then these carefully collected old weeds. Dried, dead, what was the difference? Left to sweat in the sun like prunes and raisins. Latin, was it? Latin, of course. Hoo. Mummification. He'd written down that couple's name—he had—he knew he had. It was an attack on him, all of it, everything. . . . And Pearson would come in a bit. Ah, *now* Glick was busy. His french cuffs slid from his coat sleeves. Bizz-bizz-

bizz. Well, Pearson would come in a bit. Shatteringly. Nothing up with those numbers, Mr. Pearson, I'm afraid, no, nothing up. His icicles now—they ought to increase themselves carefully. If he had time he'd just drive by during lunch—see how they were doing. Strawflowers, did he say? Aaah. They were perfectly turned, that's how nature did it. Drops gathering at the tip, then falling away. *Of course* icicles were all over. Who'd said otherwise? Climate general, conditions everywhere the same, consequences similar, very natural, who— Fender drew a deep shuddery breath. My my my, old fellow, friend, what a way really, what a way, take hold now, get a grip. When I think of you, Glick . . . *monstrosum?* is that what he said? it had the right sound. Lord. The show-off. The fake. But such a shame. They were so fragile. Such a shame.

Pearson did not come. Contrary to his custom, he did not come at all, nor did he notify them. The phone was still. After a time the typewriter ceased. Fender sat for a long while quite motionless and silent, in a kind of trance, papers spread out before him in a fan, staring down at their decorative surfaces, some pink, some cream, some yellow, most white, a pencil sticking like a twig from his fingers, the warmth coming and going, the worry too, causing his brows to clench and the corners of his mouth to wrinkle, until the remarkable storm of feeling that had burst upon him the moment he had drawn aside the office door passed off, he cooled, and his heart began to slow and settle. Then his gaze regained its content. He heard the humming of the fluorescent lights. Something—jewelry?—clicked. The image of Glick's vase was squatting in the wax, and Fender, able to speak, though overloudly, said: where's Pearson this morning? what's the matter? is he sick? Riding his chair from behind his desk, Glick spun gayly around.

Isn't it nice? Fender tried to smile. He'd be a good fellow.
But the office, for some reason, wasn't safe this morning,
it didn't feel right. He didn't feel right himself. He was,
for one thing, a good deal smaller than his skin. Your body
owns you; another house, isn't it? Fender came up cautiously to the ports of his eyes: lady's hanky in a wad,
string of clips, glistening pen stem, ringlet of phone wire,
pamphlets bent back savagely . . . wrong, wrong, wrong,
everything wrong . . . a golden row of pencils coming to
points, then Glick, bluish, turning gently, smiling, pretending to raise his ribs with his hands, inhaling noisily, isn't
it nice? . . . dull green cabinets covered with sideswipes,
darkly indented caster tracks on the asphalt tile, the stainless tube of a chair, while across the window the Gothically
lettered name of the agency in black, and beyond that the
bright sun littering the street with reflection.

What's the white stuff? This? that's honesty. *What,* demanded Fender, who was prepared to be angry again. It's
called honesty, Fen . . . *Lunaria annua.* Glick laughed
the hearty joker's laugh and Fender grew uneasy. It's also
called the money plant. And this is amaranth, *Gomphrena.*
Glick tilted, his shoes rose gleaming. Glick, ah, how . . .
how do you make them, I mean, get them so dry? His
voice seemed strange and distant, mechanized, as though
it came from a speaker. The office was edging away, pen,
pencils, paper; the phone drew back, the punch, the sta-
pler; and Glick sang on without him. Maybe Pearson's got
the word, Glick said—the sheet's sneaked down from the
statue; or maybe he hasn't any pennies for the papers, he's
broke finally, flindered, his pockets bulge with his pieces;
or maybe he sold a property and swooned clean away like
the slope on a steeple. Flies of his fingers, Glick flew them
in spirals. It was all for Isabelle, and Fender couldn't bear

it. Where *was* Pearson? Bake . . . do you bake them somehow? Fender asked. But Glick was handing himself to Isabelle, smiling his soul out. Fender couldn't bear it. No, Izzy—no, Glick said, I see it quite plainly now—now suddenly I see it all. He was peering between his fingers. In a moment—god!—he'd be a guide on a bus. Do you do them like raisins? Glick pushed both his palms forward like a traffic policeman. Here's how the news got through —I'm certain—no other way, really—he saw it in the socials. Prunes? like prunes? The socials! Isabelle was giggly. You could have hung her clothes on the line between them. Eee-hee-hee, sweetie. All sorts of dried things these days: fruit, milk, peas, beans, eggs even, potatoes. He saw it in the socials or in the financials. The financials, says Isabelle, sweetie! How could she? Fender heard himself getting loud. Surprise invaded their faces. He had determined on an answer; he had to head them off; he could not endure their duet today or scale the cruel peaks of their hilarity. *Cut when young, bound in loose bunches, hung upside down, cold dry place, where a breeze would be helpful . . .* The chance was gone, Glick spoke so swiftly. Then in the funnies, Glick said, beginning the recital, when Pearson was blue-penning the balloons, there he read it—a dog said it. Isabelle flounced. There was a sound of settling sand and sliding paper. Fender shut his eyes. He could not bear it. Surely the financial page, she said, but Glick was on—spinning his chair, bouncing, pointing, wagging his head and making faces.

The owner of the house and lot at seventeen eleven Pierce; of the duplex that backs up to the alley at four seventy-seven Chauncey, formerly the family home and now a house divided . . .

Fender peeked where their glee, in beaded strings, divided: Glick's fists were turtling toward his knees, the thumbs were heads. . . .

. . . of lots at six oh five North Erie and two twenty-three Scott, both vacant except for ashes, cans, and native weeds . . .

Such a saddens story, sweetie, says Isabelle, such a sorry story . . .

. . . a beaten path across Billswool Place . . .

I know the one.

Do you, dearie? Well . . . renter of dingy office space at ninety-eight South Main near the Central Station and close to the bus . . .

Maybe, thought Fender, he should scream them under, throw a fit, have some sort of frothing seizure. How many peas, Glick, do you suppose are contained in the average pot pie? the beef? He might ask that.

. . . sordid work room . . .

Yes indeedy, says Isabelle.

. . . a ratty-off-hole . . .

Don't we know it, says Isabelle.

. . . a god damn grave . . .

Oh now, Leo, exclaims Isabelle.

. . . but handy . . .

Very handy, says Isabelle.

. . . to the bus . . .

To the bus, yes, says Isabelle.

. . . and to the railroad . . .

Just as you say, says Isabelle, the railroad.

What was epilepsy, Fender thought, but a struggle with the powers of the air.

. . . holder in fee simple of Leo Glick and Charlie Fender . . .

And also me-oh, says Isabelle.

. . . holder of expired guarantees, depression script, forfeited bail bonds . . .

Eeee . . .

. . . holder of mortgages . . .

How many peas? he might ask that. Go ahead, Glick, guess.

. . . tennis courts, Coke machines, car lots, traffic islands, circus tents, cat houses . . .

Reelee, I wouldn't know, says Isabelle.

. . . holder of options in addition . . .

Fender had chosen to wallow in the gravy and the steam.

. . . fire escapes, dumbwaiters, clothes chutes, letter drops, elevators . . .

Guess, how many peas? I'm not green like you, Glick, not countably discrete, not caught between tines, not raised, not even bitten through or mashed against the teeth.

. . . pee-bins and squat-closets . . .

Leo, *hon*estly, says Isabelle.

Fender remembered the census had missed him. He'd had to call attention to himself. How bitter he'd been about that.

. . . furthermore landlord in London-like absentia of slums in the country and yard-farms in town . . .

Fender began fumbling for his figures—the gently purple card—and Pearson perhaps would come; please lord to let him.

. . . acres of scrub and eroding gullies, mud flats, river islands . . .

Look, Glick, jesus, stop, cease, *end*—get off!

. . . erstwhile . . .

Dearie, exclaims Isabelle.

. . . erstwhile, I say, though still at times trader in lamp-wick stock and photo booths . . .

Okay, okay, okay, okay, consider it over . . .

. . . as well as salt swamps in Florida, pine barrens in Canada, sand boxes and cliff sides in New Mexico and Arizona . . .

O-*kay* . . .

. . . in Kentucky: caves; in Montana: butte tops; all over the country—the appropriate clip; for hire, let, lease, rent, charter, or sale: cattle-tittle ranches in Idaho, for instance (pardon me, Isabelle) . . .

You're forgiven, honey.

Wait'll you're dead, you'll see. It's the physical they'll respect—only right.

. . . yessiree, Pearson of the Pearson Agency *and* the Pearson Agency itself are all washed up, done for; they've gone pop, kaflooey, bang . . .

You sing so sweetly, like a thrush, says Isabelle.

Most bodies outlast the souls that rent them—know that? I read it somewhere. True.

. . . yup, this same Pearson Agency, after years of splendid service to the community, is absolutely bussst (pardon me, Isabelle, but busssssssst!) . . .

Think nothing of it, honey, you were carried away.

You know, Fender, a person gets his living room for a low fee. It's something to think about. On the nose. Smacko.

. . . and Pearson, in arrears up to his assets . . .

Oh Leo—that's good, that's *always* good, says Isabelle.

. . . in bitter shame, in low despair, all sour-mouthed and quite thoroughly quinced, has fallen *not* on the sword of his lodge . . .

Not, wonders Isabelle.

. . . but on the—on the impertinent pick of an icicle . . .

What, exclaims Isabelle.

. . . so when it's melted itself from the puncture, everyone will wonder—like in the mystery books and pictures—

Oooo, says Isabelle.

. . . as much at how he lowered the lid on his life . . .

Closed the cover on his career . . .

Hush now, honey—let *me* . . . so I say that everyone will wonder, when it's melted itself from the puncture,
as much at how he let the air out of his life as they ever
had before at how he'd pumped it in her.

Leo, you're simply fabulous, I mean really fabulous.

Yeah, you're one of the wisemen, Glick, you know? one
of the wisemen.

3

As Fender slowly approached, they got out of their car
and waited for him on the sidewalk. She seemed terribly
small and muffled up, and when he drew near he saw that
she was both. Her hat was covered with fur, she wore a
fur coat that seemed to have been stained mahogany, and
there were tattered strips of fur around the tops of her
overshoes that had been dipped in a similar color. Her
hands were hidden in a fur muff that almost matched her
coat and she stood very formally, the muff at her middle,
like a figure in a print or display in a shop. She was even
smaller than he'd thought: the furs of her coat were long
and coarse, the collar closed across her chin, her overshoes had high thin heels. The man said something. Fender
greeted him; his words were gay. The moist lips, the movement of the arm, the grip, the crinkle at the edge of the

eye, the bob he gave to his head—all were there, performing for him, working their spell as he liked to think, for even if it was Ringley he was selling, he owed it to Pearson, and after this morning he felt his loyalty more deeply, perhaps, than he ever had before. He gratefully acknowledged his debt, because Pearson was far better than . . . far better than Glick and all the other people who regularly jeered at him. He was better absolutely. He had a beautiful belief. And although it was true that he sold badly—he had too much momentum, it carried him past the sale—still . . . Fender smiled at the woman, who blinked. She had swollen eyes, and her nose, which surprised Fender by being huge and angular, was raw beneath the nostrils. That's the way it goes, he thought, turning away; she's got the flu or something, and I'll catch it. Fender couldn't blame people for hating Pearson. Pearson *was* a bully. Fender had felt his anger and contempt often enough; had heard him brag at length and failed his challenges. With a pencil pulled suddenly from his pocket, Fender wrote figures in the snow. Needs a bit of paint of course . . . but sits well back. These fine old homes . . . there's no other way to purchase space these days, the space one requires for gracious living. It was true: he sold badly, he bragged, well, yes, he lied too, he was a bully. He was impossibly vain, an incurable gossip. But he could drive a street and tell its fortune like a Gypsy. *Your body owns you; another house, isn't it?* Old souls in them, old souls like aged widow women, watching through the windows Pearson coming, helpless, unable, even, to crawl their stairs. There'd be embalming in the basement if it wasn't damp. He threw the woman a ferocious glare but she seemed quite oblivious to him, swallowed in her animal. Fender led the way up the unshoveled walk, gallantly raking his feet from side to side to make a path, and as he mounted the steps a breeze moved up beside him and the sun bloomed so brilliantly that the snow seemed to leap with the light. Icicles hung from the high eaves of the house, fantastically twisted, enormously long, and all around the porch smaller ones grew in great profusion. They certainly disfigure a place, he said, and the key was still cold in his pocket. Prop-purr-tee. A lovely sound. He hauled the door open.

Another thing I do—I always remember to bring along a coat hanger.

This is the entrance hall. We are diseases entering it. We are three diseases. We differ among ourselves: which of us shall be the reigning sickness in this grand old body —the muff, the muff's man, or I? The corners of the ceiling have risen since I saw them last. Note please the grandeur of the stair. Because it curves. Curvature has grandeur. The pillar is Corinthian. And see the lathe-carved gewgaws. Now then if Pearson has the power to predict for streets and houses, for all sorts of property, reading their futures from the patches to their paint and shingles, couldn't he . . . couldn't he do it for a face for instance, maybe, or an elbow—Fender's own, he realized, was caked—for an employee? This is a window seat. You don't find many of these any more. And Fender sat heavily. Of course one's nose seldom got its name in the papers—no clue there. Kids love window seats. The seats come up. Lids—look. Lots of storage underneath. But Fender didn't budge, mastered by his overcoat. In Pearson's face, morning after morning, when full of lordly entrance he had leaned over Fender's phone and basket, what had Fender seen but just such a judgment? There's no one to help you, Fender, you have no history, remember? Log in the stream. The house was so empty, so silent, he could hear them breathing, and their three breaths, in lease to the spirit, drifted across their collars and spilled on their sleeves. The poisons of pneumonia are heaviest. Fading in her furs like a mist in a forest. So the Agency would fold; perhaps it had, for it was bound to—when had they sold something? And here is Ringley—the walrus-jawed. And here was his responsibility. He rose wearily. Sizes! He stretched out his arms. A tape measure magically spanned the doorway. Unkinked, the masterful metal presided.

And this is the living room. See the high windows. He drove up the shades and the sun flashed through, frightening the woman in her furs, whose hairs, Fender now noticed, were split at their ends and raggedly combed. Fine floors. He stamped his foot thunderously, flouring snow around his shoe. Should a mouse run up the wall or a wasp appear from the attic, what would she do—disappear in her skins? He ran his pencil rat-a-tat-tat along the radiator. Nothing beats steam. He placed a reverent finger on the paper. Fleur-de-lis, he said. It wasn't a mew she made, but she moved to touch her husband. Royal, he said, and rapped the wall with a knuckle. It was true: he sold badly; he was a braggart and a liar. He had cheated his clients, often dodged taxes, falsified documents, behaved like a fool in front of Isabelle, like a child, like a . . . Were they coming along? What did they want, for the love of god, what did they expect? When you think what the owner's asking, he said, twisting his neck . . . well, it's a shame. Romance, was it? was that the cat at the bottom of the basket? Can you recall those better days, madam and mister, when the chandeliers blazed here, and down

that stair the hostess dragged her gown? With all the sliding doors drawn in, the Ringleys danced.

This used to be called the parlor. They read in here on
Sundays from edifying books and during the week practiced the piano, but you could use it as a family room:
hobbies, card games, the TV, toys—have a regular romp.
Because of a torn blind, a splintery tree. He turned slowly,
lifting his arms. Isn't it wonderful—what a place for kids!
The left hand had come from the muff and was caught
now on the coat sleeve of the muff's friend and male companion. Very suddenly there were alarming quick steps on
the porch. Fender lifted the front shade and a small boy
turned toward him and stared in, an icicle every bit as big
as he was cradled in his arms. By god, Fender gasped, running toward the door, the nerve! The boy was standing
in the snow looking at the house apprehensively when
Fender burst upon the porch. Whatdoyoumean, whatdoyoumean, he yelled, as the child made off. Those icicles,
boy, you ought to know, they come with the house! They're
a part of the property! Fender gave chase, but at once lost
his quarry behind the garages. The child moved quickly,
and in the deep snow and on the slippery drives and ter-
races, Fender, awkward under the best of circumstances,
fell twice. Worst of all, the thief had held on to his prize.
Fender returned slowly, winded, brushing his coat and
trousers. The way kids carry on these days—they've no
respect—why they'll do anything—imagine—right under
our noses—with our sign out front, too—THE PEARSON
AGENCY, big as life—but what do they care? not these kids
—they steal the signs—you'd be surprised. Fender shook
his head. By george what nerve, he said. However when
Fender looked up he could not see either of his clients,
and after a moment when his eyes sought them wildly

everywhere, he discovered them entering their car, which almost immediately, though the rear wheels whined, moved rapidly off.

At home, for that is where Fender, in a panic, had taken himself at once, he first shoveled the walk. It was pleasant work, his body was accommodating, and its movements made him calm. He would frequently rest to watch his icicles, the whole line, firing up, holding the sun like a maiden in her sleep or a princess in her tower—so real, so false, so magical. It was his own invention, that image, and he was proud of it. The walk completed, he sat at ease in his window, examining them carefully from that side, observing their spiral rings and ridges, the cloudy, the grainy, the cellular places, as well as the fair new ice and its queer, surprising turns, the warts and dimples which appeared on some, the threadlike quality of others, in short, every particular of their formation, imagining himself suddenly to possess a most piercing scientific eye, cold and ruthless as a knife, yet in warmth and kindness as philosophic as a blanket, taking everything in and absorbing their natures as wholly as warmer weather one day would. The melting snow ran down them, cooling as it went, until, little by little, it froze, though a drop might collect at the point sometimes and make its escape from there. Across considerable distances they bent, on occasion, to touch, or they threw out lateral shoots like vines, with minuscule fingers eagerly crooked. When he saw the postman coming, Fender hurried out and stood in front, painfully screwing a smile on, terrified lest the man push by him suddenly and knock them off. Humbly he received his mail and when the postman seemed well on his way and there was no chance he might have forgotten something and turn back, Fender, worn and sighing, thought it safe to go in. He idly shuffled through the letters—bills, ads, nothing much. You've no job, Fender, he said, and you haven't eaten lunch.

The beauty of the icicles was a sign of the beauty of their possessor, Fender thought. They were a mark of nature's favor like fair skin, fair hair, blue eyes. Only the icicles mattered. What was lunch when he was nourishing the spirit? If he could grow them inside himself, if he could swallow them like a carnival performer and put their beauty in his body . . . He dreamed, but he was disturbed, fully and honestly anxious. The sun itself would destroy them, or they would be torn off in the night by the wind, or fall helplessly in the weight of their armor. But property endures. . . . Pearson doubtless had his cemetery lot all paid for. He would attend first to his last address—that would be like him. This crypt is the site of the great man's grave. Within, a casket, bronze, with scrolling handles, holds a plastic coffin like a Thermos liner. Rolled in a sling of satin, even beneath the earth, in his hollow body cavity, the embalming liquids sway. Momentarily Fender didn't give a damn; he put a kiss on the glass and saw the paper boy approaching. Ah, god, he would smash— Then Fender went to the door again to greet the boy with his best hypocrisy, but the boy passed sullenly, thank heaven, with scarcely a nod. He, Fender, would not be in the papers. No blue line would pass over him. But on the front page was a picture of a grimacing, pork-cheeked little girl no more than three or four who was the measure of an immensely twisted, knotty, threatening icicle like the root of a tree, and it did what it was meant to—it engulfed her. SOME PLEASURE IN ICE THAT GRIPS CITY. Egh. Disgusting.

But Fender, what foolishness are you believing about

yourself? These laws that build beauty out of change, what
have they to do with you? In a dull way, you're ugly, certainly deceitful, cowardly and disloyal, cheap and thin like
the overpressed and cleaned out clothes you're standing in.
But Fender did not feel the remorse of the guilty. There
is another law, he said, the law that passes beauty into
me, for I am growing like them, I am coming to deserve
them, I have lost my job today and had no lunch. Fender,
these are icicles. Perishing is the word for them. He flew
the paper to a table and paced about the room attempting
various formulations. Well then, he said, my soul shall
have to grow agreeable to its end. How grand, Fender,
how grand you are, trembling so badly you can scarcely
stand, to speak like this. What have you done with your
life? With a vulgar *houf,* Fender sank wearily in a chair.
They should be spectacular tonight, he thought. He would
see them from all sides, observe from every angle. They
could capture his eyes, for all he cared, and grind them
like lenses. What would color be like? He'd put a rosy bulb
in the porch light.

Fender. You have no job. He had no job. He shrugged.
So. The weather was lousy, dinner not so hot again, bed
would be . . . as always. But he had an address. My god,
those are the world's worst words, the world's worst, I
mean when you read in the papers where it says that so and
so of no fixed address was picked up for loitering or pinching purses or was arrested for drunk and disorderly and it
says: of no fixed address. Imagine. Pearson keens; he wails
with his arms. Such a person has *no place.* He can't be
found. He's like one of those unphysical things they talk
about in science now—like one of those things that's moving, you know, always moving on, but through no space.
Jesus. Who can understand? I leave that sort to them like

I leave these vagrants to police; but imagine a man without a place to be, a place that's known, that has a name, is some way fixed; why that's like being alone at sea without a log to hang on—and the sharks at your toes. Fender shrugged. Fender: you have no job. You lack an occupation, Fender—a position, Fender—a spot to johnny on. He shrugged. Yeah. He lacked. And Fender—Charlie Fender—of such and such a number, such and such a road, in such and such a town and state, has quit, is fired, is out, at his age, after so, so many years. . . . Yes, he thought, I do not even occupy myself.

In the arms of the chair he felt a great distance from everything. His arms on the arms of the chair embraced him, squeezed. And he was not in the space his toes turned up in. It could, he supposed, have happened to him any time: a terrible accident like a plane crash, dividing limbs and luggage up indifferently, scattering toiletries. Planes were property. He saw his socks softly falling; they'd snag eventually on wires and trees. Everything was property— Pearson was correct—yet pouf! and it's snowing shirts and business papers. The chair . . . the chair's arms were weariless. Pouf, Fender. Can you restrain your bacteria? No, you're freezerless. So pouf! One day it's done. Even now you're melting down. True—but those icicles gather the snow as it softens, oppose their coldness to the sun, and turn their very going into . . . Isabelles. Look, Fender: feet flat on the floor. Keep. Them. There. Arms in the arms of the chair. Armchair. Oh hug, and hold hard, and be beloved! But Fender did not stir. His inner exclamations were like advertising signs—for gasoline and colas—the worst kind. Chair arms were property. They would enwooden him; reskin him in something floral, a disposition of designs as in a dance to decorate his coverings. He'd be . . .

tattooed. It was stupid. He tried to drive himself into word-lessness. There were so many words which worried him. Phrases. Voices. Scenes. It was stupid. Ah, finally you're For Sale, Fender. Yeah. He lived in his pie like the peas. That's very funny. I hope—I trust you see the humor in it—for you to be For Sale. Held in the chair he could not move to any music. He was tattooed. The legs fold over on the dotted line. Tat. Tat. Tat. He stared at his knees . . . where fell like trousered water . . . what? They played colored lights on the wall of Niagara. His icicles gleamed. That boy had taken such a big one—god—so carelessly— and carried it away. What did he know! what did he feel! the pain to that poor house! the wrench! Yet Fender did not shout; he did not move. He was falling away toward his feet nonetheless . . . softly, still. Like socks scattered from a suitcase in an air crash . . . lightly snowing. In each pie there are how many? how many? how many? . . . peas.

So finally you're For Sale, Fender. That's very funny. I hope you see the humor in it. It makes a fellow's job a whole lot easier—I mean, if there's humor in it and the humor's seen, it's easier all around. Be happy, eh? Does that check? How long do you plan to stay listed? Well it was fart smart to stand empty through the winter, that's all I say. What I mean, it was dumb—bum dumb. Come to think of it, you were vacant longer than that. You're bound to be badly shit up. Now if I were you, considering your kind of case, what's best by and large and everything, why I'd try multiple listing. That way, if a good thing turns up, maybe you can close the deal on your own— after all, you're with an agency—Pearson—jesus, he's piss bliss, Pearson is. Anyway, you can't expect anybody to make you their main concern—I mean, you know, that's the way it goes, it's a tough business, and five percent of you—well it won't run to much. Okay? It's good that's clear—a happy thing. Now what are your sizes? How much room do you have around the ribs there—there in the cage? Many kidney malfunctions? They come on often, about your age. Your shoulders slope and we ought to burn that wart off your chin. Why the hell—if I had a wart on my chin like that— Look, I've got the usual things to check out. . . . Um, your skin is sort of fibrous looking, I'm afraid, and pretty splotchy—poor stuff—scaly, thin— a sour diet. How long have those bruises been in? and that spread of blood along the shin? broken capillaries, are they? Say, Fender, no bull, we're in the same business, man to man, eh? why take the trouble? Hell, you know the list's the same for everybody: sinus, spleen, intestines, all those glands. . . . Should we start with the palate and drop straight down: teeth, tonsils, tongue, lungs, liver, bronchial tree? would it be worth the bother? And after that, let's see, going up it's rectum, colon, stomach, heart, and so on, all the soft goods, and then the skull, spine, pelvis, ribs, et cetera, et cetera—but there's little point—I mean, consider your chances calmly a minute. Well look, fellow, there's no charm to your entrances. Like I say— we've got to face the facts, and an old place is an old place. You know the business. No surprises. Right? So let's concentrate on good points if we can—jolly buttocks maybe— we've customers for them. But I don't like that loosening hair. Jesus, look what you've done to your knuckles. And how about the light in there? Dammit, you *know* it's the first thing they ask. They come in—they want to see where the light falls. Say, I'll tell you a trick. I always take a yardstick with me, and times like that, when the sun's pouring pleasantly in, I just measure it up for them—so many feet of it. You can figure the effect. Selling's not all fuck luck, nossir. Not all fuck luck . . . fuckaluck. What? you're cool? no crap now, how could you be cool? you've no shade. Hey—isn't that right? Nothing to say—right? Fender, you haven't any answer—right? How will they look with a colored bulb in your porch light, the walls of Niagara? Had your heart flushed recently or your bowels scrubbed? I like to have the dates. Well no harm, no harm, we're friends in business—but let's look at some stools before I leave, on the off chance, just the same. . . .

Shoes, the rug—he saw the rug—and the foot of a table rising from the weave, thickening as it treed its top—was it rosily wooded?—waxed featureless and gleaming. Prop-purr-tee: a lovely sound. Was he an organ looking out? was this how it seemed to the liver, lying . . . where? He knew where peas were likely in pot pies, but he could not imagine his liver—did not wish—the way he dreamed of women, always smudged across the crotch. Prop-purr-tee. They shone. He could not watch. Fender—why not rent? All right, all right then, I'd like to give you a break, but it's not up to me, a sale's no certain thing, not everybody's hunting, it isn't like you were a honey-sweet piece, they're not anxious, they've no itch. Oh sure, to live *above* themselves, but not, you know, to . . . Hey, does that check? Now—damage to the skin? property your vintage, some crazing's likely—but, yeah, we've covered that. Drafts get in? I don't know, Fender. Honestly. You're in a bad district. It's the slack season. Things are slow all over. You might try lodgers. . . .

Deposit of paper on the table, slick painted wall—he saw the wall—it went up nowhere, sight ran like water over it. Prop. Prop. Look, Fender, it's a busy time, a busy time. . . . Sure they'll laugh—pee hee hee—that's how they'll laugh. What can I do? If they laugh, they laugh. A dog's house is a dog's house, to be cunt blunt, and so they'll laugh. You bet there'll be a lot of traipsing in and out. They'll want to know what you see from where you are; they'll ask how's the view . . . should this be news? Like my boss says: it ain't funny but it's money. Okay. Let's trot along. Feet flat, I suppose? bladder patched? . . . yeah? often? how much will it hold in a pinch? Hah hah. Just came to me like that—they do. Elbows next. Knees, then? Joints of the toes? You're all bones and belly, the style's not in fashion. Well, it's not my fault, Fender, but they're going to want a good stiff prick and a stony cod, you know, the kind that lays back warm against the belly when it's up, what the kids call nowadays a real hot rod. They'll want one if they're eighty—and who can blame them? Perhaps if you were to try the market another time, or place yourself in the hands of some bright young fellow, a real comer. There's that guy in your office—Glick. He'll be off on his own soon and happy for your business. . . .

The wall went into ceiling at the wall's fold. He gave his head a crank to follow; saw the ceiling: gray white similarities of space, quite grayish, sunless, not about to snow, undappled, white, weighted, heaven, up and down, so far, so low, his whole height, lengthy, heavy as a purchase—the same unsagging same. Listen, I'm trying to tell you, Fender. We all come to it. That's the way it goes. It's simple. You got a place and nobody wants to live in it. Okay, okay, it's just a job—with me it's just a job. Let's see you swallow. Fine. Now spit.

There were figures moving at the top of the street, dark spots swimming in his eyes, cinders from somewhere. The light was bad for him—the terrible glare—his whole head was burning. He blinked, and then for a moment he could

see plaid lumberjackets, red caps and boots and shining
buttons, yellow corduroy. A whole company of children—
boys mostly—were milling about, hurling snow and yelling
on the hill. You've no right to weep, Fender, whose fault
is it? His chair held him; he had no energy; he would never
sell again; certainly he was sick. What'll you do, then,
Fender? What'll you do tomorrow? Tomorrow, he thought.
God. The coming hour, the minute following, the second
next. Should he sneeze? lift his left hand? laugh? He tried
to clear his head for the children. For a time, while he
watched, they churned and circled aimlessly on the crest,
but gradually their movements grew purposive, and they
began uniting more often, then parting regularly, like a
pulse. At last they stood fixed for an instant, brightly, in a
red knot. He saw them point toward him—point directly
—and he heard them shout. In his anguish, groaning, he
gripped the arms of the chair that held him, yet he made
no attempt to rise and intercept. He was conquering himself for the third time that day. Stripes, boots, buttons,
squares, yellow—he stared at them—sleds and plastic pails
and metal shovels, tassels, mittens, bells, plaids, furries, the
branch of a spruce, clouds of upended snow, catcalls, piercing whistles, a fluttering scarlet-and-dark-green scarf behind a child's throat like a military banner. Then it was as
though, suddenly, a fist had opened, and they came down
the hill like a snowfall of rocks.

Order of Insects

We certainly had no complaints about the house after all we had been through in the other place, but we hadn't lived there very long before I began to notice every morning the bodies of a large black bug spotted about the downstairs carpet; haphazardly, as earth worms must die on the street after a rain; looking when I first saw them like rolls of dark wool or pieces of mud from the children's shoes, or sometimes, if the drapes were pulled, so like ink stains or deep burns they terrified me, for I had been intimidated by that thick rug very early and the first week had walked over it wishing my bare feet would swallow my shoes. The shells were usually broken. Legs and other parts I couldn't then identify would be scattered near like flakes of rust. Occasionally I would find them on their backs, their quilted undersides showing orange, while beside them were smudges of dark-brown powder that had to be vacuumed carefully. We believed our cat had killed them. She was frequently sick during the night then—a rare thing for her—and we could think of no other reason. Overturned like that they looked pathetic even dead.

I could not imagine where the bugs had come from. I am terribly meticulous myself. The house was clean, the cupboards tight and orderly, and we never saw one alive. The other place had been infested with those flat brown fuzzy roaches, all wires and speed, and we'd seen *them* all right, frightened by the kitchen light, sifting through the baseboards and the floor's cracks; and in the pantry I had nearly closed my fingers on one before it fled, tossing its shadow across the starch like an image of the startle in my hand.

Dead, overturned, their three pairs of legs would be delicately drawn up and folded shyly over their stomachs. When they walked I suppose their forelegs were thrust out and then bent to draw the body up. I still wonder if they jumped. More than once I've seen our cat hook one of her claws under a shell and toss it in the air, crouching while the insect fell, feigning leaps—but there was daylight; the bug was dead; she was not really interested any more; and she would walk immediately away. That image takes the place of jumping. Even if I actually saw those two back pairs of legs unhinge, as they would have to if one leaped, I think I'd find the result unreal and mechanical, a poor try measured by that sudden, high, head-over-heels flight from our cat's paw. I could look it up, I guess, but it's no study for a woman . . . bugs.

At first I reacted as I should, bending over, wondering what in the world; yet even before I recognized them I'd withdrawn my hand, shuddering. Fierce, ugly, armored things: they used their shadows to seem large. The machine sucked them up while I looked the other way. I remember the sudden thrill of horror I had hearing one rattle up the wand. I was relieved that they were dead, of course, for I could never have killed one, and if they had been popped, alive, into the dust bag of the cleaner, I believe I would have had nightmares again as I did the time my husband fought the red ants in our kitchen. All night I lay awake thinking of the ants alive in the belly of the machine, and when toward morning I finally slept I found myself in the dreadful elastic tunnel of the suction tube where ahead of me I heard them: a hundred bodies rustling in the dirt.

I never think of their species as alive but as comprised entirely by the dead ones on our carpet, all the new dead manufactured by the action of some mysterious spoor— perhaps that dust they sometimes lie in—carried in the air, solidified by night and shaped, from body into body, spontaneously, as maggots were before the age of science. I have a single book about insects, a little dated handbook in French which a good friend gave me as a joke—because of my garden, the quaintness of the plates, the fun of reading about worms in such an elegant tongue—and my bug has his picture there climbing the stem of an orchid. Beneath the picture is his name: *Periplaneta orientalis L. Ces répugnants insectes ne sont que trop communs dans les cuisines des vieilles habitations des villes, dans les magasins, entrepôts, boulangeries, brasseries, restaurants, dans la cale des navires, etc.,* the text begins. Nevertheless they are a new experience for me and I think that I am grateful for it now.

The picture didn't need to show me there were two, adult and nymph, for by that time I'd seen the bodies of both kinds. Nymph. My god the names we use. The one was dark, squat, ugly, sly. The other, slimmer, had hard sheath-like wings drawn over its back like another shell, and you could see delicate interwoven lines spun like fossil gauze across them. The nymph was a rich golden color deepening in its interstices to mahogany. Both had legs that looked under a glass like the canes of a rose, and the nymph's were sufficiently transparent in a good light you thought you saw its nerves merge and run like a jagged crack to each ultimate claw.

Tipped, their legs have fallen shut, and the more I look at them the less I believe my eyes. Corruption, in these bugs, is splendid. I've a collection now I keep in typewriter-ribbon tins, and though, in time, their bodies dry and the interior flesh decays, their features hold, as I suppose they held in life, an Egyptian determination, for their protective plates are strong and death must break bones to get in. Now that the heavy soul is gone, the case is light.

I suspect if we were as familiar with our bones as with our skin, we'd never bury dead but shrine them in their rooms, arranged as we might like to find them on a visit; and our enemies, if we could steal their bodies from the battle sites, would be museumed as they died, the steel still eloquent in their sides, their metal hats askew, the pro-tective toes of their shoes unworn, and friend and enemy would be so wondrously historical that in a hundred years we'd find the jaws still hung for the same speech and all the parts we spent our life with tilted as they always were—rib cage, collar, skull—still repetitious, still defiant, angel light, still worthy of memorial and affection. After all, what does it mean to say that when our cat has bitten through the shell and put confusion in the pulp, the life goes out of them? Alas for us, I want to cry, our bones are secret, showing last, so we must love what perishes: the muscles and the waters and the fats.

Two prongs extend like daggers from the rear. I suppose I'll never know their function. That kind of knowledge doesn't take my interest. At first I had to screw my eyes down, and as I consider it now, the whole change, the recent alteration in my life, was the consequence of finally coming near to something. It was a self-mortifying act, I recall, a penalty I laid upon myself for the evil-tempered words I'd shouted at my children in the middle of the night. I felt instinctively the insects were infectious and their own disease, so when I knelt I held a handkerchief over the lower half of my face . . . saw only horror . . . turned, sick, masking my eyes . . . yet the worst of angers held me through the day: vague, searching, guilty, and ashamed.

After that I came near often; saw, for the first time, the gold nymph's difference; put between the mandibles a tinted nail I'd let grow long; observed the movement of the jaws, the stalks of the antennae, the skull-shaped skull, the lines banding the abdomen, and found an intensity in the posture of the shell, even when tipped, like that in the gaze of Gauguin's natives' eyes. The dark plates glisten. They are wonderfully shaped; even the buttons of the compound eyes show a geometrical precision which prevents my earlier horror. It isn't possible to feel disgust toward such an order. Nevertheless, I reminded myself, a roach . . . and you a woman.

I no longer own my own imagination. I suppose they came up the drains or out of the registers. It may have been the rug they wanted. Crickets, too, I understand, will feed on wool. I used to rest by my husband . . . stiffly . . . waiting for silence to settle in the house, his sleep to come, and then the drama of their passage would take hold of me, possess me so completely that when I finally slept I merely passed from one dream to another without the slightest loss of vividness or continuity. Never alive, they came with punctures; their bodies formed from little whorls of copperish dust which in the downstairs darkness I couldn't possibly have seen; and they were dead and upside down when they materialized, for it was in that moment that our cat, herself darkly invisible, leaped and brought her paws together on the true soul of the roach; a soul so static and intense, so immortally arranged, I felt, while I lay shell-like in our bed, turned inside out, driving my mind away, it was the same as the dark soul of the world itself—and it was this beautiful and terrifying feeling that took possession of me finally, stiffened me like a rod beside my husband, played caesar to my dreams.

The weather drove them up, I think . . . moisture in the tubes of the house. The first I came on looked put together in Japan; broken, one leg bent under like a metal cinch; unwound. It rang inside the hollow of the wand like metal too; brightly, like a stream of pins. The clatter made me shiver. Well I always see what I fear. Anything my eyes have is transformed into a threatening object: mud, or stains, or burns, or if not these, then toys in unmendable metal pieces. Not fears to be afraid of. The ordinary fears of daily life. Healthy fears. Womanly, wifely, motherly ones: the children may point at the wretch with the hunch and speak in a voice he will hear; the cat has fleas again, they will get in the sofa; one's face looks smeared, it's because of the heat; is the burner on under the beans? the washing machine's obscure disease may reoccur, it rumbles on rinse and rattles on wash; my god it's already eleven o'clock; which one of you has lost a galosh? So it was amid

the worries of our ordinary life I bent, innocent and im-
properly armed, over the bug that had come undone. Let
me think back on the shock. . . . My hand would have
fled from a burn with the same speed; anyone's death or
injury would have weakened me as well; and I could have
gone cold for a number of reasons, because I felt in motion
in me my own murderous disease, for instance; but none
could have produced the revulsion that dim recognition
did, a reaction of my whole nature that flew ahead of understanding and made me withdraw like a spider.

I said I was innocent. Well I was not. Innocent. My god
the names we use. What do we live with that's alive we
haven't tamed—people like me?—even our houseplants
breathe by our permission. All along I had the fear of what
it was—something ugly and poisonous, deadly and terrible
—the simple insect, worse and wilder than fire—and I
should rather put my arms in the heart of a flame than in
the darkness of a moist and webby hole. But the eye never
ceases to change. When I examine my collection now it
isn't any longer roaches I observe but gracious order,
wholeness, and divinity. . . . My handkerchief, that time,
was useless. . . . O my husband, they are a terrible disease.

The dark soul of the world . . . a phrase I should laugh
at. The roach shell sickened me. And my jaw has broken
open. I lie still, listening, but there is nothing to hear. Our
cat is quiet. They pass through life to immortality between
her paws.

Am I grateful now my terror has another object? From
time to time I think so, but I feel as though I'd been en-
trusted with a kind of eastern mystery, sacred to a dreadful
god, and I am full of the sense of my unworthiness and
the clay of my vessel. So strange. It is the sewing machine

that has the fearful claw. I live in a scatter of blocks and children's voices. The chores are my clock, and time is every other moment interrupted. I had always thought that love knew nothing of order and that life itself was turmoil and confusion. Let us leap, let us shout! I have leaped, and to my shame, I have wrestled. But this bug that I hold in my hand and know to be dead is beautiful, and there is a fierce joy in its composition that beggars every other, for its joy is the joy of stone, and it lives in its tomb like a lion.

I don't know which is more surprising: to find such order in a roach, or such ideas in a woman.

I could not shake my point of view, infected as it was, and I took up their study with a manly passion. I sought out spiders and gave them sanctuary; played host to worms of every kind; was generous to katydids and lacewings, aphids, ants and various grubs; pampered several sorts of beetle; looked after crickets; sheltered bees; aimed my husband's chemicals away from the grasshoppers, mosquitoes, moths, and flies. I have devoted hours to watching caterpillars feed. You can see the leaves they've eaten passing through them; their bodies thin and swell until the useless pulp is squeezed in perfect rounds from their rectal end; for caterpillars are a simple section of intestine, a decorated stalk of yearning muscle, and their whole being is enlisted in the effort of digestion. *Le tube digestif des Insectes est situé dans le grand axe de la cavité générale du corps . . . de la bouche vers l'anus . . . Le pharynx . . . L'œsophage . . . Le jabot . . . Le ventricule chylifique . . . Le rectum et l'iléon . . .* Yet when they crawl their curves conform to graceful laws.

My children ought to be delighted with me as my husband is, I am so diligent, it seems, on their behalf, but they have taken fright and do not care to pry or to collect. My hobby's given me a pair of dreadful eyes, and sometimes I fancy they start from my head; yet I see, perhaps, no differently than Galileo saw when he found in the pendulum its fixed intent. Nonetheless my body resists such knowledge. It wearies of its edge. And I cannot forget, even while I watch our moonvine blossoms opening, the simple principle of the bug. It is a squat black cockroach after all, such a bug as frightens housewives, and it's only come to chew on rented wool and find its death absurdly in the teeth of the renter's cat.

Strange. Absurd. I am the wife of the house. This point of view I tremble in is the point of view of a god, and I feel certain, somehow, that could I give myself entirely to it, were I not continuing a woman, I could disarm my life, find peace and order everywhere; and I lie by my husband and I touch his arm and consider the temptation. But I am a woman. I am not worthy. Then I want to cry O husband, husband, I am ill, for I have seen what I have seen. What should he do at that, poor man, starting up in the night from his sleep to such nonsense, but comfort me blindly and murmur dream, small snail, only dream, bad dream, as I do to the children. I could go away like the wise cicada who abandons its shell to move to other mischief. I could leave and let my bones play cards and spank the children. . . . Peace. How can I think of such ludicrous things—beauty and peace, the dark soul of the world —for I am the wife of the house, concerned for the rug, tidy and punctual, surrounded by blocks.

In the Heart of the Heart of the Country

A PLACE

So I have sailed the seas and come . . .

to B . . .

a small town fastened to a field in Indiana. Twice there have been twelve hundred people here to answer to the census. The town is outstandingly neat and shady, and always puts its best side to the highway. On one lawn there's even a wood or plastic iron deer.

You can reach us by crossing a creek. In the spring the lawns are green, the forsythia is singing, and even the railroad that guts the town has straight bright rails which hum when the train is coming, and the train itself has a welcome horning sound.

Down the back streets the asphalt crumbles into gravel.

There's Westbrook's, with the geraniums, Horsefall's, Mott's. The sidewalk shatters. Gravel dust rises like breath behind the wagons. And I am in retirement from love.

WEATHER

In the Midwest, around the lower Lakes, the sky in the winter is heavy and close, and it is a rare day, a day to remark on, when the sky lifts and allows the heart up. I am keeping count, and as I write this page, it is eleven days since I have seen the sun.

MY HOUSE

There's a row of headless maples behind my house, cut to free the passage of electric wires. High stumps, ten feet tall, remain, and I climb these like a boy to watch the country sail away from me. They are ordinary fields, a little more uneven than they should be, since in the spring they puddle. The topsoil's thin, but only moderately stony. Corn is grown one year, soybeans another. At dusk starlings darken the single tree—a larch—which stands in the middle. When the sky moves, fields move under it. I feel, on my perch, that I've lost my years. It's as though I were living at last in my eyes, as I have always dreamed of doing, and I think then I know why I've come here: to see, and so to go out against new things—oh god how easily— like air in a breeze. It's true there are moments—foolish moments, ecstasy on a tree stump—when I'm all but gone, scattered I like to think like seed, for I'm the sort now in the fool's position of having love left over which I'd like to lose; what good is it now to me, candy ungiven after Halloween?

A PERSON

There are vacant lots on either side of Billy Holsclaw's house. As the weather improves, they fill with hollyhocks. From spring through fall, Billy collects coal and wood and puts the lumps and pieces in piles near his door, for keeping warm is his one work. I see him most often on mild days sitting on his doorsill in the sun. I notice he's squinting a little, which is perhaps the reason he doesn't cackle as I pass. His house is the size of a single garage, and very old. It shed its paint with its youth, and its boards are a warped and weathered gray. So is Billy. He wears a short lumpy faded black coat when it's cold, otherwise he always goes about in the same loose, grease-spotted shirt and trousers. I suspect his galluses were yellow once, when they were new.

WIRES

These wires offend me. Three trees were maimed on their account, and now these wires deface the sky. They cross like a fence in front of me, enclosing the crows with the clouds. I can't reach in, but like a stick, I throw my feelings over. What is it that offends me? I am on my stump, I've built a platform there and the wires prevent my going out. The cut trees, the black wires, all the beyond birds therefore anger me. When I've wormed through a fence to reach a meadow, do I ever feel the same about the field?

THE CHURCH

The church has a steeple like the hat of a witch, and five birds, all doves, perch in its gutters.

MY HOUSE

Leaves move in the windows. I cannot tell you yet how beautiful it is, what it means. But they do move. They move in the glass.

POLITICS

. . . for all those not in love.

I've heard Batista described as a Mason. A farmer who'd seen him in Miami made this claim. He's as nice a fellow as you'd ever want to meet. Of Castro, of course, no one speaks.

For all those not in love there's law: to rule . . . to regulate . . . to rectify. I cannot write the poetry of such proposals, the poetry of politics, though sometimes—often —always now—I am in that uneasy peace of equal powers which makes a State; then I communicate by passing papers, proclamations, orders, through my bowels. Yet I was not a State with you, nor were we both together any Indiana. A squad of Pershing Rifles at the moment, I make myself Right Face! Legislation packs the screw of my intestines. Well, king of the classroom's king of the hill. You used to waddle when you walked because my sperm between your legs was draining to a towel. Teacher, poet, folded lover—like the politician, like those drunkards, ill, or those who faucet-off while pissing heartily to preach upon the force and fullness of that stream, or pause from vomiting to praise the purity and passion of their puke— I chant, I beg, I orate, I command, I sing—

Come back to Indiana—not too late!
(Or will you be a ranger to the end?)

Good-bye . . . Good-bye . . . oh, I shall always wait
    You, Larry, traveler—
                stranger,
                    son,
                        —my friend—

my little girl, my poem by heart, my self, my childhood.

But I've heard Batista described as a Mason. That dries
up my pity, melts my hate. Back from the garage where I
have overheard it, I slap the mended fender of my car to
laugh, and listen to the metal stinging tartly in my hand.

PEOPLE

Their hair in curlers and their heads wrapped in loud
scarves, young mothers, fattish in trousers, lounge about
in the speedwash, smoking cigarettes, eating candy, drinking pop, thumbing magazines, and screaming at their children above the whir and rumble of the machines.

At the bank a young man freshly pressed is letting himself in with a key. Along the street, delicately teetering,
many grandfathers move in a dream. During the murderous
heat of summer, they perch on window ledges, their feet
dangling just inside the narrow shelf of shade the store has
made, staring steadily into the street. Where their consciousness has gone I can't say. It's not in the eyes. Perhaps
it's diffuse, all temperature and skin, like an infant's,
though more mild. Near the corner there are several large
overalled men employed in standing. A truck turns to be
weighed on the scales at the Feed and Grain. Images drift
on the drugstore window. The wind has blown the smell
of cattle into town. Our eyes have been driven in like the
eyes of the old men. And there's no one to have mercy on
us.

VITAL DATA

There are two restaurants here and a tearoom. two bars. one bank, three barbers, one with a green shade with which he blinds his window. two groceries. a dealer in Fords. one drug, one hardware, and one appliance store. several that sell feed, grain, and farm equipment. an antique shop. a poolroom. a laundromat. three doctors. a dentist. a plumber. a vet. a funeral home in elegant repair the color of a buttercup. numerous beauty parlors which open and shut like night-blooming plants. a tiny dime and department store of no width but several floors. a hutch, home-made, where you can order, after lying down or squirming in, furniture that's been fashioned from bent lengths of stainless tubing, glowing plastic, metallic thread, and clear shellac. an American Legion Post and a root beer stand. little agencies for this and that: cosmetics, brushes, insurance, greeting cards and garden produce—anything—sample shoes—which do their business out of hats and satchels, over coffee cups and dissolving sugar. a factory for making paper sacks and pasteboard boxes that's lodged in an old brick building bearing the legend OPERA HOUSE, still faintly golden, on its roof. a library given by Carnegie. a post office. a school. a railroad station. fire station. lumberyard. telephone company. welding shop. garage . . . and spotted through the town from one end to the other in a line along the highway, gas stations to the number five.

EDUCATION

In 1833, Colin Goodykoontz, an itinerant preacher with a name from a fairytale, summed up the situation in one Indiana town this way:

Ignorance and her squalid brood. A universal dearth of intellect. Total abstinence from literature is very generally practiced. . . . There is not a scholar in grammar or geography, or a *teacher capable* of *instructing* in them, to my knowledge. . . . Others are supplied a few months of the year with the most antiquated & unreasonable forms of teaching reading, writing & cyphering. . . . Need I stop to remind you of the host of loathsome reptiles such a stagnant pool is fitted to breed! Croaking jealousy; bloated bigotry; coiling suspicion; wormish blindness; crocodile malice!

Things have changed since then, but in none of the respects mentioned.

BUSINESS

One side section of street is blocked off with sawhorses. Hard, thin, bitter men in blue jeans, cowboy boots and hats, untruck a dinky carnival. The merchants are promoting themselves. There will be free rides, raucous music, parades and coneys, pop, popcorn, candy, cones, awards and drawings, with all you can endure of pinch, push, bawl, shove, shout, scream, shriek, and bellow. Children pedal past on decorated bicycles, their wheels a blur of color, streaming crinkled paper and excited dogs. A little later there's a pet show for a prize—dogs, cats, birds, sheep, ponies, goats—none of which wins. The whirlabouts whirl about. The Ferris wheel climbs dizzily into the sky as far as a tall man on tiptoe might be persuaded to reach, and the irritated operators measure the height and weight of every child with sour eyes to see if they are safe for the machines. An electrical megaphone repeatedly trumpets the names of the generous sponsors. The following day they do not allow the refuse to remain long in the street.

MY HOUSE, THIS PLACE AND BODY

I have met with some mischance, wings withering, as Plato says obscurely, and across the breadth of Ohio, like heaven on a table, I've fallen as far as the poet, to the sixth sort of body, this house in B, in Indiana, with its blue and gray bewitching windows, holy magical insides. Great thick evergreens protect its entry. And I live *in*.

Lost in the corn rows, I remember feeling just another stalk, and thus this country takes me over in the way I occupy myself when I am well . . . completely—to the edge of both my house and body. No one notices, when they walk by, that I am brimming in the doorways. My house, this place and body, I've come in mourning to be born in. To anybody else it's pretty silly: love. Why should I feel a loss? How am I bereft? She was never mine; she was a fiction, always a golden tomgirl, barefoot, with an adolescent's slouch and a boy's taste for sports and fishing, a figure out of Twain, or worse, in Riley. Age cannot be kind.

There's little hand-in-hand here . . . not in B. No one touches except in rage. Occasionally girls will twine their arms about each other and lurch along, school out, toward home and play. I dreamed my lips would drift down your back like a skiff on a river. I'd follow a vein with the point of my finger, hold your bare feet in my naked hands.

THE SAME PERSON

Billy Holsclaw lives alone—how alone it is impossible to fathom. In the post office he talks greedily to me about the weather. His head bobs on a wild flood of words, and I take this violence to be a measure of his eagerness for speech. He badly needs a shave, coal dust has layered his face, he spits when he speaks, and his fingers pick at his tatters. He wobbles out in the wind when I leave him, a paper sack mashed in the fold of his arm, the leaves blowing past him, and our encounter drives me sadly home to poetry—where there's no answer. Billy closes his door and carries coal or wood to his fire and closes his eyes, and there's simply no way of knowing how lonely and empty he is or whether he's as vacant and barren and loveless as the rest of us are—here in the heart of the country.

WEATHER

For we're always out of luck here. That's just how it is— for instance in the winter. The sides of the buildings, the roofs, the limbs of the trees are gray. Streets, sidewalks, faces, feelings—they are gray. Speech is gray, and the grass where it shows. Every flank and front, each top is gray. Everything is gray: hair, eyes, window glass, the hawkers' bills and touters' posters, lips, teeth, poles and metal signs—they're gray, quite gray. Cars are gray. Boots, shoes, suits, hats, gloves are gray. Horses, sheep, and cows, cats killed in the road, squirrels in the same way, sparrows, doves, and pigeons, all are gray, everything is gray, and everyone is out of luck who lives here.

A similar haze turns the summer sky milky, and the air muffles your head and shoulders like a sweater you've got caught in. In the summer light, too, the sky darkens a moment when you open your eyes. The heat is pure distraction. Steeped in our fluids, miserable in the folds of our bodies, we can scarcely think of anything but our sticky parts. Hot cyclonic winds and storms of dust crisscross the country. In many places, given an indifferent push, the wind will still coast for miles, gathering resource and edge as it goes, cunning and force. According to the season, paper, leaves, field litter, seeds, snow, fill up the fences. Sometimes I think the land is flat because the winds have leveled it, they blow so constantly. In any case, a gale can grow in a field of corn that's as hot as a draft from hell, and to receive it is one of the most dismaying experiences of this life, though the smart of the same wind in winter is more humiliating, and in that sense even worse. But in the spring it rains as well, and the trees fill with ice.

PLACE

Many small Midwestern towns are nothing more than rural slums, and this community could easily become one. Principally during the first decade of the century, though there were many earlier instances, well-to-do farmers moved to town and built fine homes to contain them in their retirement. Others desired a more social life, and so lived in, driving to their fields like storekeepers to their businesses. These houses are now dying like the bereaved who inhabit them; they are slowly losing their senses—deafness, blindness, forgetfulness, mumbling, an insecure gait, an uncontrollable trembling has overcome them. Some kind of Northern Snopes will occupy them next: large-familied, Catholic, Democratic, scrambling, vigorous, poor; and since the parents will work in larger, nearby towns, the children will be loosed upon themselves and upon the hapless neighbors much as the fabulous Khan loosed his legendary horde. These Snopes will undertake makeshift repairs with materials that other people have thrown away; paint halfway round their house, then quit; almost certainly maintain an ugly loud cantankerous dog and underfeed a pair of cats to keep the rodents down. They will collect piles of possibly useful junk in the back yard, park their cars in the front, live largely leaning over engines, give not a hoot for the land, the old community, the hallowed ways, the established clans. Weakening widow ladies have already begun to hire large rude youths from families such as these to rake and mow and tidy the grounds they will inherit.

PEOPLE

In the cinders at the station boys sit smoking steadily in darkened cars, their arms bent out the windows, white shirts glowing behind the glass. Nine o'clock is the best time. They sit in a line facing the highway—two or three or four of them—idling their engines. As you walk by a machine may growl at you or a pair of headlights flare up briefly. In a moment one will pull out, spinning cinders behind it, to stalk impatiently up and down the dark streets or roar half a mile into the country before returning to its place in line and pulling up.

MY HOUSE, MY CAT, MY COMPANY

I must organize myself. I must, as they say, pull myself together, dump this cat from my lap, stir—yes, resolve, move, do. But do what? My will is like the rosy dustlike light in this room: soft, diffuse, and gently comforting. It lets me do . . . anything . . . nothing. My ears hear what they happen to; I eat what's put before me; my eyes see what blunders into them; my thoughts are not thoughts, they are dreams. I'm empty or I'm full . . . depending; and I cannot choose. I sink my claws in Tick's fur and scratch the bones of his back until his rear rises amorously. Mr. Tick, I murmur, I must organize myself. I must pull myself together. And Mr. Tick rolls over on his belly, all ooze.

I spill Mr. Tick when I've rubbed his stomach. Shoo. He steps away slowly, his long tail rhyming with his paws. How beautifully he moves, I think; how beautifully, like you, he commands his loving, how beautifully he accepts. So I rise and wander from room to room, up and down, gazing through most of my forty-one windows. How well this house receives its loving too. Let out like Mr. Tick, my eyes sink in the shrubbery. I am not here; I've passed the glass, passed second-story spaces, flown by branches, brilliant berries, to the ground, grass high in seed and leafage every season; and it is the same as when I passed above you in my aged, ardent body; it's, in short, a kind of love; and I am learning to restore myself, my house, my body, by paying court to gardens, cats, and running water, and with neighbors keeping company.

Mrs. Desmond is my right-hand friend; she's eighty-five. A thin white mist of hair, fine and tangled, manifests the climate of her mind. She is habitually suspicious, fretful, nervous. Burglars break in at noon. Children trespass. Even now they are shaking the pear tree, stealing rhubarb, denting lawn. Flies caught in the screens and numbed by frost awake in the heat to buzz and scrape the metal cloth and frighten her, though she is deaf to me, and consequently cannot hear them. Boards creak, the wind whistles across the chimney mouth, drafts cruise like fish through the hollow rooms. It is herself she hears, her own flesh failing, for only death will preserve her from those daily chores she climbs like stairs, and all that anxious waiting. Is it now, she wonders. No? Then: is it now?

We do not converse. She visits me to talk. My task to murmur. She talks about her grandsons, her daughter who lives in Delphi, her sister or her husband—both gone—obscure friends—dead—obscurer aunts and uncles—lost—ancient neighbors, members of her church or of her clubs —passed or passing on; and in this way she brings the ends of her life together with a terrifying rush: she is a girl, a wife, a mother, widow, all at once. All at once—appalling —but I believe it; I wince in expectation of the clap. Her talk's a fence—a shade drawn, window fastened, door that's locked—for no one dies taking tea in a kitchen; and as her years compress and begin to jumble, I really believe in the brevity of life; I sweat in my wonder; death is the dog down the street, the angry gander, bedroom spider, goblin who's come to get her; and it occurs to me that in my listening posture I'm the boy who suffered the winds of my grandfather with an exactly similar politeness, that I am, right now, all my ages, out in elbows, as angular as badly stacked cards. Thus was I, when I loved you, every man I could be, youth and child—far from enough—and you, so strangely ambiguous a being, met me, heart for spade, play after play, the whole run of our suits.

Mr. Tick, you do me honor. You not only lie in my lap, but you remain alive there, coiled like a fetus. Through your deep nap, I feel you hum. You are, and are not, a machine. You are alive, alive exactly, and it means nothing to you—much to me. You are a cat—you cannot understand—you are a cat so easily. Your nature is not something you must rise to. You, not I, live in: in house, in skin, in shrubbery. Yes. I think I shall hat my head with a steeple; turn church; devour people. Mr. Tick, though, has a tail he can twitch, he need not fly his Fancy. Claws, not metrical schema, poetry his paws; while smoothing . . .

smoothing . . . smoothing roughly, his tongue laps its neat-
ness. O Mr. Tick, I know you; you are an electrical penis.
Go on now, shoo. Mrs. Desmond doesn't like you. She
thinks you will tangle yourself in her legs and she will fall.
You murder her birds, she knows, and walk upon her roof
with death in your jaws. I must gather myself together for
a bound. What age is it I'm at right now, I wonder. The
heart, don't they always say, keeps the true time. Mrs.
Desmond is knocking. Faintly, you'd think, but she pounds.
She's brought me a cucumber. I believe she believes I'm a
woman. Come in, Mrs. Desmond, thank you, be my company, it looks lovely, and have tea. I'll slice it, crisp, with
cream, for luncheon, each slice as thin as me.

POLITICS

O all ye isolate and separate powers, Sing! Sing, and sing
in such a way that from a distance it will seem a harmony,
a Strindberg play, a friendship ring . . . so happy—happy,
happy, happy—as here we go hand in handling, up and
down. Our union was a singing, though we were silent in
the songs we sang like single notes are silent in a symphony.
In no sense sober, we barbershopped together and never
heard the discords in our music or saw ourselves as dirty,
cheap, or silly. Yet cats have worn out better shoes than
those thrown through our love songs at us. Hush. Be patient—prudent—politic. Still, Cleveland killed you, Mr.
Crane. Were you not politic enough and fond of being
beaten? Like a piece of sewage, the city shat you from its
stern three hundred miles from history—beyond the loving
reach of sailors. Well, I'm not a poet who puts Paris to his
temple in his youth to blow himself from Idaho, or—fancy
that—Missouri. My god, I said, this is my country, but

must my country go so far as Terre Haute or Whiting, go
so far as Gary?

When the Russians first announced the launching of their
satellite, many people naturally refused to believe them.
Later others were outraged that they had sent a dog around
the earth. I wouldn't want to take that mutt from out that
metal flying thing if he's still living when he lands, our own
dog catcher said; anybody knows you shut a dog up by
himself to toss around the first thing he'll be setting on to
do you let him out is bite somebody.

This Midwest. A dissonance of parts and people, we are
a consonance of Towns. Like a man grown fat in everything but heart, we overlabor; our outlook never really ur-
ban, never rural either, we enlarge and linger at the same
time, as Alice both changed and remained in her story.
You are blond. I put my hand upon your belly; feel it
tremble from my trembling. We always drive large cars in
my section of the country. How could you be a comfort
to me now?

MORE VITAL DATA

The town is exactly fifty houses, trailers, stores, and miscel-
laneous buildings long, but in places no streets deep. It
takes on width as you drive south, always adding to the
east. Most of the dwellings are fairly spacious farm houses
in the customary white, with wide wraparound porches and
tall narrow windows, though there are many of the grander
kind—fretted, scalloped, turreted, and decorated with clap-
boards set at angles or on end, with stained-glass windows
at the stair landings and lots of wrought iron full of fancy
curls—and a few of these look like castles in their rarer

brick. Old stables serve as garages now, and the lots are large to contain them and the vegetable and flower gardens which, ultimately, widows plant and weed and then entirely disappear in. The shade is ample, the grass is good, the sky a glorious fall violet; the apple trees are heavy and red, the roads are calm and empty; corn has sifted from the chains of tractored wagons to speckle the streets with gold and with the russet fragments of the cob, and a man would be a fool who wanted, blessed with this, to live anywhere else in the world.

EDUCATION

Buses like great orange animals move through the early light to school. There the children will be taught to read and warned against Communism. By Miss Janet Jakes. That's not her name. Her name is Helen something—Scott or James. A teacher twenty years. She's now worn fine and smooth, and has a face, Wilfred says, like a mail-order ax. Her voice is hoarse, and she has a cough. For she screams abuse. The children stare, their faces blank. This is the thirteenth week. They are used to it. You will all, she shouts, you will all draw pictures of me. No. She is a Mrs. —someone's missus. And in silence they set to work while Miss Jakes jabs hairpins in her hair. Wilfred says an ax, but she has those rimless tinted glasses, graying hair, an almost dimpled chin. I must concentrate. I must stop making up things. I must give myself to life; let it mold me: that's what they say in *Wisdom's Monthly Digest* every day. Enough, enough—you've been at it long enough; and the children rise formally a row at a time to present their work to her desk. No, she wears rims; it's her chin that's dimple-

less. Well, it will take more than a tablespoon of features
to sweeten that face. So she grimly shuffles their sheets,
examines her reflection crayoned on them. I would not dare
. . . allow a child . . . to put a line around me. Though now
and then she smiles like a nick in the blade, in the end
these drawings depress her. I could not bear it—how can
she ask?—that anyone . . . draw me. Her anger's lit.
That's why she does it: flame. There go her eyes; the pink
in her glasses brightens, dims. She is a pumpkin, and her
rage is breathing like the candle in. No, she shouts, no—
the cartoon trembling—no, John Mauck, John Stewart
Mauck, this will not do. The picture flutters from her
fingers. You've made me too muscular.

I work on my poetry. I remember my friends, associates,
my students, by their names. Their names are Maypop,
Dormouse, Upsydaisy. Their names are Gladiolus, Callow
Bladder, Prince and Princess Oleo, Hieronymus, Cardinal
Mummum, Mr. Fitchew, The Silken Howdah, Spot. Sometimes you're Tom Sawyer, Huckleberry Finn; it is perpetu-
ally summer; your buttocks are my pillow; we are adrift on
a raft; your back is our river. Sometimes you are Major
Barbara, sometimes a goddess who kills men in battle,
sometimes you are soft like a shower of water; you are
bread in my mouth.

I do not work on my poetry. I forget my friends, associates, my students, and their names: Gramophone, Blow-
gun, Pickle, Serenade . . . Marge the Barge, Arena, Uber-
haupt . . . Doctor Dildoe, The Fog Machine. For I am
now in B, in Indiana: out of job and out of patience, out
of love and time and money, out of bread and out of body,
in a temper, Mrs. Desmond, out of tea. So shut your fist
up, bitch, you bag of death; go bang another door; go die,
my dearie. Die, life-deaf old lady. Spill your breath. Fall

over like a frozen board. Gray hair grows from the nose of your mind. You are a skull already—*memento mori*—the foreskin retracts from your teeth. Will your plastic gums last longer than your bones, and color their grinning? And is your twot still hazel-hairy, or are you bald as a ditch? . . . bitch . . . . . . bitch . . . . bitch. I wanted to be famous, but you bring me age—my emptiness. Was it *that* which I thought would balloon me above the rest? Love? where are you? . . . love me. I want to rise so high, I said, that when I shit I won't miss anybody.

BUSINESS

For most people, business is poor. Nearby cities have siphoned off all but a neighborhood trade. Except for feed and grain and farm supplies, you stand a chance to sell only what one runs out to buy. Chevrolet has quit, and Frigidaire. A locker plant has left its afterimage. The lumberyard has been, so far, six months about its going. Gas stations change hands clumsily, a restaurant becomes available, a grocery closes. One day they came and knocked the cornices from the watch repair and pasted campaign posters on the windows. Torn across, by now, by boys, they urge you still to vote for half an orange beblazoned man who as a whole one failed two years ago to win at his election. Everywhere, in this manner, the past speaks, and it mostly speaks of failure. The empty stores, the old signs and dusty fixtures, the debris in alleys, the flaking paint and rusty gutters, the heavy locks and sagging boards: they say the same disagreeable things. What do the sightless windows see, I wonder, when the sun throws a passerby against them? Here a stair unfolds toward the street—dark, rickety, and treacherous—and I always feel, as I pass it, that

if I just went carefully up and turned the corner at the
landing, I would find myself out of the world. But I've
never had the courage.

THAT SAME PERSON

The weeds catch up with Billy. In pursuit of the hollyhocks, they rise in coarse clumps all around the front of
his house. Billy has to stamp down a circle by his door
like a dog or cat does turning round to nest up, they're so
thick. What particularly troubles me is that winter will find
the weeds still standing stiff and tindery to take the sparks
which Billy's little mortarless chimney spouts. It's true that
fires are fun here. The town whistle, which otherwise only
blows for noon (and there's no noon on Sunday), signals
the direction of the fire by the length and number of its
blasts, the volunteer firemen rush past in their cars and
trucks, houses empty their owners along the street every
time like an illustration in a children's book. There are
many bikes, too, and barking dogs, and sometimes—hal-
leluiah—the fire's right here in town—a vacant lot of weeds
and stubble flaming up. But I'd rather it weren't Billy or
Billy's lot or house. Quite selfishly I want him to remain
the way he is—counting his sticks and logs, sitting on his
sill in the soft early sun—though I'm not sure what his
presence means to me . . . or to anyone. Nevertheless, I
keep wondering whether, given time, I might not someday
find a figure in our language which would serve him faith-
fully, and furnish his poverty and loneliness richly out.

WIRES

Where sparrows sit like fists. Doves fly the steeple. In mist
the wires change perspective, rise and twist. If they led to

you, I would know what they were. Thoughts passing often, like the starlings who flock these fields at evening to sleep in the trees beyond, would form a family of paths like this; they'd foot down the natural height of air to just about a bird's perch. But they do not lead to you.

> Of whose beauty it was sung
> She shall make the old man young.

They fasten me.

If I walked straight on, in my present mood, I would reach the Wabash. It's not a mood in which I'd choose to conjure you. Similes dangle like baubles from me. This time of year the river is slow and shallow, the clay banks crack in the sun, weeds surprise the sandbars. The air is moist and I am sweating. It's impossible to rhyme in this dust. Everything—sky, the cornfield, stump, wild daisies, my old clothes and pressless feelings—seem fabricated for installment purchase. Yes. Christ. I am suffering a summer Christmas; and I cannot walk under the wires. The sparrows scatter like handfuls of gravel. Really, wires are voices in thin strips. They are words wound in cables. Bars of connection.

WEATHER

I would rather it were the weather that was to blame for what I am and what my friends and neighbors are—we who live here in the heart of the country. Better the weather, the wind, the pale dying snow . . . the snow— why not the snow? There's never much really, not around the lower Lakes anyway, not enough to boast about, not enough to be useful. My father tells how the snow in the Dakotas would sweep to the roofs of the barns in the old days, and he and his friends could sled on the crust that would form because the snow was so fiercely driven. In Bemidji trees have been known to explode. That would be something—if the trees in Davenport or Francisville or Carbondale or Niles were to go blam some winter—blam! blam! blam! all the way down the gray, cindery, snow-sick streets.

A cold fall rain is blackening the trees or the air is like lilac and full of parachuting seeds. Who cares to live in any season but his own? Still I suspect the secret's in this snow, the secret of our sickness, if we could only diagnose it, for we are all dying like the elms in Urbana. This snow—like our skin it covers the country. Later dust will do it. Right now—snow. Mud presently. But it is snow without any laughter in it, a pale gray pudding thinly spread on stiff toast, and if that seems a strange description, it's accurate all the same. Of course soot blackens everything, but apart from that, we are never sufficiently cold here. The flakes as they come, alive and burning, we cannot retain, for if our temperatures fall, they rise promptly again, just as, in the summer, they bob about in the same feckless way. Suppose though . . . suppose they were to rise some August, climb and rise, and then hang in the hundreds like a hawk through December, what a desert we could make of ourselves—from Chicago to Cairo, from Hammond to Columbus—what beautiful Death Valleys.

PLACE

I would rather it were the weather. It drives us in upon ourselves—an unlucky fate. Of course there is enough to stir our wonder anywhere; there's enough to love, anywhere, if one is strong enough, if one is diligent enough, if one is perceptive, patient, kind enough—whatever it takes;

and surely it's better to live in the country, to live on a prairie by a drawing of rivers, in Iowa or Illinois or Indiana, say, than in any city, in any stinking fog of human beings, in any blooming orchard of machines. It ought to be. The cities are swollen and poisonous with people. It ought to be better. Man has never been a fit environment for man—for rats, maybe, rats do nicely, or for dogs or cats and the household beetle.

And how long the street is, nowadays. These endless walls are fallen to keep back the tides of earth. Brick could be beautiful but we have covered it gradually with gray industrial vomits. Age does not make concrete genial, and asphalt is always—like America—twenty-one, until it breaks up in crumbs like stale cake. The brick, the asphalt, the concrete, the dancing signs and garish posters, the feed and excrement of the automobile, the litter of its inhabitants: they compose, they decorate, they line our streets, and there is nowhere, nowadays, our streets can't reach.

A man in the city has no natural thing by which to measure himself. His parks are potted plants. Nothing can live and remain free where he resides but the pigeon, starling, sparrow, spider, cockroach, mouse, moth, fly and weed, and he laments the existence of even these and makes his plans to poison them. The zoo? There *is* the zoo. Through its bars the city man stares at the great cats and dully sucks his ice. Living, alas, among men and their marvels, the city man supposes that his happiness depends on establishing, somehow, a special kind of harmonious accord with others. The novelists of the city, of slums and crowds, they call it love—and break their pens.

Wordsworth feared the accumulation of men in cities. He foresaw their "degrading thirst after outrageous stimulation," and some of their hunger for love. Living in a city, among so many, dwelling in the heat and tumult of incessant movement, a man's affairs are touch and go—that's all. It's not surprising that the novelists of the slums, the cities, and the crowds, should find that sex is but a scratch to ease a tickle, that we're most human when we're sitting on the john, and that the justest image of our life is in full passage through the plumbing.

> That man, immur'd in cities, still retains
> His inborn inextinguishable thirst
> Of rural scenes, compensating his loss
> By supplemental shifts, the best he may.

Come into the country, then. The air nimbly and sweetly recommends itself unto our gentle senses. Here, growling tractors tear the earth. Dust roils up behind them. Drivers sit jouncing under bright umbrellas. They wear refrigerated hats and steer by looking at the tracks they've cut behind them, their transistors blaring. Close to the land, are they? good companions to the soil? Tell me: do they live in harmony with the alternating seasons?

It's a lie of old poetry. The modern husbandman uses chemicals from cylinders and sacks, spike-ball-and-claw machines, metal sheds, and cost accounting. Nature in the old sense does not matter. It does not exist. Our farmer's only mystical attachment is to parity. And if he does not realize that cows and corn are simply different kinds of chemical engine, he cannot expect to make a go of it.

It isn't necessary to suppose our cows have feelings; our neighbor hasn't as many as he used to have either; but think of it this way a moment, you can correct for the human imputations later: how would it feel to nurse those strange tentacled calves with their rubber, glass, and metal lips, their stainless eyes?

PEOPLE

Aunt Pet's still able to drive her car—a high square Ford —even though she walks with difficulty and a stout stick. She has a watery gaze, a smooth plump face despite her age, and jet black hair in a bun. She has the slowest smile of anyone I ever saw, but she hates dogs, and not very long ago cracked the back of one she cornered in her garden. To prove her vigor she will tell you this, her smile breaking gently while she raises the knob of her stick to the level of your eyes.

HOUSE, MY BREATH AND WINDOW

My window is a grave, and all that lies within it's dead. No snow is falling. There's no haze. It is not still, not silent. Its images are not an animal that waits, for movement is no demonstration. I have seen the sea slack, life bubble through a body without a trace, its spheres impervious as soda's. Downwound, the whore at wagtag clicks and clacks. Leaves wiggle. Grass sways. A bird chirps, pecks the ground. An auto wheel in penning circles keeps its rigid spokes. These images are stones; they are memorials. Beneath this sea lies sea: god rest it . . . rest the world beyond my window, me in front of my reflection, above this page, my shade. Death is not so still, so silent, since silence implies a falling quiet, stillness a stopping, containing, holding in; for death is time in a clock, like Mr. Tick, electric . . . like wind through a windup poet. And my blear floats out to visible against the glass, befog its country and bespill myself. The mist lifts slowly from the fields in the morning. No one now would say: the Earth throws back

its covers; it is rising from sleep. Why is the feeling foolish?
The image is too Greek. I used to gaze at you so wantonly
your body blushed. Imagine: wonder: that my eyes could
cause such flowering. Ah, my friend, your face is pale, the
weather cloudy; a street has been felled through your chin,
bare trees do nothing, houses take root in their rectangles,
a steeple stands up in your head. You speak of loving;
then give me a kiss. The pane is cold. On icy mornings
the fog rises to greet me (as you always did); the barns and
other buildings, rather than ghostly, seem all the more sub-
stantial for looming, as if they grew in themselves while I
watched (as you always did). Oh my approach, I suppose,
was like breath in a rubber monkey. Nevertheless, on the
road along the Wabash in the morning, though the trees
are sometimes obscured by fog, their reflection floats serenely on the river, reasoning the banks, the sycamores in
French rows. Magically, the world tips. I'm led to think
that only those who grow down live (which will scarcely
win me twenty-five from *Wisdom's Monthly Digest*), but I
find I write that only those who live down grow; and what
I write, I hold, whatever I really know. My every word's
inverted, or reversed—or I am. I held you, too, that way.
You were so utterly provisional, subject to my change. I
could inflate your bosom with a kiss, disperse your skin
with gentleness, enter your vagina from within, and make
my love emerge like a fresh sex. The pane is cold. Honesty
is cold, my inside lover. The sun looks, through the mist,
like a plum on the tree of heaven, or a bruise on the slope
of your belly. Which? The grass crawls with frost. We
meet on this window, the world and I, inelegantly, swim-
mers of the glass; and swung wrong way round to one another, the world seems in. The world—how grand, how
monumental, grave and deadly, that word is: the world, my

house and poetry. All poets have their inside lovers. Wee penis does not belong to me, or any of this foggery. It is *his* property which he's thrust through what's womanly of me to set down this. These wooden houses in their squares, gray streets and fallen sidewalks, standing trees, your name I've written sentimentally across my breath into the whitening air, pale birds: they exist in me now because of him. I gazed with what intensity . . . A bush in the excitement of its roses could not have bloomed so beautifully as you did then. It was a look I'd like to give this page. For that is poetry: to bring within about, to change.

POLITICS

Sports, politics, and religion are the three passions of the badly educated. They are the Midwest's open sores. Ugly to see, a source of constant discontent, they sap the body's strength. Appalling quantities of money, time, and energy are wasted on them. The rural mind is narrow, passionate, and reckless on these matters. Greed, however shortsighted and direct, will not alone account for it. I have known men, for instance, who for years have voted squarely against their interests. Nor have I ever noticed that their surly Christian views prevented them from urging forward the smithereening, say, of Russia, China, Cuba, or Korea. And they tend to back their country like they back their local team: they have a fanatical desire to win; yelling is their forte; and if things go badly, they are inclined to sack the coach. All in all, then, Birch is a good name. It stands for the bigot's stick, the wild-child-tamer's cane.

Forgetfulness—is that their object?

Oh, I was new, I thought. A fresh start: new cunt, new climate, and new country—there you were, and I was pioneer, and had no history. That language hurts me, too, my dear. You'll never hear it.

FINAL VITAL DATA

The Modern Homemakers' Demonstration Club. The Prairie Home Demonstration Club. The Night-outers' Home Demonstration Club. The IOOF, FFF, VFW, WCTU, WSCS, 4-H, 40 and 8, Psi Iota Chi, and PTA. The Boy and Girl Scouts, Rainbows, Masons, Indians and Rebekah Lodge. Also the Past Noble Grand Club of the Rebekah Lodge. As well as the Moose and the Ladies of the Moose. The Elks, the Eagles, the Jaynettes and the Eastern Star. The Women's Literary Club, the Hobby Club, the Art Club, the Sunshine Society, the Dorcas Society, the Pythian Sisters, the Pilgrim Youth Fellowship, the American Legion, the American Legion Auxiliary, the American Legion Junior Auxiliary, the Gardez Club, the Bridge for Fun Club, the What-can-you-do? Club, the Get Together Club, the Coterie Club, the Worthwhile Club, the Let's Help Our Town Club, the No Name Club, the Forget-me-not Club, the Merry-go-round Club . . .

EDUCATION

Has a quarter disappeared from Paula Frosty's pocket book? Imagine the landscape of that face: no crayon could engender it; soft wax is wrong; thin wire in trifling snips might do the trick. Paula Frosty and Christopher Roger accuse the pale and splotchy Cheryl Pipes. But Miss Jakes, I *saw* her. Miss Jakes is so extremely vexed she snaps her pencil. What else is missing? I appoint you a detective, John: search her desk. Gum, candy, paper, pencils, marble, round eraser—whose? A thief. I can't watch her all the time, I'm here to teach. Poor pale fossetted Cheryl, it's determined, can't return the money because she took it home and spent it. Cindy, Janice, John, and Pete—you four who sit around her—you will be detectives this whole term to watch her. A thief. In all my time. Miss Jakes turns, unfists, and turns again. I'll handle you, she cries. To think. A thief. In all my years. Then she writes on the blackboard the name of Cheryl Pipes and beneath that the figure twenty-five with a large sign for cents. Now Cheryl, she says, this won't be taken off until you bring that money out of home, out of home straight up to here, Miss Jakes says, tapping her desk.

Which is three days.

ANOTHER PERSON

I was raking leaves when Uncle Halley introduced himself to me. He said his name came from the comet, and that his mother had borne him prematurely in her fright of it. I thought of Hobbes, whom fear of the Spanish Armada had hurried into birth, and so I believed Uncle Halley to honor the philosopher, though Uncle Halley is a liar, and neither the one hundred twenty-nine nor the fifty-three he ought to be. That fall the leaves had burned themselves out on the trees, the leaf lobes had curled, and now they flocked noisily down the street and were broken in the wires of my rake. Uncle Halley was himself (like Mrs. Desmond and history generally) both deaf and implacable, and he shooed me down his basement stairs to a room set aside there for stacks of newspapers reaching to the ceiling, boxes of leaflets and letters and programs, racks of photo albums, scrapbooks, bundles of rolled-up posters and maps, flags and pennants and slanting piles of dusty magazines devoted mostly to motoring and the Christian ethic. I saw a bird cage, a tray of butterflies, a bugle, a stiff straw boater, and all kinds of tassels tied to a coat tree. He still possessed and had on display the steering lever from his first car, a linen duster, driving gloves and goggles, photographs along the wall of himself, his friends, and his various machines, a shell from the first war, a record of "Ramona" nailed through its hole to a post, walking sticks and fanciful umbrellas, shoes of all sorts (his baby shoes, their counters broken, were held in sorrow beneath my nose—they had not been bronzed, but he might have them done someday before he died, he said), countless boxes of medals, pins, beads, trinkets, toys, and keys (I scarcely saw—they flowed like jewels from his palms), pictures of downtown when it was only a path by the railroad station, a brightly colored globe of the world with a dent in Poland, antique guns, belt buckles, buttons, souvenir plates and cups and saucers (I can't remember all of it—I won't), but I recall how shamefully, how rudely, how abruptly, I fled, a good story in my mouth but death in my nostrils; and how afterward I busily, righteously, burned my leaves as if I were purging the world of its years. I still wonder if this town —its life, and mine now—isn't really a record like the one of "Ramona" that I used to crank around on my grandmother's mahogany Victrola through lonely rainy days as a kid.

THE FIRST PERSON

Billy's like the coal he's found: spilled, mislaid, discarded. The sky's no comfort. His house and his body are dying together. His windows are boarded. And now he's reduced to his hands. I suspect he has glaucoma. At any rate he can scarcely see, and weeds his yard of rubble on his hands and knees. Perhaps he's a surgeon cleansing a wound or an ardent and tactile lover. I watch, I must say, apprehensively. Like mine-war detectors, his hands graze in circles ahead of him. Your nipples were the color of your eyes. Pebble. Snarl of paper. Length of twine. He leans down closely, picks up something silvery, holds it near his nose. Foil? cap? coin? He has within him—what, I wonder? Does he know more now because he fingers everything and has to sniff to see? It would be romantic cruelty to think so. He bends the down on your arms like a breeze. You wrote me: something is strange when we don't understand. I write in return: I think when I loved you I fell to my death.

Billy, I could read to you from Beddoes; he's your man perhaps; he held with dying, freed his blood of its arteries; and he said that there were many wretched love-ill fools like me lying alongside the last bone of their former selves, as full of spirit and speech, nonetheless, as Mrs. Desmond, Uncle Halley and the Ferris wheel, Aunt Pet, Miss Jakes, Ramona or the megaphone; yet I reverse him finally, Billy, on no evidence but braggadocio, and I declare that though my inner organs were devoured long ago, the worm which swallowed down my parts still throbs and glows like a crystal palace.

Yes, you were younger. I was Uncle Halley, the museum man and infrequent meteor. Here is my first piece of ass. They weren't so flat in those days, had more round, more juice. And over here's the sperm I've spilled, nicely jarred and clearly labeled. Look at this tape like lengths of intestine where I've stored my spew, the endless worm of words I've written, a hundred million emissions or more:

oh I was quite a man right from the start; even when un-conscious in my cradle, from crotch to cranium, I was erectile tissue; though mostly, after the manner approved by Plato, I had intercourse by eye. Never mind, old Hols-claw, you are blind. We pull down darkness when we go to bed; put out like Oedipus the actually offending organ, and train our touch to lies. All cats are gray, says Mr. Tick; so under cover of glaucoma you are sack gray too, and cannot be distinguished from a stallion.

I must pull myself together, get a grip, just as they say, but I feel spilled, bewildered, quite mislaid. I did not re-store my house to its youth, but to its age. Hunting, you hitch through the hollyhocks. I'm inclined to say you aren't half the cripple I am, for there is nothing left of me but mouth. However, I resist the impulse. It is another lie of poetry. My organs are all there, though it's there where I fail—at the roots of my experience. Poet of the spiritual, Rilke, weren't you? yet that's what you said. Poetry, like love, is—in and out—a physical caress. I can't tolerate any more of my sophistries about spirit, mind, and breath. Body equals being, and if your weight goes down, you are the less.

HOUSEHOLD APPLES

I knew nothing about apples. Why should I? My country came in my childhood, and I dreamed of sitting among the blooms like the bees. I failed to spray the pear tree too. I doubled up under them at first, admiring the sturdy low branches I should have pruned, and later I acclaimed the blossoms. Shortly after the fruit formed there were falls—not many—apples the size of goodish stones which made me wobble on my ankles when I walked about the yard. Sometimes a piece crushed by a heel would cling on the shoe to track the house. I gathered a few and heaved them over the wires. A slingshot would have been splendid. Hard, an unattractive green, the worms had them. Before long I realized the worms had them all. Even as the apples reddened, lit their tree, they were being swallowed. The birds preferred the pears, which were small—sugar pears I think they're called—with thick skins of graying green that ripen on toward violet. So the fruit fell, and once I made some applesauce by quartering and paring hundreds; but mostly I did nothing, left them, until suddenly, overnight it seemed, in that ugly late September heat we often have in Indiana, my problem was upon me.

My childhood came in the country. I remember, now, the flies on our snowy luncheon table. As we cleared away they would settle, fastidiously scrub themselves and stroll to the crumbs to feed where I would kill them in crowds with a swatter. It was quite a game to catch them taking off. I struck heavily since I didn't mind a few stains; they'd wash. The swatter was a square of screen bound down in red cloth. It drove no air ahead of it to give them warning. They might have thought they'd flown headlong into a summered window. The faint pink dot where they had died did not rub out as I'd supposed, and after years of use our luncheon linen would faintly, pinkly, speckle.

The country became my childhood. Flies braided themselves on the flypaper in my grandmother's house. I can smell the bakery and the grocery and the stables and the dairy in that small Dakota town I knew as a kid; knew as I dreamed I'd know your body, as I've known nothing, before or since; knew as the flies knew, in the honest, un-

chaste sense: the burned house, hose-wet, which drew a
mist of insects like the blue smoke of its smolder, and
gangs of boys, moist-lipped, destructive as its burning. Flies
have always impressed me; they are so persistently alive.
Now they were coating the ground beneath my trees. Some
were ordinary flies; there were the large blue-green ones;
there were swarms of fruit flies too, and the red-spotted
scavenger beetle; there were a few wasps, several sorts of
bees and butterflies—checkers, sulphurs, monarchs, com-
mas, question marks—and delicate dragonflies . . . but
principally houseflies and horseflies and bottleflies, flies and
more flies in clusters around the rotting fruit. They loved
the pears. Inside, they fed. If you picked up a pear, they
flew, and the pear became skin and stem. They were everywhere the fruit was: in the tree still—apples like a hive
for them—or where the fruit littered the ground, squashing
itself as you stepped . . . there was no help for it. The
flies droned, feasting on the sweet juice. No one could go
near the trees; I could not climb; so I determined at last
to labor like Hercules. There were fruit baskets in the barn.
Collecting them and kneeling under the branches, I began
to gather remains. Deep in the strong rich smell of the
fruit, I began to hum myself. The fruit caved in at the
touch. Glistening red apples, my lifting disclosed, had
families of beetles, flies, and bugs, devouring their rotten
undersides. There were streams of flies; there were lakes
and cataracts and rivers of flies, seas and oceans. The hum
was heavier, higher, than the hum of the bees when they
came to the blooms in the spring, though the bees were
there, among the flies, ignoring me—ignoring everyone.
As my work went on and juice covered my hands and
arms, they would form a sleeve, black and moving, like

knotty wool. No caress could have been more indifferently complete. Still I rose fearfully, ramming my head in the branches, apples bumping against me before falling, bursting with bugs. I'd snap my hand sharply but the flies would cling to the sweet. I could toss a whole cluster into a basket from several feet. As the pear or apple lit, they would explosively rise, like monads for a moment, windowless, certainly, with respect to one another, sugar their harmony. I had to admit, though, despite my distaste, that my arm had never been more alive, oftener or more gently kissed. Those hundreds of feet were light. In washing them off, I pretended the hose was a pump. What have I missed? Childhood is a lie of poetry.

THE CHURCH

Friday night. Girls in dark skirts and white blouses sit in ranks and scream in concert. They carry funnels loosely stuffed with orange and black paper which they shake wildly, and small megaphones through which, as drilled, they direct and magnify their shouting. Their leaders, barely pubescent girls, prance and shake and whirl their skirts above their bloomers. The young men, leaping, extend their arms and race through puddles of amber light, their bodies glistening. In a lull, though it rarely occurs, you can hear the squeak of tennis shoes against the floor. Then the yelling begins again, and then continues; fathers, mothers, neighbors joining in to form a single pulsing ululation—a cry of the whole community—for in this gymnasium each body becomes the bodies beside it, pressed as they are together, thigh to thigh, and the same shudder runs through all of them, and runs toward the same release.

Only the ball moves serenely through this dazzling din. Obedient to law it scarcely speaks but caroms quietly and lives at peace.

BUSINESS

It is the week of Christmas and the stores, to accommodate the rush they hope for, are remaining open in the evening. You can see snow falling in the cones of the street lamps. The roads are filling—undisturbed. Strings of red and green lights droop over the principal highway, and the water tower wears a star. The windows of the stores have been bedizened. Shamelessly they beckon. But I am alone, leaning against a pole—no . . . there is no one in sight. They're all at home, perhaps by their instruments, tuning in on their evenings, and like Ramona, tirelessly playing and replaying themelves. There's a speaker perched in the tower, and through the boughs of falling snow and over the vacant streets, it drapes the twisted and metallic strains of a tune that can barely be distinguished—yes, I believe it's one of the jolly ones, it's "Joy to the World." There's no one to hear the music but myself, and though I'm listening, I'm no longer certain. Perhaps the record's playing something else.

A Note on the Author

Born in Fargo, North Dakota in 1924, William Gass was educated at Kenyon College, Ohio Wesleyan, and Cornell. He has taught philosophy at Purdue University and at Washington University (St. Louis) where he is now a professor. His books include the novel *Omensetter's Luck*, the novella *Willie Masters' Lonely Wife*, two volumes of criticism *Fiction & the Figures of Life* and *The World Within the Word*, and *On Being Blue: A Philosophical Inquiry*. He is married and the father of three children.